"What did I do or say that was wrong?" Declan asked.

"You didn't do or say anything." Alethea swallowed. "It's not you. It's your mindset. Your impulsiveness. I look at you sometimes and I just get..." She stopped, searching for the words as she waved her hand in the air.

"Angry. The word is *angry*."

"It isn't you," she repeated. "It's what you represent."

"Success? Financial stability?" Time to lighten the mood. "Romantic temptation? Come on." He flashed the smile that had landed him on the cover of national magazines. "You've thought about it." He slipped his fingers through hers and watched as her chin dipped, as she looked at the way their hands joined.

Her lips twitched. "Being around you is nice, Declan. It's really nice."

"There's a *but* coming, isn't there?"

"A big one." She took a deep breath. "You're a risk. And seeing how you are, it hurts."

Dear Reader,

Since the first book, Butterfly Harbor has served as a healing haven. Over the course of the series, the small town has welcomed newcomers to its West Coast shores with open arms, offering refuge, affection and, for many, a new start. It has become, in a way, a character.

When Alethea Costas arrived, she was close to broken. Losing her lifelong best friend to a battle so many people have fought left her drifting and feeling more alone than she ever believed possible. How can she think about a future when she knows just how easily it can be taken away? The answer is simple: she can't.

Race car driver Declan Cartwright knows better than most how fragile life can be. He barely survived a crash that left his own future in the industry in serious doubt. But he's determined to make a comeback in every possible way. Nothing is going to stop him, even if the odds are stacked against him.

I've finally discovered what I love most about this small town I created years ago: Butterfly Harbor does the impossible, time after time. It heals broken hearts, uplifts and inspires.

Anna

HEARTWARMING

Worth the Risk

—

Anna J. Stewart

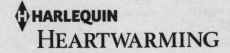

ⒽHARLEQUIN®
HEARTWARMING™

Recycling programs for this product may not exist in your area.

ISBN-13: 978-1-335-42655-0

Worth the Risk

Copyright © 2021 by Anna J. Stewart

All rights reserved. No part of this book may be used or reproduced in any manner whatsoever without written permission except in the case of brief quotations embodied in critical articles and reviews.

This is a work of fiction. Names, characters, places and incidents are either the product of the author's imagination or are used fictitiously. Any resemblance to actual persons, living or dead, businesses, companies, events or locales is entirely coincidental.

This edition published by arrangement with Harlequin Books S.A.

For questions and comments about the quality of this book, please contact us at CustomerService@Harlequin.com.

Harlequin Enterprises ULC
22 Adelaide St. West, 40th Floor
Toronto, Ontario M5H 4E3, Canada
www.Harlequin.com

Printed in U.S.A.

CHAPTER ONE

How was it, after nearly two years of living in the small town of Butterfly Harbor, California, Alethea Costas could still get lost?

The tires on Flutterby Wheels ground through the dirt and gravel of the unfamiliar winding road. She eased her foot off the gas, and slowed, her heart rate increasing as she realized she had absolutely no idea where she was.

She pulled the food truck over and stopped beneath a thick grove of eucalyptus and redwoods and sat back with a heavy sigh. "This is just ridiculous." It wasn't like she couldn't find her way back to town. All roads inevitably led there. It just irritated her how easily this had happened.

She reached up and tugged her ponytail tighter on top of her head, trying to shake loose the nerves that descended whenever she took a wrong turn in life. *Okay, get a grip.*

This wasn't a complete disaster. At least she'd gotten lost at the end of her deliveries and after she'd served the lunch rush at the butterfly sanctuary construction site this time.

Even if she was still on the clock, Chef Jason Corwin wasn't going to fire her. She'd made herself indispensable to her boss, especially now that Jason and his wife, Abby, had welcomed their baby boy. Little David Corwin, named after Jason's late twin brother, was proving to be a colic-prone handful and giving his parents a lot of sleepless nights.

On the bright side, the baby's arrival had given Alethea the chance to step up and prove herself. So far she'd been able to handle anything Jason had thrown at her, which left her boss to deal primarily with his restaurant at the Flutterby Inn. That could all change, however, if Jason decided the business plan for expansion, which Alethea had presented to him a few weeks before, moved forward.

Nerves of an entirely different kind fluttered to life. He had yet to respond to her proposal and sure, he'd had a lot on his mind and she definitely hadn't wanted to push, but they needed to strike now if they were going to locally expand Jason's brand and his offerings to a ravenous customer base.

She loved the hard work, the distracting work. The work that at times exhausted her to the point of oblivion and the need to think. Plus the overtime meant she'd just about saved enough money to finally move out of her brother and sister-in-law's place. With Xander and Calliope expecting their first child later this year and with Calliope's little sister living in the stone cottage on Duskywing Farm, things were getting quite cramped.

It was time, Alethea told herself, to move beyond the pain of what had brought her to Butterfly Harbor in the first place and begin again.

All she needed to do was get out of her own way.

"Easier said than done," she muttered and squinting into the late afternoon sun, leaned over the steering wheel and attempted to get her bearings. Her cell phone was stuck in perpetual search mode which meant she'd ended up in one of Butterfly Harbor's infamous dead zones. No surprise considering the dense trees growing up and around her. Her adopted town was known for its out-of-the-way areas, well off the beaten track, and hidey-holes far removed from anything resembling busy intersections and bustling crowds.

"Makes perfect sense I'd find this spot." Alethea tried to sound upbeat. "Okay, let's turn this puppy around and find our way home." With the engine rumbling again, she hit the gas and turned the wheel. Only to hear a heart-dropping double *pop* a second later.

Her foot came up slowly. The truck drifted to a stop. She held her breath. Nothing happened. Until the back of the vehicle lurched, sagged and slowly sank down and back.

"Oh, no," she whispered, fumbling with her seat belt, then, slid open the door to drop to the ground. She hurried around to the back of the truck. "No, no, no." She stood there, staring unblinkingly at the driver's side dual rear tires. "Okay, now you're just messing with me," she accused the universe at large. She knew how to change out a flat. On her own car. But she couldn't manage alone on this behemoth of a truck.

She took a long, deep breath. Nothing else she could do except find a signal for her cell phone, call Cal Mopton and pray he'd chosen today to actually come into the only garage and mechanic service Butterfly Harbor had to offer.

She jumped back into the truck and grabbed a light sweatshirt to tug on over her tie-dyed pink Flutterby Dreams T-shirt and jeans. Better safe than sorry. Even in mid-August, West Coast weather could be unpredictable, especially these days.

At least she was out in the middle of nowhere and didn't have to worry about blocking any traffic. The road was wide enough to get around the truck if any cars came by and judging by the state of the road, that hadn't happened in ages. She locked up Flutterby Wheels, took one last sorrowful look at her cell screen, then, turned and headed up the winding road.

Fifteen minutes later the road dead-ended. The shrubbery and trees had gotten thick enough that the sun could barely peek through. "Xander is never going to let me live this one down." Her brother was always making fun of her lack of direction. The older she got, the less funny she found it. Her learning curve on this subject was about as steep as an anthill.

She checked her watch. She wasn't due

home for dinner for another few hours, so no one would miss her before then. Alethea caught sight of her truck in the distance and hurried forward. Her foot caught on a tree root and sent her sprawling, facefirst, onto the ground. Her phone flew out of her hand. Her chin knocked hard against the earth. The sigh that erupted this time sounded more like a groan of frustration. She rolled onto her back, lying there, mortified, her chin throbbing, and stared up into the sky beyond the swaying treetops.

Someone up there, and she knew exactly who the someone would be, was definitely laughing at her. *Talia*. Tears that should have dried up ages ago burned in her throat. Alethea's vision blurred as grief escaped her control. Sometimes she missed her best friend so much she ached.

When she shoved herself up, she found leaves and debris caught in her ponytail and coating her shirt and sweatshirt. She grabbed her phone, stood and brushed herself off just as she heard the sound of an engine rumbling nearby. Alethea watched as up ahead, a delivery truck emerged from a thicket of trees so dense, it all but obscured the worn makeshift gravel road.

"Wait!" She raced forward, only to trip once again, although this time she stayed on her feet. By the time she caught her balance, the delivery truck was already heading down the hill and rumbling out of sight. She planted her hands on her hips and blew out a frustrated breath. "Clearly today is not the day to buy a lottery ticket."

Still, where there was a delivery, there was an address—an occupied address. She checked her cell phone one more time, then, when no bars appeared, watched where she stepped as she headed down the hill. She ducked into the cover of the trees, feeling a bit like she'd stepped into a storybook when, at the far end of the property, she spotted the house.

No wonder she'd missed it on her way up the hill. With the overgrown foliage, the area was as gloomy, dreary and sun-starved back here as the road she'd just come up. But that house…there was something other than the possibility of a phone that drew her closer.

Weeds and shrubs looked desperately thirsty as she crunched her way through the overgrown and neglected grass. It was such a shame, she thought, as she reached the musty pebbled path at the end of the flora. She brushed off burs and clinging dandelion puffs and sent them soaring into the air. This house, like so many others in town, was filled with potential and yet caught in time accentuated by neglect.

There was no sign of a car and, judging by the boxes stacked on the front porch, the occupant probably wasn't home.

The wraparound porch seemed oddly detached from the rest of the derelict area with a surprising bloom of healthy wisteria accenting the weathered white paint. The comforting roar of the ocean beckoned her forward, as if confirming she was safe.

The ocean, this town, had yet to steer her wrong. If she'd found this place, there was a reason and, even as she stepped up onto the creaky porch and found the door slightly ajar, cautious hope bloomed inside her.

She knocked, winced at the stark sound echoing through the silence. "Hello?" Hesitant but determined, Alethea took a solitary step inside, listening for a response or some sign of life. It would be easy enough to explain her presence here and even as she told herself to hurry, she couldn't help but let her curiosity about the place take over.

The wood floors were worn, stained and slightly warped. The flowered-and-striped paper covering the walls had turned yellow with age and sagged in spots, as if the house had given up. The staircase spindles on the steps leading to the second level were delicately turned and stained a dark brown to match the floors. The air was coated with the smell of dust, age and more than a recent hint of coffee and…was that chocolate? Her stomach rumbled.

"I'm not here to break in!" she called again and winced as her voice echoed back at her. "I just need a…phone." She spotted one on an old-fashioned stand at the base of the stairs. The cordless was probably older than she was, but when she picked it up and got a dial tone, she let out a breath she hadn't realized she'd been holding.

After accessing her cell's contact list, she called Cal Mopton's garage number. One ring. Four. Nine. When the voice mail picked up, she left a short message, but any hope she had of help from the town's only mechanic vanished. Hovering near defeat, she scrolled for another number and dialed. "Hi, Luke. It's Alethea." She plowed in before the town's sheriff had a chance to answer. "I hate to do this to you, but Cal isn't at his garage and the food truck blew both back left tires. There are spares at the inn by the back loading area. But I can't come get them and I can't change them out myself."

"Not a problem," Luke's usually calm tone managed to soothe some of her nerves. "I've got Matt and Fletcher both here. I'll grab one of them and the tires and head up your way. Where are you?"

"Um." She cringed again. "Hang on." She cupped the phone against her shoulder and glanced out the grimy window. "I honestly have no idea. If you know of some dead-end road at the top of a hill—wait. Hang on." She ducked down and opened the tiny cabinet door, rifled through it. "There's a phone book here." The spine cracked when she opened it. "Howser? I can't read the first name."

"The old Howser... Alethea? How did you end up all the way up there?"

"Talent?" For being an only child, Luke had mastered the irritated big brother tone. "I'll wait for you at the truck."

"Give us about a half hour."

Relieved, Alethea hung up, set the address book back in its spot and quickly left the house. At least she wouldn't be caught trespassing. Inside at least. She left the door as she'd found it.

She stepped off the porch and froze. She'd been hanging out with Jo and Kendall too long. She could swear she heard the whir of an electric drill. She walked to the edge of the porch, spotted the weathered oversize workshop shed that was bigger than the house. As she moved closer, music beat from inside, almost in tempo to the pulse of the power tools.

She curled her toes against the desire to explore further. She should just leave before anyone realized she'd been here. It wasn't the polite thing to do, especially now that she knew someone was actually here. And, well, there were few things in life that entertained her as much as a mystery or a surprise. And this house, this place and its invisible resident, was both.

"What's the worst that could happen?" The worst was she'd get thrown off the property for trespassing. The best? She'd make a new friend and Alethea was the kind of woman who could never have enough friends.

Moving across the large front yard was an adventure in tetanus avoidance. The property was a mess, from the overgrown yard to the tarp-covered something that had probably been a car in a previous life. Junk and debris, from car parts to plywood scraps, had piled up to the point of merging into an unidentifiable blob. Add in some nuclear waste and it would probably form into a comic book super villain.

The whirring continued, this time accompanying an energetic, male and very off-key declaration to "shake it off." Stifling a laugh, she approached the door and poked her head just inside.

A dark figure dropped straight down like a giant spider splayed on an industrial metal web.

Alethea yelped and jumped back. She'd have landed right on her butt if a large, rough hand hadn't reached out and caught hers. Rather than steadying her, she found herself yanked forward and into the solid embrace of her caterwauling mystery man.

"Oh, wow." She grabbed hold of his shoulders as he swayed, feet dangling a good few feet off the ground, at the end of a harness and pullied rope. His hold on her was steady, sturdy, and, as he shifted his grip, seemed to be sending tiny little shock waves rocketing through her system. She blinked, clearing the surprise from her eyes, and drew him into focus.

Long, shoulder-length, dark blond hair. A good three days' growth of beard covering what she suspected was a stone-carved jaw. His gray eyes reminded her of a summer storm, with lightning bolt sparks of amusement curving his full lips into an entertained smile. "Wow." She said again as the flush warmed her face.

"Sorry to scare you." He released her, reached down to unhook himself from the rope and still hung on to it while he lowered his feet to the ground. "Lost my hold on the rope. You all right?"

"I'm fine." She stepped back, tucked an invisible curl behind her ear and shoved her suddenly shaky hands into her pockets. His voice carried a hint of the South and coated her roughened heart like smooth molasses. She took a deep breath and wondered when the combination of leather, sawdust and sweat had become appealing? "I called out from the house." She had to shout over the music. "But I guess you didn't hear me." She inclined her chin toward the Bluetooth speaker that continued to blare. "Nice music."

He tapped his watch and the music stopped. "I get easily sucked in." He unholstered his drill from his waistband as if it were a sidearm and blew on the bit, set it on a nearby crate. "But the job's nearly done. What do you think?"

"About what?" She blinked again. Had she missed their introductions?

"That." He pointed behind her and when she turned away from the miasma of tools and yet another hodgepodge of debris and what she assumed was discarded junk, she found half of the east wall covered in plywood and what looked like dozens of handles in varying sizes, colors and shapes. The fact the man continued to dangle from a rope that extended down from the rafters didn't seem to phase him one bit.

Alethea looked up the length of the wall. "It's a rock climbing wall." The boards reached all the way to the roofline, a good twenty feet off the ground. Her head spun at the thought. "A really big one."

"It is indeed." His grin had her swallowing hard. Good-looking men didn't normally throw her; half the time she was too busy to notice or care, but this man...whew. He could stop traffic with that smile of his. "I've pre-drilled holes so I can readjust the climbing holds when it gets too easy. Need to keep it challenging. Want to give it a try?"

"Not particularly." Personally, Alethea had never really seen the point of rock climbing inside. Not that she understood the appeal of climbing outside. Both seemed unnecessarily risky to her. "I'm sorry to intrude. My food truck blew two tires and I needed a phone to call for help. My cell doesn't work up here."

"Food truck?" His eyebrows arched and disappeared beneath the smooth hair that swept over his eyes. "What brings you up to my little corner of the world?"

Hearing echoes of her conversation with the local sheriff, Alethea kept her sigh to herself. "I took a wrong turn."

"Must be my lucky day, then."

Alethea found herself locked into that

million-watt smile of his. Either she was seriously out of touch or he was flirting with her.

If he found her silence to be a deterrent, it didn't show. He lowered himself to the ground and, after a moment, found his footing before he sat on a nearby stool. "At least if you'd gotten stranded out here you wouldn't have starved." He unbuckled himself from the line and cast it away. "There's a phone in the house. You're welcome to—"

"I already used it." She grimaced at his raised brow. "Sorry. I saw the door was open and didn't want to…"

He waved her off, grabbed a bottle of water and slugged half of it down. "Don't worry about it. Glad I could help. I'm Declan, by the way." He set the water down, offered the same hand he'd caught her in before. "Declan Cartwright. And my mama and sisters always taught me to help a lady in distress."

Her eye twitched. She hadn't been in distress. Exactly. "Alethea. Costas," she said, adding her last name when his expression clearly asked for more information. "I should be heading back to my truck. The sheriff's coming up to help me change the tires so… thanks for the unwitting assist." He got to his feet as she turned to leave. It took that long for his name to sink in. "Declan Cartwright." She spun around as he reached for the telescopic walking stick he tucked around his arm. "But he's…you're—" Alethea trailed off as he adjusted the cane's cuff around the back of his arm, grasped the handle. "I thought I heard—"

"I'm not dead." That smile of his dimmed. "Should be from what the doctors said. A testament to modern medicine but if you ask my sisters, it's due to a stubborn streak that only a baby brother can have."

Declan Cartwright. One of the most successful race car drivers of the past decade. If it had an engine and a steering wheel, he could drive it. And drive it fast. And fast was not limited to the racetrack. The man had a reputation for collecting girlfriends like she collected recipes. At least he'd had that reputation until last year. He'd not only crashed shortly after the start of the first race of the season, he'd left the entire world wondering if he'd be extricated from the wreck alive. Even nonracing fans like herself had been glued to social media waiting for word of his condition, only to have him fade from the headlines when it became clear his future in the sport was over.

She repressed a shudder. The video of the crash had gone viral. Rumor had it Vegas had been laying odds on his chance for survival. When even Vegas bets against you, your future is seriously in doubt. "What are you doing in Butterfly Harbor?"

"Recovering." He lifted his cane off the ground. "Don't let this fool you. It's more for mental security than physical stability. I'll walk you out."

She was already scrambling for an excuse. "No, that's okay, you don't have—"

"I'll walk you out." It was like watching a snowstorm freeze everything in its path as he moved past her. That tone left no room for argument and it wasn't one she felt comfortable challenging. His limp was barely noticeable, but after a year, it was evident his extensive injuries were still just that.

"I'm sorry," she said as she joined him outside. "I didn't mean—"

"Forget it." And just like that, his welcoming expression was back in place. "I've been alone up here for too long. Clearly I've forgotten how to interact with people."

"How long have you been here?"

"A couple of weeks. I'm only staying until I can go back on the circuit."

"You're going back?" Shocked, Alethea stopped walking. Arms crossed over her chest, she balked. "To driving? After what happened to you? But you almost died."

"The key word is *almost*." He pivoted, far more elegantly than she would have anticipated.

He was a beautifully made man and while he displayed the telltale signs of a significant weight loss, there was a surprising, healthy quality about him.

"I'm still here," Declan continued. "Which means I have a second chance. I don't plan on wasting it."

Wasting it would be tempting fate and possibly getting himself killed. Alethea bit the inside of her cheek. It wasn't any of her business if the man wanted to squander all the possibilities a second chance brought with it. Second chances were a rare thing. Most people who deserved them didn't get them. Clearly he was grateful for his, but that wouldn't stop her from thinking he was dead wrong about what he was going to do with it.

They were standing in front of the house now and here, in the late afternoon sun of a perfect California summer's day, she could see what had made Declan Cartwright such a success both on and off the track. Charisma and affability aside, and he had truckloads of both, his entire presence was charged, like a force field he could flip on and off. She could only imagine what the Butterfly Harbor rumor mill was going to do with and about him once word leaked out who was living in their midst. And it would leak out. It was only a matter of time.

"It was nice to meet you." She didn't offer her hand. Instead, she tightened her hold on her waist and squeezed harder. "Thank you again for the assist."

He leaned on his cane and tilted his head, that glorious hair of his falling rakishly over one eye. "Feel free to fall into my arms at any time."

She would not blush. She would not… Her cheeks went bonfire hot.

She forced herself to keep her eyes front and center as she moved through the weeds and overgrown grass, to not look back. But she could feel his eyes on her. Incredible eyes.

Deep. Teasing. Entrancing. Ridiculous, she told herself. She didn't understand daredevils, risk-takers who dived in headfirst for nothing more than the thrill. But her reticence didn't stop the pressure from building inside her, like a balloon of attraction being inflated by the desire to see those eyes again.

She surrendered, and glanced over her shoulder.

He grinned, as if he'd been waiting for her to do just that, then, waved and made his way up the porch steps.

THE LAST THING Declan had expected to deal with today was an armful of feminine temptation.

Clearly his time in Butterfly Harbor was looking up to be more entertaining than expected.

Humming on his way into the house, he made a mental note to retrieve his deliveries after he'd brewed a new batch of iced tea. He'd need the caffeine boost to return the latest round of text messages from his sisters. One of the good things about spotty cell reception up here—he had an excuse as to why he wasn't getting their calls.

The soreness in his muscles began to settle in. He'd overdone it again. He'd been lectured by his PTs and his doctors about the hazards of doing too much too soon, but after almost a year…

There was no too soon. No matter how much his body pushed back.

As long as he was in this forced holding pattern, he was going to keep going, even if he paid for it at night.

He'd wanted to accomplish something of substance while he was here, although his definition of substance probably differed from most other people's. He'd wanted to get the climbing wall finished so he could start his new workout routine. Building up his upper body strength as well as his dexterity with his legs was going to get him into better shape for when he met with a specialist in a few weeks. He needed off the cane, off the meds and back on his own two feet. It was the only way he was going to get to where he belonged: behind the wheel.

Driving, and only driving would make him feel whole again. And he was darn tired of feeling like half himself.

Not that a pretty woman wouldn't help motivate him along the way.

He had some time to qualify for the season finale race. Some, but not a lot. Hopefully enough to leave the last year and a half completely in the rearview mirror for good and move forward. He had team members, family members and his own future riding on a return. Failure was definitely not an option.

He flexed his stiff hands. It would just take more work but work and Declan were old friends.

While he'd leased the place for three months, his plan had been to be here a week, maybe two. But waiting for an appointment with one of the best thoracic surgeons in the country meant waiting on the doctor's schedule and for the last month and a half, that doctor was making her way home to San Francisco through Africa where she was visiting various medical clinics to offer her expertise.

An appointment could come tomorrow, or it could come next week or even next month. And while there were other doctors he could see in the meantime, Dr. Yvonne Kenemen's word was gold. If he got her approval to return to racing, they'd have to let him back in. Whatever treatment she recommended, whatever he needed to do to pass her inspection, he was darn well going to get it done.

In the meantime, rather than going home to Illinois and dealing with his family and friends coddling and placating him, he'd called an old friend and asked for a recommendation on where he could recuperate in relative peace and wait.

Said accommodations also came with a warning about the interest his arrival in Butterfly Harbor would cause. According to his friend, they could ferret out new residents like a bloodhound after a deer. They could be just as tenacious when it came to uncovering and unearthing every little detail about new residents, which meant his solitary confinement was definitely over.

Gossip and small towns. He chuckled and shook his head. They were all the same. He'd spent a good deal of his early life dreaming of escaping the one he'd grown up in. When his father had died and his mother found a job just outside Chicago, their lives—and Declan's world perspective—had changed. Ironic he'd chosen another small town to recuperate. And wait for his life to get back on track.

That said, if he'd known the welcoming committee would be anything like Alethea Costas, he might have been more eager to engage. He added sugar to the oversize mason jar, tasted, added a bit more, along with some lemon slices, then, feeling pretty secure that his left leg would support his weight, abandoned the walking stick and moved the jar into the fridge.

The strain had his hands shaking, but he pushed through, flexing his fingers even as he retrieved his stick and, after trudging to the door, his deliveries. His body definitely had its own ideas. He could go days at a stretch sometimes without a twinge of discomfort while other days it felt as if he'd been lit on fire from the inside. It was his legs that worried him the most. Mobility and agility were key to racing. Without those two things, his career, his life, would be over.

He opened the box that contained climbing gloves, a new harness, and collection of ropes and carabiners. The helmet had been in acquiescence to his oldest sister, Marcy's, concern about him being determined to break his neck—one of the parts of him that hadn't been damaged in the crash. Only after the threat of not one, or even two, but *all* of his sisters turning up on his doorstep had he surrendered and promised not only to order one, but to wear it.

One thing his sisters knew; if he promised something, he meant it. Not that he had a choice. He'd always been incapable of lying to them. Whatever tell he had, those six women knew if even the tiniest fib crossed his lips, and they refused to let him in on the secret.

The familiar pang of loneliness and a longing for his family struck quick, but he dismissed it with practiced ease. Long stretches on the road, traveling the circuit and earning his racing stripes had meant weeks, but more likely months went by before he saw his family. It was part of the grind, and one of the deals you make getting into the sport. His sending the emotion away didn't mean he didn't love them any less, only that he appreciated them even more when he did see them.

He'd definitely gotten his fill of sisterly protection and attention over the past year. Enough that he had stored up that appreciation to get him through multiple future racing seasons.

Picking up the second box—a new WiFi router and circuit board for his ancient laptop, he found himself looking back toward the path his visitor this afternoon had walked down.

Watching Alethea Costas stroll away from him was as close to a dream state as he'd let himself entertain in recent months and he'd definitely enjoyed the moment. Not to mention the view.

He'd wondered if those sparks he'd felt when he'd held her hand had been one-sided. One thing that hadn't been damaged in the crash was his ego. He'd been this close to convinced she wasn't interested until she looked back at him before she hurried out of sight.

Even from a distance, that blushing color on her cheeks would warm him on cold nights. Not that this part of California, a hop, skip, and a jump from Monterey, got particularly chilly. She didn't wear a ring, but these days that didn't mean anything. Although he felt pretty secure in believing she was on the single lady list. And didn't that just make his entire day.

He was a man who appreciated faces and figures and hers were classic, curvy and downright stunning. Her thick, curling and slightly frizzy black hair had been caught back from her face and strewn with leaves and twigs. Her chin was scraped as if she'd had a tussle with the ground and lost. Her rainbow-bright T-shirt and worn jeans placed her somewhere between the girl next door and curvaceous Hollywood ingenue with star potential bursting beneath the surface.

But it was those eyes of hers—those ocean blue eyes flashing with distant recognition that, had he not been suspended from a rope hanging from the ceiling, he might have been knocked off his feet from the sight. She had layers, endless deep layers of complexity he wanted to peel back and uncover.

He wanted to memorize the image, but focused on being able to remember the feel of the rough skin of her hand that spoke of hard work. She'd gripped his hand so tightly, so perfectly, he hadn't been in any rush to let go. Even now, his fingers tingled at the prospect of touching her again. It was a nice change from the pinprick tingles that had been excruciating when he'd first woken up in the hospital. Nerve damage, the doctors had said. Temporary, they'd hoped. There hadn't been a part of him that didn't hurt, even after two weeks in a coma.

Days like this, days that offered up an introduction to a woman like Alethea had him feeling even more lucky to be alive. Up until now all his time and effort had been spent pushing through his recovery, regaining his strength, mobility and dexterity and being in top form for whenever he met with Dr. K.

Now he could add another goal to his growing list: finding an excuse to see Alethea Costas again.

"You two are my heroes." Alethea pushed off the hood of the sheriff's SUV as Deputy Fletcher Bradley and Sheriff Luke Saxon tightened the final lug nut on the second replacement tire they'd brought with them. "Seriously, that probably would have cost me a fortune if Cal had answered his phone."

"Won't argue on that point." Luke, rising to his full height, swiped a hand over his damp forehead. Grease smudges dotted the khaki uniform shirt he wore and coated his hands.

"Cal's gotten a little cost prohibitive with his repairs and service calls."

"Man's been running that service station longer than I've been alive," Fletcher, a life-long resident of Butterfly Harbor, agreed. Taller, lankier and more easygoing than his boss, Fletcher had a natural way of evoking smiles and cheery conversation. "Cal's hoping if he prices himself out of business he can retire free and clear."

"Yeah, well, no one's going to buy his business if he's lost all his customers," Luke added. "It's not the building people invest in—it's the clientele. Not to mention the convenience and as much as I'm happy to help, the sheriff's department isn't set up for vehicular assistance on a long-term basis."

"Personally I'm glad Cal didn't answer," Alethea declared. "And you guys get free lunch from the truck for a week. It's the least I can do," Alethea added at Luke's coming protest.

"Is that offer transferable?" Fletcher asked with hope in his California-blue eyes when he looked at her. "I would love to get Paige out of the house with the baby if at all possible."

"Absolutely." She always had plenty of food

left over after her lunch rush and the idea of seeing Fletcher and Paige's new baby girl would be a bonus. "I'll even toss in a few nights of Charlie-sitting if you two are so inclined." Fletcher's eleven-year-old stepdaughter was one of her favorite distractions and Alethea, having earned her share of big sister rights with a number of the kids in town, took every opportunity she could to spend time with the red-headed little sprite.

"You do know an evening with you creates more problems than it solves, right?" Fletcher gathered up their tools and stashed them in the back of the SUV. "Every time she hangs out with you she's ready to become a chef. Our kitchen can't survive another attempt at her learning to cook. Last time she set off the smoke alarm boiling pasta."

"Sounds like she's been taking lessons from her Aunt Abby, not me." Alethea laughed. Her boss's wife was notorious for her rather indelicate ineptitude in the culinary aspect of life and had earned the nickname Five Alarm Manning. Personally Alethea thought the woman's kitchen ineptitude would make for an endlessly entertaining TV series or movie. "I'll recruit Jo or Sienna to join us for a girls' night," Alethea volunteered. "Maybe expand Charlie's interest in construction or event planning and invite some of her friends." She made a mental note to put it on her to do list.

"Jo's going to need a replacement herself pretty soon," Luke said. "Ozzy said she's about ready with that baby of hers."

"Six weeks and counting," Alethea confirmed, a bubble of excitement bursting inside her for her friends. Butterfly Harbor had attracted a lot of different people in recent years, herself included. Jo Bertoletti, who had quickly become the focus of firefighter Ozzy Lakeman's affection, had been the most recent. She frowned. That wasn't true anymore, was it?

"That reminds me, I need to call Holly." Luke pulled out his phone, started to dial.

Alethea jumped on that statement. "Is Holly pregnant again?" He was a great husband and dad.

"What?" For a town sheriff, the man could sure pale in a panic. "No, my wife is not pregnant. At least, I don't think…" His throat actually tightened to the point Alethea could see him swallow. For an instant he looked like he'd been caught in headlights. "I just need to touch base about the twins. I'm supposed to pick them up at the diner in about a half hour. Darn." He lifted the phone, turned in a circle. "No signal." He frowned at Alethea. "What magic phone do you have that you could call me?"

"Oh, um. There's a phone at the Howser place." She shrugged. "I used that one."

"The old Howser place?" Fletcher slammed the back of the department's SUV closed. "No one's lived in that house for years."

"New tenant," Luke said a bit too absently. "Friend of mine leased it for a few months."

Alethea started to respond, but realized Luke hadn't elaborated or given any details. Any pleasure she might have gotten from sharing new gossip and information faded as she realized Declan Cartwright had come here to recover, not be the subject of town rumors and chitchat. "Since when?" Fletcher balked, his sun-kissed handsome face clouding with surprise. "Did it sell? I didn't realize Gil put it on the market."

"He didn't. Not yet." Luke still wasn't looking either of them in the eye. "The renter's a friend of a friend of mine and he needed a place to crash. I'm sure you'll meet him soon.

He's a people person, so he'll be starving for some societal interaction." Now he looked at Alethea with a silent plea, asking her to back him up.

"Guy got a name?" Fletcher asked, clearly not fooled by the looks Alethea and Luke were exchanging.

"He does," Alethea confirmed. Then pressed her lips into a tight line and smiled.

"Riiiight." Fletcher sighed. "Guess I'll just have to wait and see along with everyone else." But it was clear the idea of being out of the loop didn't appeal. "You're all set to go," he told her as he and Luke climbed back into their SUV. A few minutes later, engine rumbling and new tires fully inflated, she followed them down the hill.

CHAPTER TWO

"KNOCK KNOCK."

The rap of knuckles on the door of the workshop had Declan tightening his grip on one of the holds of his climbing wall. He carefully craned his neck and looked down to see who it was. "Hey, Luke." He glanced at his watch and realized he'd been at this for a few hours. No wonder his arms were burning and his back was throbbing. "Give me a sec."

Declan grabbed hold of his safety harness and pushed himself off the wall with both feet, using the latch on one of the pulleys to lower himself to the ground.

"What on earth is all this?" Luke Saxon looked every bit his sheriff self, from his uniform khakis, to his baseball cap displaying the Butterfly Harbor Police Department logo. To the concern marring his brow. "You turning this place into a gym? You aren't overdoing things, are you?"

"You sound like Marcy," Declan grumbled, thinking of the text exchange he'd had with his oldest sister last night. "And yes on the gym, actually." Declan looked around the cluttered area. "The space needs a bit of a cleanout, but I started with that. You said it was okay to add in some amenities."

Luke shrugged, scrubbed a hand across his chin. "Obviously our definitions of amenities differ."

"What brings you by?"

"A few things, but this first." Luke reached into his back pocket, pulled out a folded-up piece of paper and handed it to Declan. "His name's Christopher Russo. We've had some trouble with him around town. Vandalism, assault. He's wanted in questioning for arson."

"Arson?" Declan's eyes went wide as he accepted the person-of-interest flyer. "Small-town surprises, huh?"

"Something like that." Luke didn't look amused. "It's complicated, but just so you're aware. Up here, it's pretty isolated. Would make for a good place for him to hide out. You haven't noticed anything odd around here since you moved in, have you? Broken locks? Busted windows? Stolen food or provisions?"

"No. The place is so quiet I can hear my cells multiplying." He stared at the man's picture, memorized the face. "If I see him, I'll definitely let you know."

"Thanks."

"You want coffee?"

Luke's sigh of gratitude was beyond familiar. "Always."

"Great. Come on in to the house." Declan led the way, again, using the walking stick as a precaution rather than for actual balance. Sometimes after climbing, stairs or walls, he had vertigo issues.

"This place really is like a time warp, isn't it?" Luke followed him out of the workshop and into the house, where they were greeted with the scarred wooden floors and oddly striped flowered wallpaper. "That pattern must give you a headache."

"It has its charm." More importantly, the house had what Declan needed: privacy and a place to focus on getting back in shape. "Getting around has definitely been a workout of its own." The hallways were narrow, the stairs steep and the rooms on the small size, especially for a man of his six foot plus height. Rather than finding it all annoying, the situation made him laugh. One side effect of having nearly died was being able to put all of life's little annoyances firmly out of mind.

While Declan put a pot of coffee on to brew—none of those silly single serving pods for him, Luke stood at the sink and gazed out the window overlooking the wilderness of the surrounding yard. It was replete with a broken-down, fixer-upper car that Declan was pretty sure had been parked out by the workshop for longer than he had been alive. That car's restoration...if he had his way, was going to be his reward for reaching his next therapy milestone.

"You talk to Marcy lately?" Luke's unreadable expression didn't shift as he turned to accept a steaming mug.

Declan shrugged. "Does texting count? Why?" Knowing his sister would go out of her way to prevent him from worrying about her—yet another spot of irony in his life, he frowned. "Have you heard from her? Did something happen? Is she okay? The kids? Roscoe?"

Luke waved off his concern. "She called last night to check in. She's fine. Husband and kids are fine. Loud from what I heard."

He grinned as Declan used his good hand to pull out his own chair. "She's got a houseful, doesn't she?"

"Five of them. All under eight." Declan felt an odd pang of…something chime deep inside his chest. One of the first thoughts he'd had after the crash was that he regretted not being a father. Being an uncle was one thing, but he wanted that connection. More than he'd realized. But one lesson he'd learned early in his career: racing and having a family was a mix he did not want to experiment with. "Marcy always wanted a big family. At one point I think she planned to give our mother a run for her money, but that would take things too far, even for Marcy"

Luke's eyes took on a somewhat glazed look. "I only have three. I give thanks for the woman I married every single day. Especially now that the twins are running around at warp speed. Good thing their big brother is an expert wrangler."

"How old is Simon now?"

"Almost twelve. And that's no joke of an age," Luke chuckled. "He's turned his big brotherhood into a long-term school science experiment. He constantly devises new containment plans and the twins just zip right past or through them." The affectionate smile on the sheriff's face made Declan's stomach tighten. "My boy does love a challenge. He also spends all his spare time with his nose in a book or a screen." His smile dimmed a bit. "Wish I could get him out and doing more physical activities, but I've learned to pick my battles."

His boy. Declan's lips twitched at the obvious affection Luke held for his stepson. Declan didn't know much about Luke's life here in Butterfly Harbor other than the fact that he'd accepted the town sheriff's position a few years ago and soon after married the local diner owner. Now he had those three children and seemed as content and happy as any man had a right to be. "So why did Marcy call you to check up on me?"

Luke shrugged. "She's worried about you. And I've never known your sister to be an alarmist."

Declan had to agree. Marcy had worked with Luke on an after-school program in Chicago back when Luke had been on the community's police detail. They'd given dating a shot, which was how Declan and Luke met, but Marcy had lamented on more than one occasion that she and Luke were destined to be just friends. That didn't mean, however, that his sister didn't get an entertaining tint to her cheeks whenever the topic of Luke Saxon came up.

"Marcy can't be what brought you out here. If it's to tell me my cover's been blown, I am well aware."

"Yeah, Alethea." Luke sighed and scrubbed a hand against the side of his neck. "Sorry about that."

"Don't be." Declan shrugged again. Alethea. A beautiful name. Matched the beautiful young woman with all those curls and curves and a smile that could light up a moonless midnight. She had a mouth that was made for sweet kisses on a hot summer's evening. "I guess that means you're here to tell me she's outed me to the rest of the town."

"No, actually." Luke seemed surprised himself. "That would be due to one of my deputies, who got a bee in his bonnet and did some poking around. He doesn't have your name. Yet," Luke warned. "But your presence has definitely been the main topic of conversation at the diner which means the rest of the town isn't far behind."

"Being diner gossip has always been a dream of mine. Seriously, Luke. Don't worry about it." Declan shrugged it off. "I'm looking forward to meeting everyone. Just hope none of them get too attached to me."

Luke laughed at Declan's grin. "Well, that's one attitude to take. You hear from the doctor's office?"

"Not yet." Declan had never been good with waiting, which meant he needed distractions. Good thing this property, house and workshop needed repair. He hadn't even been given the all clear to drive on regular streets yet, which meant wherever he went, he was trapped.

There was a reason Declan felt most comfortable in a vehicle—any kind of vehicle. Because they were how you got places beyond where you were. And Declan was a man who was always looking to the horizon. "I'm better now than I was when I got here. I can feel it." He knocked a fist against his thigh as if to wake it up. "I don't need that thing quite so much." He gestured to the cane standing by the door. "As long as I get the okay from

Dr. Kenemen in the next six weeks or so, I should be able to get back up and training for the final qualifying run in November." It wasn't a lot of time, but it was enough. That was all Declan asked for. "You're really going to go for that comeback after what happened?"

It wasn't disbelief Declan heard in Luke's voice, but concern. The same concern he heard from his sisters, from his doctors, and most recently, Alethea Costas.

"A man's got to have goals," Declan told him. "Racing's all I know, Luke. It's not only home, it's where I belong. I know that as surely as I know that refrigerator of mine is about running on empty. Aiming to get back on the circuit gives me something to work on. Work toward."

The rest of that thought would remain his secret. When he didn't have something to focus on, that's when the doubt crept in. Doubt and the unbridled terror of what his life would be without the sport that had given him the life and financial security he had.

"You've done a lot more than race. You have your charity and foundation. Not to mention your patent on that new hybrid engine that's set a new standard and level of conservation to anyone coming into the sport. There's more to you than what you do behind the wheel."

Including new regulations and medical guidelines racing officials had put in place because of his accident. But Declan didn't want to think about those. He wanted to focus on the one thing that made him feel alive.

"That patent was a fluke." A fluke that had set him up well enough that he could take care of himself, along with his sisters and their families for the rest of their lives. "I blew up more engines than the number that ended up working out."

All this talk about racing had memories circling like a pace car. Even now, he could smell that ghostly, adrenaline inducing, air-clinging scent of hot oil on the asphalt track. He missed it. So much. Racing to him had been like oxygen to the lungs. From sunup to sundown, the only things he'd thought about, the only things he'd dreamed about, were cars, racing, and that addictive checkered flag.

Chills raced down his spine, reminding him of the adrenaline rush waiting for him when he got back onto that speedway. "At least I found out that I do like that side of things. The mechanics of it. The puzzling things out. Making things work that shouldn't or don't want to. It's a challenge."

"That actually brings me to the main reason I stopped by." Luke finished his coffee and got to his feet, carried his cup to the sink. "Something Alethea said the other day got me to thinking. Back when I spoke to the mayor about you renting this place, he mentioned some plans he'd been making for it. Refurbishing it, inside and out. I bet I can talk him into turning it into a rental property for the town, use it for promotional and advertising opportunities."

"It would be ideal for that." Declan agreed. "Let me guess. Now your mayor wants me out."

"No. No, Gil was more than happy to have three months' lease on the place. Especially with what you paid. He's already agreed to set that money aside to put toward the rehab. So to speak," Luke added with a quick grin. "The thing is, he kind of jumped ahead and already talked to someone about doing the work. And I don't exactly have time to oversee the project."

"With a wife and three kids and your job?" Declan shook his head and rolled his eyes. "I wouldn't think so."

"Exactly," Luke said. "Kendall and Jo, it's their company that'll be doing the updates. They're both great and don't need much oversight, just a point person on the planning stages. Since we don't have to worry about them inflating the costs or cutting corners or whatever, I was thinking, given you've been living here, and know it better than anyone. So you'd have valuable feedback for changes that could help make it be accessible for everybody. You'd be great for the job. Construction wouldn't start until after you move on. So no dust, dirt or noise."

Tempting. Surprisingly so. It would give him something additional to focus on, something new to challenge himself with. Even better, it gave him the opportunity to be something he hadn't been in months: useful. "The only restoration or refurbishment experience I have is limited to under the hood of a car."

"You won't need any. Kendall and Jo are

experts. You present your ideas, they decide if they'll work. It might mean a little preliminary work and a few visits from both of them and some of their crew—"

"I've dealt with worse. It would also throw me right into the community fire. How soon are we talking?"

"This week, maybc? Jo's expecting a baby pretty soon so I can't imagine they'll be here every day." Luke added, "I'd consider it a personal favor if you'd say yes."

"Now that's just firing the big guns at me." Declan sighed overdramatically and shook his head. "You know a good Southern boy like myself isn't going to say no to a friend asking a favor."

"Yeah." Luke smiled. "Marcy might have mentioned something about that."

His entire life was the result of impulsive, sometimes reckless decisions; it made sense that he'd agree to this on the spot. "Since you've opened the door, I'm going to jump right in and mention the cell service up here is nonexistent. And don't get me started on internet and WiFi."

"Yeah, not much we can do about the cell phones," Luke murmured. "Internet, on the other hand, it's just a matter of calling around and—"

"Just making sure we're on the same page. I'll start calling around about installation tomorrow."

"And just like that the pressure is off." Luke held out his hand. "I appreciate this more than I can say."

Declan could see that; he could feel it in the handshake they exchanged before Luke left. A few minutes after the door closed, Declan was wandering around the lower level of the house, seeing things with a new, critical eye. The narrow hallways and doorways were definitely a problem and would need to be addressed. Fortunately, there was room to expand, to knock down walls, to make it far more livable for anyone who might want to stay here.

It wasn't until he'd circled back to the kitchen and poured himself another cup of coffee that he realized Luke had given him a gift. Something that gave him what everyone needed in their life: purpose.

It wasn't a huge thing; it was barely a little thing. This wouldn't change his life or his world or much of anything else, but helping with this project would give him a reason to get up in the morning.

And for now that would be more than enough.

"OKAY, LET'S SEE how this goes." With mild trepidation, Alethea slid the chipped crock-cry bowl draped with a towel, into the oven to allow her latest attempt at dough to rise. While she'd mastered many things in the kitchen, yeast had proven to be her nemesis.

Conquering breads, rolls and buns was close to the top of the self-challenge portion of her to-do list; a list she'd been keeping for the better part of two years. A list that gave her something to focus on when the nights were sleepless, long, and at times, unending.

"See you in an hour," she whispered to the dough before closing the oven door. Her distraction and focus on her list and prep work for tomorrow's menu for the truck had absolutely nothing to do with her unabated curiosity about one Declan Cartwright. That darned curiosity streak of hers just wouldn't let it—or him—be. His friendship with Luke seemed odd; she couldn't fathom where the two of them might have met given Declan had no connection to law enforcement that she'd ever heard. Of course it wouldn't take much time to do an internet search and find out one way or the other, but she was not going to waste her time looking into the past of a man who held absolutely no interest for her.

"Keep telling yourself that," she practically sang under her breath as she gathered up the ingredients for tomorrow's selection of sauces. She wasn't so detached from reality that she didn't notice her long-dormant hormones had reignited the second he'd touched her. Dating anyone had dropped far off her radar even before she'd left school. Before... She swallowed hard. Before Talia had died. She hadn't had any inclination to even consider a social life outside the trusted circle of friends she'd formed.

She blew out a breath, gave herself a hard mental shake. Irritation pushed the tingle of attraction out of her system. Despite her determination to put him completely out of her mind, Declan Cartwright had managed to wiggle his way into her overactive and sleep-starved brain.

As she chopped and sorted and began to sauté, she found herself once again giving thanks that her brother had taken that design job in Butterfly Harbor a few years back. Saving Costas Architecture had been first and foremost in his mind, and he'd certainly never had any intention of moving here permanently let alone getting married and settling down with Calliope Jones. For purely selfish reasons, she was thrilled life had taken some turns for him. She'd not only found a place to start over, she'd expanded her sister circle by two, and found a career she'd never expected to have.

A career working as a sous-chef for one of the top chefs in the country: a chef who had himself started over in this town. Jason Corwin had taken her in, taught her, guided her and now trusted her with helping him expand his business into the food truck industry. The nerves she kept in check during the day escaped in the dead of night. If the business plans she'd submitted to him were approved, a new casual restaurant to complement the more elegant fare of Flutterby Dreams could be her next big project.

She stopped chopping, looked up and out of the large window over the counter and kitchen sink. The moon shone down on her, bathing her in the promise of a new day, and, hopefully, new possibilities.

After a long week, she was taking it easy on herself tomorrow with, among her usual fare, a slow-cooker pulled pork with a choice of sauces, one of which was beginning to simmer now.

Wrist deep in garlic and onions, she felt rather than heard Calliope step into the kitchen. There was a certain charge that struck whenever Calliope entered a room. Electric and calming at the same time. Alethea glanced over her shoulder and up at the clock. "Oh, no." One thirty in the morning. "I didn't wake you, did I?"

"No." Her sister-in-law, tall, curvy, barefoot as usual, and wearing tiny fairy bells woven through her long, curly red hair, drifted into the room as if on a cloud, her usual peaceful, comforting expression in place. "No, your future niece or nephew did that all on their own." Her rounded stomach that stretched her sleeveless white nightdress should have prevented her from moving gracefully, but there was little Calliope Costas didn't do with a touch of elegance and poise.

There wasn't a hint of pregnancy stress

about her, not from the tip of her nose to the tops of her slightly swollen bare toes. She approached, rested a hand on Alethea's arm and took a deep breath. "Although it does appear as if the baby has an affinity for..." She narrowed her eyes at the ingredients lining the kitchen counter. "Barbecue sauce?"

Alethea grinned. "Two sauces, actually. One will have a bit of jalapeño kick."

"I'm having plenty of those these days." Calliope retrieved the kettle from the back of the stove and set it to heat. "These late nights of yours are becoming a habit."

Her sister-in-law had a way of loading a casual statement with observation, amusement and concern. Alethea glanced at the clock over the stove. "Sorry about that. Lately I think better at night."

"Some might call this morning," Calliope said with a knowing smile. "Trouble sleeping again? You know I have some herbs to help with that if you'd like."

Alethea didn't answer and instead focused her attention on sautéing the veggies, then, on measuring out the dried herbs and spices. It wasn't that she couldn't sleep. Exactly. It was more that she didn't want to. The last time she'd slept through the night she'd awakened sobbing and clinging to a past that had turned to fog in her mind. A past she would give anything in the world to change. All the more reason for her to move into her own place. She didn't like the idea of worrying Calliope, especially during this time. "I'm fine."

"Of course you are." Calliope retrieved one of her homemade tea bags from the shelf near the sink, pulled down her favorite mug, a crooked turquoise one with too thick a handle and a sagging lip. Stella, Calliope's twelve-year-old sister, had made one for all of them shortly after Alethea had moved to Butterfly Harbor. While Alethea kept hers filled with freshly clipped flowers by her bed and Xander kept his in his office in town, Calliope drank from hers every day yet took such care of it one would think it was cast from gold and studded with rare jewels. "Xander said you have something to talk to me about," Calliope mentioned. "Perhaps talking now would help ease your mind?"

"Oh. Yeah, well. Maybe I guess." Alethea turned down the heat under the pot. She wiped her hands on the towel tucked into the tie of her apron. "It's no big deal. It's just…"

she should have prepared better for this. She should have realized Calliope—whether aided by Xander or not—would know something was up. "With the baby coming and space being what it is here, it's time I found a place of my own. Out from under your feet."

"I see." Calliope pulled the kettle from the flame before it could whistle. "I thought you liked babies."

"I love babies and you know it." Alethea rolled her eyes. Sometimes Calliope was so much like Alethea's mother and other older sisters back in Chicago it was, well, almost irritating. "And I already love this one." She reached out and touched her fingers to Calliope's stomach, felt a flutter that had her heart tightening. "It's just my room is perfect for the nursery and you'll be wanting to get that in order. And, well." She shrugged.

"And you'd love to be able to cook in the middle of the night without being interrogated by your nosy sister-in-law." Calliope steeped her tea, dunking the strainer in and out of the boiling water while Alethea dumped the rest of the ingredients into the pot and put the lid on. "Let's discuss this further." It was typical Calliope style: more of an order than a suggestion, tempered by understanding and steeled with guidance. They sat and before Alethea could use her calendar and notebook as a distraction, Calliope shifted both out of reach. "It's been nearly two years since you came to Butterfly Harbor."

Alethea wished she'd poured her own cup of tea now. Not because she was thirsty, but because it would give her hands something to do. "Two years too long to have lived with my brother and his family."

The joke, as she expected, didn't land and only seemed to strengthen Calliope's resolve. She was nearly twenty-five, plenty old enough and some would say it was far past time for her to be out on her own. That didn't mean she didn't have reservations about the possibility. She liked living here, loved her brother and his family, who had all helped her get through a few rough years. They were safe. She was safe here. But she had to take a step away at some point, didn't she? And it wasn't like she'd be moving far. There were plenty of options in town for her to consider, even with her limited budget.

"Hearts take time to mend, Alethea." Calliope sipped her tea and spoke as if she'd read Alethea's mind. "It's normal to feel like you've been knocked off-balance. Constantly spinning like a top isn't going to stop you from feeling what's necessary. All this hopping around is only going to delay it."

Is that how she'd been feeling? Off-balance? She tapped two fingers against her heart, as if that would confirm Calliope's statement. "I've grieved," she told her sister-in-law. "I've dealt with it." Even as she said the words she wasn't entirely certain she believed it.

"Grief leaves a void we sometimes don't feel until life begins to settle again." Calliope continued, "It's up to you to decide how to fill that hole inside of you. Talia was a big part of your life. She was like a sister to you. Losing her was like losing part of yourself. You've told me that on more than one occasion."

In Calliope, Alethea had found not only a sister-in-law, but also a friend she could turn to. She'd found a number of them, actually, to fill that void Calliope spoke of. She'd also been raised to believe she could have everything and anything she ever wanted; all she had to do was work for it.

But no amount of hard work was going to bring her best friend back from the dead.

If only Alethea had told someone about Talia's problems. If she'd only convinced Talia to get help instead of doing stupid things that had only caused a rift between them; a rift that had resulted in so much friction those last weeks that Talia had practically stopped talking to her.

If only she had another chance…

Another chance. Anger burned its way through grief. Chances like that weren't for people like her; they were for people like Declan Cartwright who, it seemed, was determined to squander them by throwing caution out the window and going back to the sport that had nearly killed him.

That wasn't living life, Alethea thought. That was tempting fate.

A breeze burst through the open kitchen window, causing Alethea to shiver even as the image of storm-swept gray eyes in a man who looked as lost as she felt jostled her out of her inward contemplation. Restless, curious, Alethea got to her feet and brewed her own cup of tea. "Have you heard the latest gossip?"

Calliope chuckled. "I had members of the

Cocoon Club up here this morning, so you'll have to be more specific."

"About our latest new resident." Maybe getting Calliope's take on Declan would help get him out of Alethea's head.

"Ah, yes." Calliope nodded. "Came as a bit of a surprise, actually. Normally I'm quicker to suss out new arrivals."

"I met him. Couple of days ago. At the old Howser place? I didn't even know there were houses that far up the hill," Alethea continued and came over to sit across from Calliope now. "Do you know the place?"

"Yes, of course." Calliope had been born in Butterfly Harbor. Few had the complete connection to the town that she did. Her grandmother had built the house they were currently living in and Calliope had turned the entire property into a destination organic farm and market. "It used to belong to Elisha Howser." Calliope's expression softened. "That's a name I've not thought of in a while. She was a gentle soul. A preschool teacher for most of her life, before she retired to write children's books. When she passed a few years ago, she didn't leave a will so the property reverted to the town. I believe

Luke accepted caretaker rights, no doubt at the behest of our mayor. It's lovely property. I've not been up there for a while." She drew a finger around the rim of her mug. "Perhaps it's time for a visit."

"Wear a crash helmet," Alethea muttered and earned an arched auburn brow in response. "His name's Declan Cartwright. I doubt you've heard of him. He's a—"

"Race car driver, yes." Calliope nodded, her brows knitting. "Jasper O'Neill's a fan. He and Xander used to watch races when Jasper was done with deliveries for the farm. That reminds me, I'm going to have to hire someone to help us out around here." She smoothed a hand over her stomach. "It's getting a bit difficult to do the gathering for orders. And no," Calliope said when Alethea opened her mouth. "You are not allowed to volunteer. You have enough going on and a future to build for yourself. Focus on that. I wonder." She tapped a finger against her lips, then, picked up a pen from the table and scribbled a note to herself before ripping off the paper and folding it. "In the meantime, I'll have to put together a welcome basket for Mr. Cartwright."

And hook herself another customer, Alethea thought. Duskywing Farm was renowned for its organic produce and offerings like honey and fresh eggs from the chickens Stella had begun to keep earlier this year.

Alethea could hear the sauce come up to a bubble on the stove. As she got to her feet, so did Calliope, just as a flash of silver gray streaked through the small carved archway in the back door.

Ophelia, sleek, stealthy and most definitely feline, leaped onto the bench beside her mistress and bopped her head against Calliope's arm. "Someone's been midnight mousing." Calliope tapped a finger against Ophelia's nose and earned a louder purr. "Best watch where we step in the morning. Alethea?"

"Yes?"

"The answers you're looking for will present themselves." Cup in hand, Calliope extricated herself from the table. "Slow down a bit. Take things as they come. And stop pushing yourself so hard. You'll miss the fun parts of life."

Alethea remained silent as Calliope wandered back to her room. Her sister-in-law was usually right about these things. There were fun parts of life to be lived.

But fun didn't mean they had to be unsafe.

That was where Alethea and one Declan Cartwright definitely parted ways.

CHAPTER THREE

WAKING UP THE MORNING AFTER his conversation with Luke Saxon was a bit like waking up with an improved perspective. The solitude and silence Declan had lost himself in these past few weeks hummed with a sense of promise and…positivity.

It was that optimism, along with his determination to get his morning workout over and done with, that had him climbing out of bed and heading into the kitchen just as the sun was peeking over the horizon.

Without internet access––he'd decided not to put it off and called yesterday for an installation appointment for early next week—he'd started his own list of what he needed to research as well as things he thought the remodeling team should address. As a wannabe engineer, he loved the idea of solving the issues this house presented and, as someone who, until recently, never had the funds to pursue much of an education, did best when he taught himself. He didn't plan on swinging a hammer or rewiring the electrical system, but he also didn't want to be in the way. If he could learn how to strip, repair and rebuild anything with an engine in it, he could certainly lend a critical hand and eye to the plans Luke and Mayor Gil Hamilton had.

His foot caught on a split seam in the yellowed linoleum floor and nearly sent him sprawling onto his face. He grabbed hold of the counter, took an extra few beats before righting himself. His leg screamed against the tweak, the pain settling into a dull throb that had him clenching his teeth.

He reached for his cane, only to realize he'd left it in the kitchen.

Declan knocked a fist against his thigh. Sometimes the impulse to move didn't reach down far or fast enough to keep him moving in time with his brain. It was likely, more than one doctor had told him, he'd never be where and what he was before the accident.

Challenge accepted.

He would be back in that qualifying race and on the leaderboard faster than a rookie in a roadster. Not only to prove everyone wrong, but to prove himself right. He didn't belong anywhere other than a racetrack.

He took a long drink of coffee, waited until he knew he had control of the leg that moments before had been shaky and returned to his room to get changed. The pain eased enough to have him avoid taking medication. Early on in his treatment, he'd discovered how easy they were to take. So after a serious discussion with his doctor, they'd agreed he'd only be prescribed the lowest dosage and that he was to only have one when it was absolutely necessary.

Ten minutes later he was using the weight set he'd stashed in the living room, getting in his upper body reps and not stopping until he broke a sweat and his body screamed for surrender. Stretching out those painful areas tended to be the best solution and gave his body something else to scream about.

Only after he showered and changed and poured an oversize mug of caffeine-laden octane did he step outside, into the cool, bright morning.

The second he was on the porch, his thoughts turned to Alethea. Not so long ago he might have wondered if he'd been hallucinating. He'd done that before, in the hospital, coming off the pain meds and sleeping pills, but all of those imaginary visions had to do with competitive driving, his garage, the life he'd built in the racing world. But his imagination had never been good enough to come up with someone like her.

As his relationships had been cursory, surface and more than a bit rebellious. Marriage, kids, family, that had all been so far out in the future, he hadn't felt its loss until he was told he had almost died.

Not that Alethea was the woman to focus that attention on. She clearly disapproved not only of his life choices but his lifestyle. The hostility and disbelief that had shone on her face when he'd said he was going to drive again had struck him like a crowbar.

He looked back into the house.

Thin rays of sun streamed through the narrow beveled glass pane beside the front door; tiny particles of dust drifted through the air like miniscule snowflakes.

In the time since he'd taken up residence in the old-English-cottage-inspired home, he hadn't done much more than the minimum, aside from the workshop, which he'd turned into his daily obsession. Luke had seen it. So had Alethea.

The house needed help.

That new perspective he had made her see things in a different light now. The run-down property, the landscaping calling out for attention. How had he not noticed how depressing it was before? The area outside the walls he'd inhabited, from the thigh-high decaying weeds to the curved-roof shed with some long forgotten vehicle wasting away beneath a heavy cloth tarp, was in need. Of care. Of tending to.

Of rescue.

A familiar tingle raced down his spine. Luke Saxon was giving him an opportunity he never expected. It wasn't having something to focus on during the day that brought a spark of hope back into his body. It was more the desire to be needed that required filling.

His fingers itched and flexed to grasp the tarp covering the neglected vehicle that sat between the house and shed.

One step at a time. Just like he'd taken in the hospital.

He shook his head, sucked in another deep

breath and headed back inside. When Declan closed the door, he resumed his path to the sitting room, only now when he entered it, he didn't click on the light to cut through the shadows.

He made his way around the old Victorian couch and dainty coffee table, grabbed hold of the fabric and ripped open the curtains.

"SALMON TOSTADA WITH mango salsa up!" Alethea pivoted away from the griddle inside the food truck and held out the eco-friendly paper bowl loaded with Mexican-inspired goodness. Sweat coated her face. The steam and heat bathed her skin in a film that felt detoxifying. "Give the new salsa a try," she urged construction co-foreman Jed Bishop and pointed to the condiment stand at the front of the truck. "It's got a little kick, but it's perfect with the mango."

"You've not steered us wrong yet," Jed said with an approving nod. His graying hair glinted against the sun as he made his way through the crowd of lunchtime stragglers.

Serving her customers here at the butterfly sanctuary construction site was the highlight of her day. In the past months she'd been able to witness the progress being made on what was certain to be Butterfly Harbor's biggest attraction, second only to the ocean and the kitschy hometown feel of Monarch Lane, the main thoroughfare that wove through town.

The project had had its setbacks and controversies, but the main structure was complete and only interior work left to be done. It was a sight to behold. Surrounded by countless eucalyptus trees that served as the natural habitat for the monarch butterflies that migrated to and from the area every year, the building had been designed by Alethea's brother to embrace and utilize the natural surroundings as much as possible.

That she was able to park the food truck into her own little dedicated pocket did her heart good every time she pulled into the lot. Serving the crew and observers who came to see the progress reminded her of what her father had always told his children: *do what you love to do and you'll never work a day in your life*.

Alethea gazed out the side window toward the playground that had been built by a group of town volunteers a few months prior. After school let out, dozens of kids would flood in to play out their pent-up energy and get an update from the workers as to how soon the structure would be open for exploration and business.

Alethea returned to the order window, scribbled down the next three requests, accepted payment and quickly went to the cooktop to fill the orders.

Lunchtime at the construction site guaranteed two things: one, she'd have a steady stream of customers from the second she lifted the metal awning at noon, and two, she'd be far too busy to think about anything other than making hungry people happy.

That included thinking about Declan Cartwright and that darned, irritating, bloodspiking smile of his.

She'd already served breakfast down at the beach, just a block away from the other bit of construction going on in town—the rebuilding of the town's historic pub—that, before it had burned down last Christmas, had served as the temporary city hall while that building had been undergoing refurbishment.

The two shifts made for a long day, but also doubled as a great way to keep up with all the friends she'd made since moving here.

It might have been desperation and grief that had her boarding that bus from Virginia to California, but it was acceptance and the promise of a fresh start that had her staying.

Whoever she'd been back in college, whatever life she'd been meant to have, she didn't want to contemplate now. She'd moved beyond them. And she was so much better for it. She was exactly where she was supposed to be and doing what she should be doing.

"One salmon taco, double jalapeños, one mac and grilled cheese," she called the orders out as she hefted the tray of food to the window. "Double bison burger with grilled onion jam. Come and get it!"

"Got time for a few more orders?" Ozzy Lakeman, wearing his usual black cargo pants and matching Butterfly Harbor Fire Department T-shirt, stepped up to the order window as the last of the line moved off to eat. "Frankie and Roman are both craving your short rib nachos. Double order for Roman. Jasper wants one of your chicken burritos and I'll take one of your veggie burrito bowls, light on the rice."

"You've got it." As if she needed more evidence that the truck was a success, having the town firefighters seek her out was proof positive.

"Can we talk while you cook?" Ozzy's somewhat-under-his-breath question had Alethea's eyebrows raising, but she nodded, gestured toward the door.

"Come on in." When Ozzy joined her in the surprisingly spacious kitchen area of the vehicle and stood almost at attention by the refrigerator, she inclined her head. "What's up?"

"Well, I was hoping to get your advice on something. For Jo. You know, a surprise."

"A surprise?" Alethea lifted the lid off the slow cooker containing the rich short ribs for the nachos that were fast becoming a menu favorite. She'd added some of the barbecue sauce she'd made in Calliope's kitchen to the braising liquid and sent her senses to zinging. "What kind of surprise?"

"This kind."

When Alethea glanced over her shoulder, Ozzy had reached into his pocket and pulled out a small square box. He cracked it open, revealing an intricate double woven silver band in a delicate vine pattern embracing a perfect solitaire diamond. "Oh, Ozzy." She dropped the containers on the stainless steel counter and all but dived for him, cupping his hand between hers to look at the ring more closely. "It's beautiful. Jo's going to love it."

"Yeah?" His entire body sagged in relief. "I bought it a few weeks ago when I was in Monterey. It was an impulse thing, but when I saw it." He shrugged, his lips curving as he gazed down at the box. "It just said Jo to me. It's not dainty, not delicate, but it seems elegant and strong. Just like her."

"Falling in love has turned you into a poet," Alethea teased at his blush. "Speaking on behalf of myself and the Cocoon Club, might I say it's about time."

The pink that had colored Ozzy's cheeks vanished. "The Cocoon Club?" His voice squeaked. "What does the Cocoon Club have to do with this?"

Figuring she could have some fun here, Alethea returned his earlier shrug and, after flipping the sign in the window to closed, focused her attention on his lunch order.

"Harvey and Oscar have developed quite an attachment to your Jo." She spooned a healthy serving of black beans onto the oversize whole wheat tortilla, then, topped the warm mixture with a good handful of cheese. The Cocoon Club consisted of a group of senior citizens, most of whom lived together in an old Victorian house on the other side of town. "It's not every woman who can discuss blueprints and construction as easily as the weather. Our senior contingent has been wondering when you were going to make it official. Last I heard, they planned to sic Myra and Eloise on you to push you in a matrimonial direction before Jo goes into labor."

"That's all I need." But the grimace on his round, handsome face was tinged with the promise of good things to come. The joy Ozzy displayed over becoming a husband and father—to a baby that wasn't biologically his, was practically contagious. "I'm nervous enough about asking Jo without the added pressure." Sweat beaded his brow. "They were seriously going to put Myra and Eloise on my case?"

Myra and Eloise would only be the start of Ozzy's problems if the aforementioned club had anything to say about it. Once those folks were out in full force, nothing stopped them.

"Lucky for you they've been busy raising money for a new seniors-friendly hot tub for their backyard. But now you don't have to worry." Alethea scooped chicken onto the flattop, added some of her extra cumin-spiced marinade and transported her senses to singing with the pungent aroma of garlic and jalapeños. Something was missing, though. She scanned her lineup of condiments on the back counter, grabbed a couple of limes and squeezed them over the sizzling meat. Ah, yeah. She nodded and took a deep breath. Perfect. When Ozzy didn't respond to her comment, she glanced up again. "So what did you need my help with?"

"I was thinking her baby shower would be a great time to propose."

"Oh, Ozzy." Alethea didn't hesitate to smile her encouragement, mainly because she couldn't say no to the hope in Ozzy's dark-green eyes. "I think that would make for a day she definitely wouldn't forget. I'm meeting with Leah, Sienna and Brooke tonight to finalize details for the shower next weekend. What do you need us to do?"

"I just want it to be special. Different," Ozzy said. "I have the ring obviously. She's not a 'put the ring in a cake' kind of fan, but I was thinking, I saw this idea on the internet about a photo booth. Maybe catch the moment as it happens?"

"Say no more." Alethea had plenty of information to get the idea. "We'll make it happen. You were already planning to be there, so that'll make things easier. I'll fill you in as soon as I talk to Leah and Sienna." A baby shower and a marriage proposal? Now there was a day that would go down in Butterfly Harbor history.

"That's great, thanks." Ozzy drooped in release as Alethea finished putting together his order. She followed him out, waved him off and, after chatting with a few satisfied lunch customers, returned to the truck to do a cursory cleanup before heading back to home base at the Flutterby Inn.

Once she'd parked in her usual spot in the delivery area, she finished her accustomed routine of packaging up the leftover food before doing a deep cleaning of the counters, grill, stove and sink. By the time she wheeled an oversize cooler filled with leftover produce and perishables in through the back door of the kitchen of Flutterby Dreams, she could feel the exhaustion seeping into her bones.

She found Jason Corwin, former celebrity

chef with a reputation for an attitude and a tendency toward terminal crankiness, chopping up a counter full of vegetables. His infant son, David, sat in a carrier, waving his arms and legs. That sight was sweet enough to make her forget about the exhaustion.

"Don't let me interrupt." Alethea dipped down to unload the cooler and readjusted the clip keeping her hair under control. "I'm sure David is providing much inspiration for this evening's menu. Hey there, little man." She stopped long enough to grab hold of one of David's feet and give it a quick squeeze. The baby let out a squeal of delight, followed by an excited spit bubble that had him clapping his hands toward her.

"He just lights up around you," Jason said with an impressed smile.

"It's the hair. Babies love curls." She swiped a finger against David's soft cheek and resisted the urge to nuzzle him. She'd been lucky enough to babysit a few times and David was a frequent visitor at the inn and the restaurant. The idea that he actually recognized her gave her heart a bit of a boost. "It's Natalie's day off, isn't it?" In recent years Jason had taken the restaurant from barely filled to reservations six nights a week. He and Abby, the inn's manager, now employed more than half a dozen employees for Flutterby Dreams alone. "You need help with dinner?"

"No, thanks." Jason waved her off. "Middle of the week slump plus Holly's put out her first batch of pumpkin pies."

"Can't compete with the Butterfly Diner when there's pumpkin pie," Alethea agreed even as she made plans to stop there herself.

"If you wouldn't mind making one delivery before you take the rest of the day?" He motioned to a box filled with fresh produce along with two foil containers. "We have a new customer. Calliope does, too, but she said she couldn't make it up that way for a few days."

"Oh." Alethea frowned, but quickly switched to a big smile for David. She hoped everything was okay. Calliope was usually more than eager to make her deliveries in person when she could. "Who to?"

"Declan Cartwright."

She'd known, even before Jason said the name. "He called?"

"He did. Put in a regular catering order for the next few weeks. Man sounded hungry."

"Hmmm. Well, he won't starve now." The man was definitely going to be putting the pounds back on if he planned to live on Jason's cooking.

"Be sure you leave that." Jason pointed to the basket with the fresh produce. "I can use all of it in the spiced gazpacho."

Oh, wow. If Jason was making his famous and addictive gazpacho, that meant...

She ducked over to the oven, cracked open the door and took a deep, herb dough breath. "Ah, you made focaccia. My day just became perfect." She loved just about everything Jason cooked, but his garlic and rosemary crusty Italian bread was something to behold. And to envy. Her latest dough attempt had ended up being nothing more than an oversize hockey puck that she swore laughed at her.

"I thought you might feel that way." Jason gestured to a bag on the counter next to the door. "I already packaged some up for you to take home. Maybe try replicating it this time before you eat it all."

"Fat chance of that." She resisted temptation to jump headfirst into the bag. Instead, she chose "temptation and calorie free" option number two and picked David up. Tucking him in against her, she offered her finger for him to gnaw on as he dropped his dark blonde head onto her shoulder. "Why would I try to impersonate the expert?"

"Because you won't make it through the Academy of Culinary Training if you can't bake."

Alethea froze, her entire body going clammy. "What—" Her ears buzzed as she searched for the words to respond. She could not have heard him correctly. "What are you talking about?"

"Abby suggested I take the time to find a way to surprise you, but this shouldn't wait." He motioned to a side cabinet that housed a collection of old cookbooks. They had been the property of the inn's original owners and their cook Matilda. "The paperwork arrived yesterday. Next semester starts in January. All you need to complete your acceptance is to go in for an interview before then."

"Paperwork? January? Interview?" Afraid she was going to drop the baby, Alethea set David back into his carrier and retrieved the oversize envelope. Sure enough, it was addressed to her and it was definitely from the ACT, one of the most exclusive cooking schools in the country. Her hands trembled. "But I didn't apply."

"No, but you auditioned."

Alethea frowned, first at her boss, then, at the envelope.

"Remember that night a few weeks ago where you covered for me at dinner?" Jason's tone was as casual as if they were discussing next week's menu rather than Alethea's future. "It turns out one of our guests is on the admissions board. She's always on the lookout for talent and she was impressed with the meal you made."

"A member of the admissions board just happened to come to Flutterby Dreams the night I was cooking." Suspicion crept in around the shock. "I could have cooked an eight-course meal fit for a prince. Board members of the ACT don't just admit people on a whim."

"True. Hence the interview." Jason made a goofy face at his son and set David to giggling. "It helps when said board member is friends with your boss. Plus I just taught that extension class for their honors students, remember? I might have called and suggested the board members come to the restaurant the night you were cooking, so they could get a taste of my assistant's creations. What's wrong? You've done the hard work—I just alerted them to your cooking." He set his knife down, a sudden frown marring his brow. "I figured since you presented me with that business plan a few weeks ago, you were looking for ways to broaden your experience and education. Your ideas for adding to Corwin Enterprises here in Butterfly Harbor are great, Alethea, but I can't do that all by myself. I'm going to need a partner in this new company offshoot. One I'm about ready to close a deal on with." His eyebrows arched. "Are you saying you aren't interested?"

Interested? Her head spun. In becoming Jason's partner? In going to cooking school? "I…don't know." Why did it feel as if the ocean was roaring in her ears? Things were going so well right now. She'd found a rhythm, a routine, one that didn't include going back to school. In any capacity.

School was something she'd done with Talia. And, then, had suddenly lost Talia less than halfway through her degree…

The very thought of returning to school had her late lunch threatening to reappear.

She jumped when the kitchen door swung open and Abby Corwin, the manager of the Flutterby Inn and Jason's wife, breezed in. Dressed in a full skirt and matching short-sleeved cardigan the color of ripe peaches, Abby's recently cut blond hair made her look even more like a garden pixie flitting from flower to flower. She stopped short, sniffed the air and sighed. "Ah, focaccia." She quickly scanned the room. "Where is it?"

"Latest batch is in the oven," Jason chuckled. "It'll be out in a few."

"I suppose I can wait." Abby swooped up her son and held him over her head before locking him onto her hip. She tilted her head up for a quick kiss from her husband. "Did you tell her?"

"I did." Jason wasn't one to sound uncertain, but Alethea could hear the doubt in his voice. "I don't think she's completely on board with the idea."

"What?" Abby retrieved a bottle of juice from the refrigerator and approached Alethea. "Why on earth not, Al? It's a fabulous opportunity."

"I know." Alethea couldn't explain it, either: the nearly paralyzing fear surging through her system. The nausea that continued to churn. "It isn't something…" She took a deep breath. "I'm sorry. It's just a surprise is all. I'm not entirely sure how to feel about it." It was as close to the truth as anyone was going to get from her.

"Excited would be my guess," Abby said with a quick smile and a gentle nudge of her elbow. "I don't know much about cooking academies, but from what I do know, this one is stellar. What an adventure for you."

Alethea didn't want an adventure.

She wanted the calm, quiet, uneventful life she'd created for herself here in Butterfly Harbor.

She wanted safe.

"If it's the money that has you worried—" Jason started.

"No. No, it's not that." But now that he mentioned it, she did have to wonder where she was going to come up with the tuition as well as funds to cover housing costs. The ACT was in San Francisco, where monthly rent was about as out of reach for her as a daily order of Kobe beef.

"She's just in shock," Abby said as David

grabbed hold of his bottle and shoved it into his mouth. "Take some time to drink it in, Al."

"What about Flutterby Wheels? What about the restaurant?" The fear had pushed the words free and now they came in a flood. "You need me here, not off in San Francisco learning what you've already taught me."

"We have plenty of people to cover and if we need more, I'll hire more. The program they've offered you involves the business end, as well. And while I do need you." He set his knife down and rested his hands on the counter. "I also need you educated. You've been a tremendous asset, up to a point. I'd love to rely on you for some of the more important things I've got planned."

Meaning she'd run out of things to offer as an employee.

"Give her some time to think about it, Jason." Abby rested her hand on Alethea's arm. "Read the information, okay? Take some time to think it over before you jump at it."

"What if I don't want to go?" She swallowed hard and finally met Jason's concerned gaze.

He inclined his head, as if processing information he hadn't expected to receive. "Then I'll need to rethink a few things."

"Would I still have a job?"

"Oh, holy hamburgers," Abby snorted. "Like he could run this place without you."

"You have a job with me as long as you want it," Jason said. "I just assumed you'd want to be doing something more. I know you've been saving up for a house of your own. As a partner, you'd be doing that a lot faster. You'd have your hands in a lot of different pies so to speak."

"Not with the way I make pies." Alethea forced the joke in an effort to break the tension. She could tell Jason was surprised, if not disappointed by her reaction and she certainly didn't want to seem ungrateful. He'd given her so much, both with her job and with his support, but… "I'll definitely think about it," she assured him. "Thank you. For whatever you did to make this happen. It means a lot that you have such faith in me." She gathered up the containers with her own items, shoved the envelope down the side of the basket, and plopped the bag of focaccia on top. "I should get going. I'll see you in the morning."

"All right."

Alethea could feel both Jason's and Abby's gazes on her as she hurried out the back door of the kitchen and walked around the gravel path to the side parking lot. It wasn't until she was in her car and driving away that she let the sob of fear and regret echo into the silence.

CHAPTER FOUR

EITHER DECLAN'S HEARING was getting better or the volume on his speakers was dying. Either way, he heard a car pull onto the property. He'd foregone a climb on the wall today after overexerting himself during his weight session this morning. Instead he'd occupied himself going through the endless piles of junk that had been stockpiled in the workshop for what looked like the past two decades.

Sweaty, covered in dust and grime, and feeling surprisingly agile, he headed to the door in time to see Alethea Costas climbing out of a clunker of a car. *Clunker* was an understatement. The poor ancient four-door looked held together with rust and hope. It was on the tip of his tongue to ask if he could check her alternator but, then, he reconsidered. He wasn't entirely certain how she'd take that request.

He grabbed a towel to clean off his hands,

pushed the door open a bit more to let the late afternoon breeze sweep in. Tapping off the music, he approached just as she popped out of the back, arms loaded with containers and a large wicker basket overflowing with some of the most gorgeous produce he'd ever seen in his life.

"Didn't think I'd be seeing you again so soon."

She jumped, clearly preoccupied, then, in a flash, recovered with a pleasant smile that didn't quite reach her eyes. "Delivery from Flutterby Dreams." She hefted the containers. "The basket's from my sister-in-law Calliope."

"That was nice of her. Here. Let me help."

"I've got it." She stepped out of reach as he stepped closer. "Just tell me where you want it."

Payback for the other day, he supposed, so he went with it. "Kitchen's great. Door's open."

"Of course it is." She shook her head.

"Hang on." He reached out before she passed, snagged an apple and, after an appreciative examination, bit it. The crunch exploded into the air. "Oh, man. That's good. That's a right-off-the-apple-tree snap."

"She grows the best. Be back in a sec."

She wore yellow today. A bright yellow T-shirt that smoothed over the waistband of worn jeans. The Flutterby Wheels logo was displayed on her back this time, in a rainbow of lettering. Her hair was tied back as it had been the first time they'd met, but a few more curls had sprung loose. The errant curls made his fingers itch to test one against his skin.

Alethea hurried inside and, feeling playful, he followed and stood in the doorway to the kitchen as she set things on the counter.

"I've got some home-brewed iced tea if you'd like a glass." He motioned to the fridge.

She hesitated. "Sure. Yeah. That sounds nice." She moved back and away, pushed her hands into the back pockets of her jeans. "Thank you."

"Least I can do for the delivery. Glasses are up there." He pointed to the cabinet near her head. He pulled out the oversize mason jar, grabbed a ladle out of one of the drawers and filled the tall glasses with ice before topping it off with the amber liquid. "It's sweet tea," he said before she sipped.

When she did, the surprise on her face boosted his pride.

"That's really nice." She drank more, toasted him and headed back outside. He expected, when he joined her, to find her on the porch. Instead she'd left her glass on the porch step and ducked around the side of the house and was reaching for the weathered tarp covering his future project.

"Curiosity killed the cat. Or so they say," he added when she looked at him. "Go ahead." He shrugged. "It's an eyesore now, but I've got plans for her."

"Why are cars always *hers*?" Alethea's brows knitted.

"There is no good way to answer that question." Even as he joined her, he could hear the silent roar of the car's no-doubt dead engine, hear the *creak* of its rusted shut doors; the whine of the brakes. The countless hours he'd spent under the hood or flat on his back beneath vehicles, tinkering and tightening and tuning, teaching himself everything he could about mechanics and car care surged back at him. Not now, he told himself. Not yet. "I assume it belonged to the previous owner."

"Maybe." Alethea didn't sound convinced.

"I knew it wasn't something you brought. You wouldn't let a beauty like this die such a slow death. Such a shame, leaving her to rot."

"I'm using her as my reward project." He pointed to the workshop. "Have to empty that thing out first so I have somewhere to spread out my tools and such."

She rested her palm on the hood, shook her head as if marveling at its frame just as he marveled at her. She seemed to have no idea of the effect she had on him. On any man, he'd venture a guess. The fact she had him doing mental doughnuts that left skid marks around his heart was proof enough of that.

"You don't see many '64 Chevy Impalas anymore," Alethea said. "Except on TV, of course." She flashed him that smile again, a smile that held the power of a small energy plant. "Boy, the car's gorgeous, isn't it? So much potential." She could obviously see what he did. A shine lurked beneath the dusty surface of age and neglect; the windshield's spiderweb of cracks threatened to break at any moment. Dings and dents and splotches of rust marred the black paint, while four tires sagged after giving in to exhaustion. The car sat so close to the ground that the exhaust pipes had buckled and bent beneath its weight. "That'll be quite a project."

"I'll be up for it soon." He made sure his tone left no doubt about it. She put the cover in place and headed back for her drink.

"Where in the South are you from?"

"What gave me away?" He leaned against the railing as she took a seat on the top stair. "The tea or the accent?"

"Both." Her smile was cautious and she grasped the glass with both hands as if trying to warm them.

"You mean to say you didn't google me after you left here the other day?" he teased.

"I don't google without permission." There. Her mouth relaxed a little.

"Georgia mostly. That's where I was born. We moved to South Carolina for a while before heading north to Chicago."

"Ah." She nodded. "That explains where you met Luke."

"My sister worked with him on an education project. They struck out as a couple but he and I remained friends." One of the better decisions he'd made in his life. That friendship had, after all, led him here.

She shifted and sat back, looked up at him.

"I thought your work with alternate engines sounded interesting. You're coming up with a new fuel injection system, right? Not just for racing, but for commercial, transportation and emergency vehicles, right?"

"I thought you didn't google me." He ignored the dull thudding in his leg, an early warning sign he was pushing things too far.

"I didn't have to in order to find your website. I'm surprised more automobile companies didn't want to partner with you to expand on your ideas. A vehicle with lower emissions and more reliable technology is something a lot of people, including myself, find appealing. Not that I can afford any of those cars. Yet." Now she was the one who winced as she looked at her pathetic car. "That's what's missing, I think. Making cars like that more affordable for the average person. I'd love to give up my gas guzzler, but it's just not financially feasible, you know?"

"You sound like my sister Hilda." The thought actually made him smile. "It's part of the reason she went into climate studies in school. She's of the belief that since technology is partially responsible for getting us into the mess we're in, it should be part of the solution."

"Sounds like your sister's a smart woman. How many brothers and sisters do you have?"

"Six. Sisters. All older," he added at her wide eyes. "Yeah, I know." He drank down half his tea. "Pretty wild, huh?"

"I'm the fifth of five, so I get it. Wild's just the beginning. There's the overprotection factor."

"And the rescue factor. Don't forget that one." Declan wouldn't have pegged her as the youngest. In his experience, there was a fearlessness that went along with that spot in the birth order. She was more cautious, like his oldest sister, Marcy. Alethea was curious, sure, but he wouldn't tag her with the previous moniker. Not by a long shot.

"That's where your fearlessness comes from I bet," she said with a tone bordering on judgmental. "Knowing there's always someone there to bail you out. Even when you take chances with your life."

"You mean the racing?" It was an interesting comment to make. One that intrigued him. "Racing is about controlling fear. Transforming it into acceptance. Believe me, when

I get behind the wheel I know exactly what can go wrong." Better than most. "My job is to make sure it doesn't happen."

She pressed her lips into a thin line.

"Yeah, I know." He smirked. "I need significant improvement in that area. As my team would attest."

"You must miss them."

"My team?"

"No." She shook her head. "Your family."

"I spent a lot of years wishing for silence, then, spent even more years getting my ears blasted by engine noise."

"That doesn't answer the question."

No, he thought. It really didn't. "I do miss them, actually." Even though he did not miss the attention they paid him. "The quiet has taken getting used to. And, honestly, before you turned up the other day, I hadn't realized how much I missed people." And now here he stood, playing patio confession with a woman who, from what he could tell, didn't think very much of the profession that gave him a reason to live.

"I felt the same way when I first came here," she said. "The ocean helped."

"The ocean?"

"That roaring, that constant rhythmic roaring as the waves wash up on shore, the way the water sounds so monstrous one moment and, then, tinny, plinking raindrops the next. It gets inside of you. It makes you listen to everything you've been ignoring before." Her eyes fogged over, as if she'd become lost in a moment, or perhaps in a wave. He remained silent, if only to let what she'd said wash over him like the evening tide. "It balanced me," she continued. "Just being out there on the beach, listening to the water. It's this life force I can never get enough of. I grew up in Chicago, middle of a big city. You know what it's like. Sure, there were rivers and waterways, but nothing that compares to the coast. The second I stepped foot on the beach here in Butterfly Harbor, I felt…" She hesitated. "I guess I felt embraced. Like everything was going to be okay." She pulled herself back to the moment, smiled. "Sounds like it's doing the same thing for you. Thank you for the tea." She finished her glass, stood up and handed it to him. "I need to get going."

"Oh, okay. Thanks for the delivery. I plan on getting into town soon, so I'm sure I'll see you around."

She nodded, smiled and, after a moment's hesitation, shoved her hands into her pockets and hurried off to her car. As she was driving away, he couldn't help but think he'd finally gotten a glimpse at the real Alethea Costas.

A woman who had her own secrets, her own past. Her own reasons for being who and what she was. Despite the display of friendliness and humor, she seemed—he wasn't quite sure what the word was. Lost? Those layers she was exposing tempted him to no end and wanting to erase those shadows in her eyes gave him something other than himself to focus on. The ocean and Butterfly Harbor might have helped heal Alethea.

But it was Alethea who might just help heal him.

"ANOTHER GLASS of wine, Al?" Sienna Bettencourt, a woman who looked as elegant and put-together in yoga pants and an off the shoulder burgundy sweatshirt as she did in a tailored designer dress, held the open bottle of Chardonnay over the edge of Alethea's glass.

"No, thanks." Alethea moved her glass out of reach so she wasn't tempted to say yes. Her visit with Declan Cartwright wasn't sitting well and for the life of her, she couldn't figure out why. And wine was not going to help.

It was irritating, the way he kept slipping into her thoughts. She already had enough to juggle with her job and her family, her obligations around town and now Jason's push for her to leave everything she'd built here and go back to school. She swallowed the bitter fear in her throat.

Yeah. Wine was definitely not going to help. Carbs on the other hand… She snatched up a cracker and nibbled. Now was the time for her friends to do what they did best and distract her from feeling like she was circling the drain.

The women's weekly get-together—usually nothing more than a catch-up, gossip, vent kind of gathering, had been usurped these past few weeks to plan construction supervisor Jo Bertoletti's baby shower.

The five of them—Alethea, Jo, Brooke Evans, Sienna and Jo's best friend, family attorney Leah Ellis—had formed a bond shortly after Sienna's arrival in town. They were down one member this evening, though. Planning the baby shower for Jo meant Jo didn't attend the meetings, which worked out for the best considering she'd been on semi bed rest for the past couple of months. Normally they'd have gone to Jo's cozy custom-built house on wheels, but as her pregnancy had progressed, the space in that house had lessened. Considerably.

"Seriously?" Leah looked forlornly at the half-empty bottle. "You're going to make us finish this without you?"

Alethea tapped on her phone and updated her schedule. "Busy day tomorrow. I can't risk the wine-over."

"When don't you have a busy day?" Leah had come straight from her office, and while she still wore one of her tailored suits, this one the color of a midnight sky, her mile-high heels had been discarded by the door the moment she stepped inside Sienna's houseboat. "You make the rest of us look like slackers, and coming from me, that's saying something. Top me off, please, Sienna. A hangover might actually do me some good tomorrow."

"You think you're busy now—imagine how it'll be once you're mayor." Sienna teased, then, chuckled at the glare Leah shot her. "Don't blame me. You're the one who decided to throw your name into the election ring."

"No one else was going to run," Leah grumbled. "Naive me assumed a small-town election would be, well, small. Instead I feel like I've been caught up in a zany out of control movie script. When do we eat? I missed lunch because of a meeting with my campaign managers."

Alethea and Sienna grinned at each other at Leah's air quotes.

"Problems with the Cocoon Club?" Sienna batted her lashes.

"They turned up at my office today wanting to discuss next month's debate," Leah practically whined. "Gil and I haven't even decided on a date for the debate yet and they wanted to talk strategy. Myra suggested a sit-in protest against his decision to sell the old Fampton building. *A sit-in.* Can you imagine? And I think Harold mentioned water balloons being handed out to the audience members during the debate."

Alethea bit the inside of her cheek so she wouldn't laugh. "Myra and Harold have definite feelings about getting Gil Hamilton out of office. You've become a means to an end."

"Oh, it wasn't just Myra and Harold this time. They brought the entire Cocoon Club with them. Including Alice Manning!" Leah laid her head on the back of the love seat and sighed. "She even revved her engine when Gil's name was brought up. I swear she thinks she's driving a racecar these days."

Alethea's smile faltered when an image of another race car driver invaded her thoughts. "Ever since Alice got that motorized wheelchair, she's been buzzing around town nonstop." Alethea bit back a groan and tried to think of something else.

"From what I hear," Leah said. "When it comes to the Hamiltons and the Cocoon Club, there's an ocean of history under that particular bridge."

"We should probably get the full story from an objective third party," Sienna suggested to Leah. "Maybe Jake Campbell down at the community youth center has some thoughts? Wasn't he sheriff once upon a time?"

"Before Luke Saxon, yes," Leah confirmed. "And that's not a bad idea. Jake's been supportive of my campaign. From what I understand it was Gil who shoved him out of his job as sheriff in the first place." She shook her head. "I just can't get a clear read on that mayor of ours."

"You will," Sienna mused and pulled out her own phone. "On the bright side, seeing Alice out and about like that made my day a bit better."

Alethea would have to agree. Not so long ago, Alice Manning's Parkinson's had restricted her to the group home she shared with a number of other senior citizens in town, i.e., The Cocoon Club. She'd been going downhill pretty fast until her granddaughter Abby and grandson-in-law Jason bought her the fancy wheelchair for Christmas. Now the older woman was able to zip around town all she liked as if she had a new lease on life. "Just add dealing with the club's interest to your list of good deeds," Alethea told Leah. "They have a lot of pull around town. If you've won them over, your chances of winning are pretty good."

"Yeah, I guess." Leah didn't sound either convinced or particularly happy at the prospect. "I just wish someone would find them something else to focus on other than me and the election." She eyed Alethea. "You're heading over to their place this week, aren't you?"

"Tomorrow." Once a month she helped

Ezzie Salazar, the Cocoon Club's live-in care-taker, do some advance marathon meal prep-ping.

"Couldn't you nudge them in another direc-tion of a new interest?" Leah asked.

"All the nudging in the world won't knock them off course," Alethea said. "But I'll speak to Ezzie when I'm over there. See if she has any suggestions." Ezzie, who had followed her son Roman to town when he became co-fire chief, had a super clever way about her when it came to her charges. Keeping a friendly eye on the Cocoon Club was a ride and a half given their good-natured fondness for sticking their collective nose in other peo-ple's lives. Ezzie loved her charges to death, but they had minds of their own. It didn't make for an easy job by any means.

"Awesome. Hey, Brooke." Leah sat up when Brooke Evans wobbled into the room. She grabbed hold of furniture as she passed to keep her balance. "You feeling better?"

"No." Brooke flopped down in a chair across from them. Closing her eyes, she held her head in one hand, and pressed her other hand flat against her stomach. "I know you

said houseboats don't move, but I feel sea-
sick."

"Well, sure we get the occasional bobble."
Sienna uncurled from her seat. "But you
shouldn't be feeling anything."

"Tell that to my insides. No wine." She
shook her head when Sienna lifted the bottle. "Just the smell makes me want to run,
er, walk very slowly back to the bathroom."

"I'll get you some ginger ale." Alethea was
already up and heading toward the kitchen.
Sienna and Monty's home—previously
owned by a long-time resident who moved
north to be with her family—was something
out of a storybook as far as Alethea was concerned. She'd never known anyone who lived
on a houseboat before, and this one was exquisite. From its gray-and-blue paint on the
exterior, to the comfortable decor throughout
the two-story structure, every window gave
an exquisite view of Butterfly Harbor or, in
the case of the sunporch the group currently
occupied, the ocean.

She and Sienna became instant friends the
second the other woman had hit town. After
leaving her previous life behind in a bit of a
headline-grabbing scandal, Sienna had found

a home, along with a husband, and become an integral part of the community with her event planning business that now included Brooke as one of her business partners.

A flash of color outside the kitchen window had Alethea stopping midpour. A stunningly bright parrot flapped to a smooth landing on the window ledge.

"Hey, Duchess." Alethea pushed open the window before Duchess broke her beak on the glass.

"*Squawk!* Guacamooooo-leeee!" That determined dark gaze landed on Alethea.

"No can do," Alethea said and shook her head. "Avocados aren't good for birds. And you are a bird," she added at the bird's dubious expression. "Whether you want to admit it or not."

"Drop and give me fifty!" Duchess screeched in response.

"Not in this or any other life." Alethea couldn't help but laugh. The parrot had been a second stowaway on *Nana's Dream*, Sienna and her husband's recently acquired boat. The feathered addition to Butterfly Harbor had previously belonged to an exercise instructor who, despite abandoning the bird, had definitely left a verbal impression.

"How about you head north a ways and check out our new visitor?" Alethea suggested. "I bet Declan could use a trainer about now." At Duchess's squawked response Alethea wished the words back. "Okay," she told herself. "You have *got* to stop thinking about him."

"Stop thinking about who?" Sienna joined her in the open, galley-style kitchen and reached into a cabinet for some crackers, then, retrieved a handful of strawberries out of the fridge and dropped them into the bowl attached to Duchess's window ledge.

When Sienna glanced over her shoulder in time to see the blush heating Alethea's cheeks, she stopped, turned and offered a huge, knowing and excited smile. "Oooooh, who's the guy?"

"Just…no one." She should have left her hair down, Alethea thought. It was long and thick enough she could hide her giveaway cheeks. "Someone new to town."

"Only person I've heard of is the new guy living in the old Howser place?" Sienna turned and leaned against the counter, settling in for what Alethea feared was a long conversation. "You've met him?"

"Twice." There was no use lying to Sienna Bettencourt. The woman was second only to Calliope when it came to detecting falsehoods. "What have you heard about him?" As much as she wanted to put Declan Cartwright out of her mind, she figured there was a reason his name had yet to be broadcast around town.

"Not much. Only that he's a bit of a recluse and that no one in town's seen him." Sienna blinked slowly. "Except you, it seems. Any details you want to share?"

"No." She quickly added, "I'm sure you'll meet him soon enough."

"Is he single?"

"Very. I mean, yes," she corrected herself at Sienna's grin. "Don't, Sienna."

"Don't what? Wonder what it's going to take to get you interested in someone? Now why would I do that?"

"Because you're happily ensconced in wedded bliss and think everyone else should be, too."

"Guilty as charged." Sienna shrugged. "You

don't have to get married, Al. It would just be nice to see you happy with someone."

"I'm happy by myself." Why did married people always think something was lacking in her life because she was unattached? "If that changes, I'll be sure to let you know."

Sienna's eyes lost a bit of their teasing glint. "I didn't mean to hurt your feelings."

"You didn't." Not much, anyway.

"Good." Sienna's smile returned instantly. "I still think it's interesting you were daydreaming about someone. Especially a someone everyone in town is getting very curious about."

"He's been made aware." She had no doubt Luke had filled Declan in on the curiosity his arrival would have caused. Especially since he'd been here a while and word of his presence was just leaking out.

Sienna popped open the oven door and filled the air with the distinct, and all too familiar scent of lasagna. Sienna took a deep breath, shut the door and all but swooned against the counter. "Moments like this I am so glad I stowed away on Monty's boat. Who would have thought I'd end up in a town with a world-renowned chef who does to-go orders."

"Tell me you got focaccia, too." Alethea was already more than halfway through the bag Jason had given her.

"Well, duh." Sienna tucked her hair behind her ear and grinned. "Something tells me Brooke won't be eating very much, though." She plopped the crackers and some sliced cheese onto a plate and led Alethea, who had the glass of ginger ale for Brooke in her hand. "Poor thing just can't kick that stomach…" She trailed off, stopped short and swung on Alethea. "Boy, are we not very bright."

"Speak for yourself." Alethea's frown returned.

"Here." She shoved the plate into Alethea's free hand. "I'll be right back."

Shaking her head, Alethea rejoined Leah and Brooke. "Lasagna for dinner. In case you were wondering."

"Hallelujah, carbs." Leah lifted two fists in the air. "My prayers have been answered."

Brooke managed a weak smile. "Thanks." She took the glass and sipped. "Oh, that should help."

No sooner had she bitten off the corner of a

cracker than Sienna reappeared. She whipped something out from behind her back and stuck it in Brooke's face. "Try this."

"Try what? Exactly what kind of dinner is this?" Brooke said.

Alethea sat in the nearest empty chair and craned her neck to get a better glimpse of what Sienna was holding. "Do we all get to try it…" Sienna spun and glared at Alethea as if she'd lost a significant number of brain cells in the last few minutes. "What? Oh. Oh!" She looked to Leah who, thankfully, seemed to be just as late to jump on the train.

"Oh, wow." Leah sat forward. "Oh, that's awesome."

"Not yet it isn't," Sienna warned them. "But it could be if she gets into the bathroom already."

Brooke looked down at the white stick. "Where'd you get a pregnancy kit that fast?"

"I've got a whole drawer full in my bathroom. What?" she asked when the three of them looked at her. "Monty and I have been trying. I want to know as soon as it happens."

"Sienna's right," Alethea said to Brooke, who looked not only shocked, but just a little bit scared. "Go take the test."

"I don't…" Brooke looked down at the test, then, at her wedding band set, blinked back tears. "What if it's negative?"

"And what if it's positive?" Sienna shot back. "If it's negative, then, you and Sebastian get to have more fun trying."

"Har har." Leah got to her feet. "Honey, go take the test. Then we'll figure out how to feel about it, okay?"

"That makes sense. Okay." Brooke stood, accepted the white stick and, after flipping her long blond hair back over her shoulder, headed into the bathroom. The second she was in, the three of them looked at each other, then, bolted over to stand on the other side of the door.

"Well?" Sienna called after a few minutes.

"I can't do what I need to with you all listening. Go away!" Brooke's voice echoed.

"Timer's buzzing on the oven," Alethea announced. "Let's go get dinner ready."

"I'm too excited to eat," Leah announced. "Another one of us is going to have a baby!"

"Maybe!" Brooke yelled.

"Right." Leah pressed a finger against her lips and they went into the kitchen, saving their girlfriend giggles and whispers until they were out of earshot.

Alethea took over, removing the lasagna from the oven and sliding the sheet of Jason's focaccia in. Sienna removed a bowl of salad from the fridge and set it on the table while Leah retrieved the wine.

"Jo's party is going to be great practice for us," Sienna announced. "I'm going to throw Brooke the biggest, bestest baby shower this town has ever seen!"

"She deserves it since she didn't get one with Mandy," Alethea added. Brooke and Sebastian's fifteen-year-old daughter had been born when Brooke was only eighteen. Circumstances being, well, complicated, Sebastian had raised Mandy on his own until Brooke recently returned to Butterfly Harbor and the family reunited.

"How long is that test supposed to take?" Leah asked Sienna.

"Five minutes," Alethea and Sienna answered together. Alethea laughed at their shock. "What? I can read." She heard a door open and quickly shushed them. Brooke walked in, a slightly dazed expression on her face. "Well?"

"It's positive." Brooke blinked, clearly not believing it. "I don't understand. I just had my… It's positive."

The three women encircled Brooke, crying and cheering and laughing even as Brooke stood there, unmoving.

"Okay, now we have something to celebrate. Brooke?" Alethea asked. "You staying for dinner or do you want to go home and tell Sebastian?"

"I'll stay. I need to think what… I think I want an actual doctor confirmation first, yeah?" Brooke looked to her friends for support.

"Whatever you want to do, we're here. Oh, Brooke." Sienna gave her a huge squeeze. "I'm so happy I've been hoarding pregnancy tests. We need to finish planning Jo's shower so we can talk about this one." She bent down and addressed Brooke's stomach. "Hey there, baby. You are going to be so loved and spoiled it'll be ridiculous."

"Four fantabulous aunts at least," Leah added as she dabbed at her eyes. "And as thrilled as I am about this, I am starving! Can we please eat now? I don't think I can take any more surprises tonight."

"How about one more?" Alethea asked. "Ozzy wants to propose to Jo at the shower. An official proposal. He showed me the ring. And even better? He has a plan."

"Of course he does, he's Ozzy." Sienna held up her hands and silently called for calm. "Okay, ladies, let's get to work."

Alethea stood back and watched her friends bustling about the kitchen, celebrating and rejoicing one of the better moments life had to offer. The loneliness she'd experienced, the void-creating loss she'd felt when Talia had died, would never be filled completely again, but it would be close.

She was so lucky to have found this place, found a home with Calliope and Xander and Stella, found friendship with these amazing, strong women. Found a job she loved.

She didn't need school. She didn't need to upend her safe life, the one she'd worked so hard to build here. Dating, falling in love, getting married…that was all a risk to her heart.

She was not going to spend her life worrying about when tragedy was going to strike. She had her family, her friends. Her job.

Alethea did not, contrary to Sienna's regimented and romanticized beliefs, need to be dating anyone to have a fulfilling life.

She had everything she needed.

That would have to be enough.

CHAPTER FIVE

DECLAN WAS A MAN who didn't surrender. Not to a challenge. Not to fear. Not to circumstance. And certainly not to an indefinable, unending pile of junk.

He stepped back, planted his filthy hands on his hips and tried to see what, if any, progress he'd made in the past few hours.

Forget his weight lifting routine. This, not the crash that had nearly driven him directly into the afterlife, was going to be the death of him.

The sharp shot of a car door slamming had him bending over in relief. Whoever had arrived, they'd just earned his undying gratitude.

He grabbed his cane on his way out the workshop door, resentment prickling the back of his neck. Overdoing it one day meant relying on it the next. He needed to find some balance so he could ditch the thing for good.

But given how his leg was acting up, today was not that day.

Declan had been here for weeks and yet every time he stepped foot outside and into the sunlight, he found himself marveling at the beauty of the sky and his surroundings. California, especially this part of the Golden State, held its own perfect, peaceful appeal. The clouds even seemed different here. Giant marshmallows of airiness that drifted by on a gentle breeze tinted with the faintest hint of salt air.

A dark blue pickup truck was parked haphazardly in front of the house. The metal toolbox in the bed glinted against the streaming sun.

"Hello?"

The woman who popped up near the porch offered him a tight smile of greeting. "Mr. Cartwright. Hi. I'm Kendall MacBride." She trudged through the weeds to offer her hand. She stood just at his shoulders, wore her straight dark hair tight back in a ponytail and was dressed in black cargo pants and a snug tank that left her scarred arms and neck exposed.

His stomach rolled in sympathy. If anyone recognized burn scars, he did.

"Sorry I didn't call before I headed over," she said. "I had some unexpected free time so thought I'd come up and get a first look at things."

"No, that's fine. And it's Declan. Luke said to expect you sooner than later."

"Place is a bit of a mess." Kendall planted her hands on her hips and surveyed the yard. A gold band glinted against her ring finger. "Worse than I expected."

"Everything's fixable." It wasn't a question, but a statement of fact.

"Agreed." She didn't smile like Alethea. In fact, Kendall seemed more somber, definitely more serious. Perhaps even intimidating, especially with those scars. "Luke said you're going to be our point person and may have some ideas about improvements we should make?"

"I've already started. Give me a second to grab my list." He made his way up the porch stairs.

"Take your time." She gestured to the house. "I'll keep looking around."

When he returned, list in hand, he found

Kendall standing at the side of the house, pressing her hands into the siding in various spots. "Luke didn't say if anything was off-limits."

"We've been told anything and everything is on the table," Kendall informed him. "Off the top of my head, I can see we'll need to hire some kids from the high school to help clear out the brush and debris. Once we get a better lay of the terrain, I can bring in Lori Knight for a landscaping consult." She moved across the porch, poked her head inside the door. "That woman will love the challenge this place presents. I'll get her the bare details, then, we'll come out together to flesh out a plan and decide how many folks we'll shift off the sanctuary crew to get going here."

"Right." Why did he feel as if he should know about this? "The sanctuary."

"The butterfly sanctuary." If she was surprised at his lack of knowledge, she didn't show it. "It's nearing completion and I'm in a holding pattern right now on another project, so this will be a nice side project to mull over. You mind?" She pointed toward the porch.

"Do whatever you need to." He moved back

as she stomped her way up, then, walked over each board of the porch as if testing the strength of the planks. "Since I don't own the place, I don't want to overstep."

"No way to do that," Kendall said as she continued down the porch. "Luke and Gil have said to focus on ADA compliance. They want this place available to everyone."

"Sounds good to me." That was right in line with a lot of his notes.

Kendall pulled out a small, weathered notebook and scribbled some details. "I can tell a few of these planks should be replaced." She bounced up and down to test their strength. "And the stairs aren't in great shape. Better than I expected, though, so that's good. I'm thinking we add in a ramp, down and around there." She pointed to the west side of the porch. "Did Luke mention a budget at all?"

Declan shrugged. "I got the feeling it's negotiable." Considering what he'd paid for a three-month lease, he at least knew part of what they had to spend.

"Negotiable is a workable answer." She moved on, around the house. Declan waited for her on the porch, found himself daydreaming about getting started on the car that lay hidden beneath that tarp. He'd meant to use it as a reward for going without his cane for a few weeks, but maybe…maybe he could use the project as a way to hone his fine motor skills.

"There's some dry rot around the back," Kendall called out as she circled to the front. "Some water damage to the siding and window frames. Probably where the kitchen is. Good thing we'll be updating inside, too. Got a ladder around here so I can check the roof?"

"There's about half a dozen of them in the workshop." He pointed to the structure. "I've been turning it into a workout space, and I'd love to get it cleaned out so I can do some automotive work."

"Sounds like a good plan." Kendall went to check it out, returned a few minutes later with an eight foot metal ladder slung over one shoulder. "Place is a treasure trove. You'll want to talk to Irving Drummond, in town. He owns the thrift store, does haul aways for super cheap. Sells a lot of the junk at his shop, On a Wing."

He made note of the name and planned to make Luke an offer on anything he wanted to keep for himself.

Kendall moved off to the side of the house. Even if he'd had the inclination, he wouldn't have asked if she needed help. She moved with authority and purpose, neither of which he wanted to get in the way of. She sloped the ladder against the house, climbed up to the second story.

She clomped around for a while, then, poked her head over the edge of the roofline. "This'll need replacing. The trees don't help so we'll have to talk to Luke about hiring some trimmers. Tons of debris left to rot has eaten through the shingles. It's maybe one or two major storms away from springing a leak if it hasn't already and we're due for one anytime. You see any leaks inside?"

"Not that I've noticed." The truth was, he spent most of his time on the first floor. "I haven't seen any water stains in the ceiling, though."

"Best if I take a look and know what we're getting into."

"Go right ahead."

She climbed down and disappeared into the house. When she returned, her expression hadn't changed. "Definitely some leaks in the attic. And some critters have taken up residence. Once I have a better idea about that I've got a contact at the local wildlife center. They do extractions and captures. The water stains are minimal, but replacing the roof will make for a longer lasting structure. You have ideas about the interior?"

"I do." Beginning with finding out if the narrow halls could be widened or the floor plan revamped.

"Great. We'll talk. I'm waiting on the permits on that other project I'm spearheading," she said. "Day after tomorrow work for you? For me to bring Jo out for a walk around and consult?"

"Sure." Imagine that. He had something to put on his calendar.

"Jo's already itching to write up a contract, but that's probably because she's trying to distract herself from the baby." Her lips twitched in what he assumed passed as a grin for her. "My business partner loves the paperwork side of things. Me? I'm the labor." She looked around again. "It's a nice area. Private. Quiet. If I'd known it was here I might have bought it myself. It's a good flipper."

"I was looking for private and quiet."

"Won't stay quiet for much longer. Espe-

cially once people find out we're fixing it up.
You do know you're the main topic of conversation around town."

"Luke and Alethea might have mentioned it."

"Alethea, huh?"

"She got turned around a few days ago,
blew a tire on her food truck."

Kendall laughed. "Alethea is amazing, but
not known for her sense of direction. You'll
probably find yourself dealing with visitors
from here on out. Especially once we get
going on the house reno. It'll give people an
excuse to come up."

"That's fine." Truth be told, after having
spent time with Luke and Alethea the past
few days, he realized he really had missed
people. "It's about time I show my face in
town, anyway."

"You sound more thrilled about that prospect than I did when I first moved here." Her
smile was one of understanding and amusement. "Good idea, beating them to the punch.
You can get a big start by making friends
with Harvey at the hardware store. Then
eat at the diner. Between Harvey and Holly,
you'll have broken the ice."

"Is that what you did?"

"Nope. You couldn't have blasted me out of my hovel." Her brightened smile lit up her dark eyes. "I had a few interlopers drop in on me up at the lighthouse where I was living. A photojournalist and his niece." She twisted her wedding band with her thumb. "I went from silent and peaceful to chaotic and crowded in the blink of an eye."

"That must have been annoying."

"It was. At first." She dropped her head back and looked up at the sky.

"What did you do about it?"

"I married him." The peace that crossed over her features triggered a wave of envy that had Declan glancing away. Happy and settled. He'd assumed he'd have that at some point. Now...unless he got back on the track he didn't know what the future held. And that, more than anything, terrified him.

She headed over to her truck. "I was about to head into town for lunch. If you're hungry, you're welcome to join me."

"Ah—" He hesitated. He didn't want to overstep or take advantage, but the truth was, he was dying to dive in and see what Butterfly Harbor's main area entailed.

"If you're worried about getting back—"

"I'm not." He snapped the reply out before he had a chance to think. "Sorry. I just meant—"

"You just meant you're capable of finding your own way home. Got it. How long before you can drive again?"

"Not sure. Not until a doctor clears me." He hated having to voice it. He hated even more that the decision wasn't up to him. "I had a crash last year."

"I know. I saw it." There wasn't any hint of sympathy in her voice, just mild-natured understanding. "I was watching. Glad to see you're doing better."

"Thanks." Pity was the one thing that could drive him straight into a bad mood and thankfully, he didn't sense any where Kendall was concerned. "I'm hoping to be back in time to qualify for the season finale race later this year. We'll see." It was his method of couching expectations even as he strived to exceed them. "In the meantime, I need to figure out a mode of transport into town, but for now, I'll take you up on that ride."

WITH A HALF day for the elementary and high schools, a full crew working at the sanctuary and a night that had produced more menu ideas than it had sleep, Alethea had surrendered solitary control over the food truck and asked Natalie Inigo, one of the kitchen assistants at Flutterby Dreams, to take the lead for the day. Not that she was admitting to burnout, but she knew a nonstop afternoon when it hovered and she wasn't about to let things get ahead of her.

Besides, having Natalie at the order and pickup window gave Alethea the chance to do what she loved most: cook. Easier to focus on that than the fact that Jason was waiting for an answer about the ACT.

Laughter and shouts rang out from the playground, which was teeming with kids of all ages. They scampered on the climbing structures, swings and tunnel slides like sugar-boosted ants. Natalie, her close-cropped dark hair streaked with mermaid blue, bopped around the truck like she had springs in her worn shoes.

"I've got a double burger with onion rings, Philly-style hot dog, and a spicy shrimp and grits for Darrell!" Natalie shouted above the din of the playground and roar of the truck. With the fryers, the propane burners and their vents all whirring at top speed, it made it tricky to hear sometimes.

Alethea had been churning out meals and snacks since she'd popped up the awning at ten thirty for breakfast service down at the beach. The summer heat, which had been hit-and-miss this season, had switched to full blast by noon, which meant her idea to fry homemade churros amped up the temp in the truck by a million degrees.

But the fried doughnutlike sticks were selling fast and already had her considering various new sauce options for the future. She needed to change it up, have more than just the traditional sticks. Bowls to fill with ice cream, maybe, or teardrops to scoop up more deliciousness.

She scribbled notes on the magnetic pad she kept by the cooktop: a place to jot down ideas and comments of what had been successful or not for the day. As much as she was enjoying the hustle and bustle, she was ready for a break. Her feet hurt, her back pained and she was getting a headache.

"It's slowing down," Natalie told her as she accepted a new lunch order for one of their Thai tostadas. "If you want to take that break you were due an hour ago, go for it." She pointed to the refrigerator. "Grab a water and snack and go decompress for a bit."

"Yeah?" Most days Alethea didn't take a break, but today, without one, she knew she'd be dragging. She needed a few minutes off her feet to recharge.

"I've got this, no problem. And I'll give a shout if I need you." Natalie's friendly demeanor and dedication to the work had made her one of the most reliable employees at Flutterby Dreams. As a single mom of two young boys, Natalie was definitely used to hard work. Alethea's return smile faltered. Natalie also gave Jason someone to replace her with.

It was that thought, along with a water bottle, that she took with her to the swings. It was in the Costas DNA not to want to disappoint anyone and she had no doubt Jason had gone above and beyond to get her on that list of potential students. But the idea of shifting her life completely off track, to pack up and move hours away, even if it would greatly benefit her future... She rubbed her hands up and down her suddenly chilled arms. The idea simply, and straight-up, terrified her.

The arriving flood of half-day students had familiar, friendly, excited faces. Middle-school-aged kids dumped their backpacks and parked their bikes at the entrance to the sanctuary site, then, raced over to join the younger kids at the playground.

That area was relatively new, built as part of the sanctuary experience and also to serve as a place to keep the children safely corralled as they watched the construction proceed. The more construction vehicles that arrived on-site triggered endless bouts of curiosity and not only from kids, but from a number of adults. There was something about the completion of a building that had consumed the attention of the town's residents that added to the growing excitement.

In another couple of months the crowds, hopefully, would be replaced with tourists and visitors anxious to explore and discover the scientific and educational displays focusing on the importance of protection of not just the monarch species of butterflies, but also conservation in general. Days like this, when Alethea could take a few minutes to sit on a rubber-seated swing and enjoy the beating heart of Butterfly Harbor—its citizens—were going to be few and far between.

But becoming a tourist destination would do so much good in bolstering shops and businesses and livelihoods.

Proving, unfortunately, that change was sometimes for the better.

Sipping her water, she wrapped her free hand around the coated metal chain of the swing. Growing up, she and Talia had spent countless hours at the playground near their house: a playground that by comparison had been bleak, run-down and probably downright dangerous. But they hadn't seen the splinters and the rough patches and the cracks in the cement. A sad smile curved her lips. She and Talia had seen a way to try to touch the clouds, to try to climb higher just by pumping their legs and letting out squeals of accomplishment when one of them beat the other.

Talia would have loved, absolutely loved this place. The bitter edge of resentment sliced across Alethea's heart as guilt and regret took over. Would the day ever come, Alethea wondered hopelessly, when the thought of her best friend didn't make her want to cry?

The moment the question flitted through her mind, Alethea saw Charlie Bradley, along with Calliope's little sister Stella, Kendall's daughter Phoebe MacBride and Jasper's little sister Marley O'Neill racing over. Deputy Matt Knight's son Leo Knight trailed behind, his big blue eyes locked and transfixed on Charlie.

Alethea dug her toes into the cushioning bark, swung back and forth as they divided up into groups, then, took off at top speed.

Charlie and Phoebe were heading directly for her. Her quiet time of contemplation and self-analysis had come to an end.

"Hey, guys."

"Hey!" Charlie plunked herself onto the swing next to Alethea, began reaching for those stars Alethea no longer even looked at. "I've been practicing my flips. Wanna see?"

"What kind of flips?"

"Swing flips." Charlie's matter-of-fact tone told Alethea she shouldn't have had to ask. "Phoebe's my spotter. I need to make sure no one's around for me to fall on."

Alethea stood up, held out her hand to Leo who came over to watch. He was such a cute little boy: wide eyes and wavy blond hair.

He'd really come out of his shell since being adopted out of the foster system by Lori and Matt Knight a few years ago. Leo was small for his age and serious health problems as an infant had caused him to have a prosthetic right leg. Leo looked down at himself and dusted off his rumpled T-shirt and jeans.

Alethea drew Leo to her, rested a hand on his shoulder to keep him out of the way of Charlie's swinging legs and determined stare.

"Charlie, I'm not so sure you should be doing this." Alethea shielded her eyes from the sun. "Be careful, okay? I don't want you getting hurt. Don't forget we have our big night coming up." She'd followed through with Fletcher's request and had made plans to take Charlie, Phoebe, Stella and Marley to the movies and pizza on Saturday night.

"I've done this loads of times," Charlie shouted as she whipped past.

"Yeah, but you don't always land so good," Phoebe called back. "Remember last time—"

"Robbie Peterson got in my way," Charlie announced. "And he's not here today, so." She kicked her legs out, leaned back to get more height. "There's. Nothing." She soared forward. Then back again. "To. Distract. Me."

"Charlie, that's high enough." Remembering her own past as a swing flipper, Alethea moved Leo and the other kids aside.

"Mom!" Phoebe's yell split the air. "What are you doing here?"

Alethea turned to see Kendall MacBride heading over from the parking lot, a familiar figure walking beside her. Her first thought was that he didn't have his cane and that for the first time since she'd met him, he didn't seem to be limping. The somewhat befuddled, amused and awestruck expression on Declan Cartwright's face made him look like one of the kids and brought a twitch of amusement to her own mouth. The way the man wore a pair of jeans and T-shirt, however, was another story. Nothing kid-like about that. Or him.

Phoebe abandoned Charlie as she hurried over to her mother. Kendall drew her close, touched her hair and introduced Phoebe to Declan, who bent down and said something that made Phoebe's face split into the biggest and widest smile Alethea had ever seen.

So he was great with kids, too. Then she remembered one of his charities had a focus on after-school sports programs. Not that charity work with kids was a prerequisite for getting along with young people. Then again, everything she'd read about Declan Cartwright showed he got along with, well, everyone. And that disarmingly sweet smile of his had a long-distance surge capacity that had her insides doing an unwanted little dance.

Distracted, Alethea wasn't watching Leo, who shifted closer to Charlie. "You said you'd teach me when I got bigger, Charlie."

"I said that only last week, Leo."

"But I've grown a whole half an inch," Leo announced. "You can ask Kyle," he said of his big brother. "He measured me and everything."

"Leo, be careful! Wait!" Charlie yelled, but it was too late.

The definitive sound of impact happening could be heard. The collision threw Charlie into a twist and sent Leo flying. He landed on his back, thankfully on the soft padding, the color vanishing from his face as he lay there, arms splayed. Alethea looked down in horror. "Oh, no."

Alethea dropped to her knees as Charlie propelled herself off the swing and ran up to them. "I'm sorry," Charlie said. "I didn't mean it. It was a total accident!"

"Leo, are you okay?" Alethea tried to keep him still so she could check for injuries.

"Ow." Leo's chin wobbled and he lifted a hand to the left cheek. "My face hurts." Tears exploded in his eyes.

"I'll bet it does." Declan's voice broke through the fear Alethea had for the little boy. He approached and dropped down on the other side of Leo, rested a hand on the boy's shoulder. "You should sit there for a minute. Let us make sure you're okay."

"She kicked me," Leo accused.

"You kind of stepped into her line of flight, little man." Declan nodded to Alethea, who quickly ran her hands up and down Leo's arms and legs, then, carefully touched his face where a bruise was forming. Leo winced and sucked in a breath.

"Ow. Ow ow ow ow ow."

"You are going to have some impressive bruises," Declan said.

Alethea went wide-eyed at the impressed tone in his voice. She glared at him.

"I'll get some ice," Kendall offered. She

and Phoebe hurried away, assuring the growing audience around them that Leo was okay.

"It was an accident," Charlie repeated.

"Of course it was," Alethea assured her. "Classic playground mishap. Leo knows that, don't you, Leo?"

"I guess," Leo grumbled. "It still hurts. So does my butt." He reached back and as he did so, inched his pant leg up, which revealed his prosthetic.

Declan stared for a moment, blinked as if processing the information. Then, without missing another beat, he continued his conversation with Leo. "You know what my mom used to call something like this, Leo?"

"No, what?" Leo sniffled and seemed to have gotten the tears back under control.

"A wipeout," Declan declared. "And that, my young friend, was a mega one."

Leo started to frown, then, winced and gasped. "It was?"

"Absolutely. Quite amazing really. I think you cleared two, maybe three feet off the ground."

"So I kinda flew?" Leo seemed to ponder that for a moment. "Cool."

Alethea rolled her eyes. Declan grinned.

"I didn't kick him *that* hard." Charlie clearly sounded offended.

"Maybe I should wear a cape?" Already Leo looked like he was feeling better and he let Declan and Alethea help him stand up.

Kendall returned with a plastic bag filled with ice from the food truck. "Here, Leo." She bent down, rolled it gently against his face and lifted his hand so he could hold it in place. "You keep that there for a while. How about I call your mom and dad and have them meet us at the ER?"

"Nah." Leo shrugged. "I feel better already. I can tell them later."

Like they wouldn't notice, Alethea thought with a cringe.

"If you change your mind, you come get me," Kendall told him. "I'm going to get some lunch, but I can drive you home after or any time."

"I can walk him home," Charlie announced, then, as Stella, her hair bells tinkling in the long curls that matched her sister Calliope's, and Marley joined them. "We all can."

"Me, too, Mom?" Phoebe moved around her mom to take Leo's hand. "We'll make sure to tell Lori and Matt it was an accident. We all saw."

"You did? You saw me fly?" Alethea watched Leo's eyes go wide as he looked down at Phoebe holding his hand. He immediately straightened his shoulders and puffed out his chest. "It's okay. It doesn't hurt as much anymore. I don't want to go home yet."

"All right, then." Kendall nodded and motioned to the other side of the playground. "How about you guys leave the swings alone for today. Go play in the castle."

"Okay." Leo was the first to race away, hand in hand with Phoebe as if nothing had happened.

Kendall, shaking her head, chuckled as Declan slowly got to his feet. "Something tells me I'll be seeing Leo at our house a lot more. I'm going to get something to eat." She headed off to the truck.

"Let me guess." Alethea arched a brow at Declan, who grabbed hold of his back and winced as he shifted. "That's what they call boy logic?"

"Chicks dig bruises." Declan's grin wasn't quite as bright as before. Sweat dotted his brow despite the cool breeze. Some of the color had drained out of his face. That, combined with his quick blinking and controlled breathing, told her he was in pain.

Not something he was planning to acknowledge, she'd bet.

"For the record, this chick doesn't."

"Noted." Declan laughed, then, getting a better look at her expression, sobered. "Kids get hurt sometimes, Alethea. It's what they do. It's part of life. It's how they learn to deal with it that can make a difference."

"Is that what happened to you? You get shot out of one too many cannons by your sisters and it gave you a death wish?"

The smile stayed in place, but his eyes sharpened. "No cannons. Perish the thought. But my daredevil streak started pretty early. What's life for if not filled with excitement and the unexpected?"

"Maybe some of us would just like to get through life unscathed. Your way tempts fate."

"Nah." Declan shook his head. "I just dance with it." He pivoted and headed toward her food truck, then, tossed over his shoulder, "You should try it sometime."

CHAPTER SIX

"YOU SURE YOU want me to drop you off here?" Kendall leaned forward and looked out Declan's open door as he climbed out of her truck later that afternoon. "Cal's hit-and-miss with his hours. No telling if he's even around the shop today."

Declan waved off her concern. "If he isn't here, I'll come back another day. I need the walk and want to do a little exploring."

"It's more than a hike back to your place." Kendall didn't look convinced. "And you didn't bring your cane."

No, he hadn't. And in hindsight, that was probably a mistake. "A hike would do me some good. I'll find my way back. Thanks, Kendall." He stepped aside and closed the door. "See you day after tomorrow?"

"By eight fifteen. You have my number if you need anything."

He nodded, slapped his hand against the

car and she drove off. Odd, how easy he found this place and the people who lived here. Lucky for him that he was good with names otherwise the crowd of people he'd met during his food truck excursion would have overwhelmed him.

He was happy to have tagged along with Kendall. He'd been needing a bit of adventure and unpredictability and going wherever Kendall's truck took him seemed a solid place to start. After a lunch, that Declan had to admit surpassed his expectations, he'd found himself watching Alethea as she cleaned up the truck before she and her colleague pulled out of the area.

Admiration and appreciation clung to him. Alethea was pure magic when it came to food and, if he weren't careful, he'd be needing to up his exercise in order to prevent the pounds from piling on. But it was that smile of hers, that smile that he swore overrode a sadness she wasn't aware she displayed, that had him curious. What she really needed was some excitement in her life. Some unpredictability to show her that life wasn't meant to be acted out according to confining lines that led to boredom and caution. Sometimes the best way to live was to leave those road warnings behind, accept a challenge and see what might present itself.

Take right now, for instance. He stood at the end of town, looking across the main thoroughfare, a road named Monarch Lane that wound and stretched its way far into the distance. Behind him, the almost straight road to the freeway, something that held no interest for him. No. He was ready to explore and jump in with both feet and see what Butterfly Harbor had to offer him beyond the peace and recovery he'd already found.

He waited patiently for the traffic light to change to green and, then, crossed the street. Looking up, he spied the rusted, barely attached sign telling him he'd found "Mopton's Garage." The pair of out-of-date gas pumps had probably been installed during the Eisenhower administration. A new coat of paint and a little attention here and there would brighten them up, and encourage customers to stop in, so they wouldn't drive to the quick stop for gas, located just off the freeway .

The shop was stuck in a time warp. A business that left Declan waiting for an eager attendant to pop out of the grimy glass office to offer to "fill 'er up, sir?" So much promise obscured by...what? Declan couldn't be sure. Neglect? Boredom? Frustration? "Probably all three," he muttered as he made his way around the back.

There was one large garage door, caught halfway up, and, around the side near the trash bins, two vehicles that were either waiting for service or had been abandoned. He wasn't sure what was the case.

Red and white had been the garage's original colors, but both had given way to sea grime and salt residue. Old metal signs, rust along their edges, decorated the exterior walls. There was history about the place, Declan thought, as he walked toward the banging he heard coming from the back. Too bad its owner had lost any sense of pride about it.

"Hello!" Declan rapped his knuckles on the metal door.

Muttered cursing sounded inside, followed by a rustling and a shuffling of footsteps. When the door was pulled fully open, Declan found himself looking into the aged, tanned face of a man who had spent a good number of his extensive years in the sun. Grungy, faded and ripped jeans along with a stained

T-shirt that hung from the man's thin frame certainly didn't show any professionalism or attachment to the job.

Okay, Declan thought. Definitely bored.

"What can I do for you?" The man pushed back his oil-stained STP ball cap, then, after a moment, he gaped. "Well, I'll be. Declan Cartwright." His hand shot out, then, looking down and noticing the grease, he quickly wiped his palm against his shirt. "Ha. Pinch me sideways and call me surprised. What on earth are you doing in this little hole-in-the-wall town? I'm Cal. Cal Mopton."

"Mr. Mopton." Declan shook the man's hand.

"Cal. Please, call me Cal. Come on in." He stood back and waved him inside. "Never in my life have I ever…well. Young man, I've seen just about every race you've driven. You've got an angel's touch with cars. Never seen anyone handle vehicles the way you do. Respect." Cal nodded. "That's what you've got. Respect for them."

"Yes, sir, I do. That's why I'm here."

"Oh?" Cal's overgrown brows arched up.

"Yes, sir. I've leased the old Howser property."

"Elisha's place?" Cal's green eyes sharpened like glass. "Wondered what Gil would do with it since he got his hands on it. Hmm, could be worse I guess. He could have razed the place to the ground and built some fancy new condos on the property."

Not the first time he'd heard some interesting commentary on the town's mayor. He could have corrected the misconception, but he knew word would get around soon enough about Gil and Luke's plans for the Howser property. "Do you know anything about the Impala that's parked in the yard?"

"Elisha's daddy bought her that car brand new, but Elisha never drove. Always preferred to walk everywhere. Probably why she was as skinny as a broomstick. She couldn't bear to part with it, though, not even after her daddy died. I used to keep it tuned up just in case, but well." He shrugged.

"I'd love to work on it. Get it back up and running. Restore it to original specs." And that, Declan knew, would be the hard part. "Before I went and ordered anything online, though, I thought I'd see if you have any connections for old parts? I'd always rather help out a local business than a large conglomerate."

"For a '64 Impala?" Cal scrubbed a hand across his chin. "Nah. I doubt it. Might have stuff around here, though. Did you check that workshop of hers? Her daddy used to collect car parts like Henry Ford collected cash."

"I'm in the process of digging through what's in the workshop."

"Tell you what." Cal reached for a rag to wipe off his hands. "I'll go through my stuff and see what I can come up with. Can't promise anything, of course. Not sure what I've got around this place after all these years. Get yourself one of those tech manuals for the model. Check with Sebastian Evans up at Cat's Eye Bookstore. If he doesn't have one in stock, he can get you one."

"I'll be sure to do that." The smell of oil, that clinging scent of exhaust, diesel and rubber captured his nose. He took a deep, lung-choking breath and all but sighed. It smelled like home. "How long you been in business, Cal?" He wandered over to the desk completely obscured by stacks of paper and an old analog phone/answering machine combo with a continuous blinking light. The message readout blinked a capital E, no doubt indicating an error message because the messages were full.

"Going on forty years. This here was my daddy's place but my granddaddy, now, he's the one who opened it."

"How's business?"

Cal's face clouded over. "You asking because you're curious or because that nosy mayor of ours asked you to? Because it ain't none of that man's business what I do with mine."

"No, sir." This mayor of theirs was certainly a touchy subject. "Just curious. I've yet to meet this mayor I've heard so much about."

"Well, you will soon enough." Cal straightened his cap. "When Gil Hamilton finds out he's got another celebrity in his town, you can darn tootin' believe he's going to make a friend of you. Don't say I didn't warn you. Them Hamiltons can't be trusted to walk across the street let alone run a town."

Curiouser and curiouser. "I did see a couple of cars outside. If you needed help with repairs—"

"Don't need no one's help." Cal turned his back and focused his attention on the task at hand. "In fact, not much interested in the work side of things anymore. I'm eighty-two. I love this old place, but the hours…" He looked up and around the walls. "I know every inch of this garage. Spent more time here than I did in my own house growing up. Same when I became an adult. Nowhere else I feel right, you know?"

"I do know." It was exactly how he felt in his own metal shop back home; where he'd built his first racing engine and restored his first car. There was no place, other than being on the road and living in trailers and trucks, that felt more comfortable to him. "I'll go about making that list of parts I'll be needing, stop back maybe next week to see what you might have available."

"All right." Cal frowned. "Guess I could take a look around by then. Parts like that are gonna cost you."

"As they should," Declan agreed. "Nice to meet you, Cal."

Cal grunted, a casual sound that made Declan grin. Ornery old coot. A demeanor like that was what got some people through. Declan had yet to meet someone he couldn't get along with. Some took more patience and understanding than others, but all of them were worth knowing.

He made his way back to the front of the station, guesstimating a walk into town wouldn't take him too long, especially with his leg feeling pretty good. A quarter mile down the road he found the first entry to the beach, an opening in the waist-high stone wall that meandered all the way down and through the main area of Butterfly Harbor.

With the ocean on one side and the quaint, bustling little shopping and business area across the street, he couldn't help but pull out his phone and snap a few pictures to send to his sisters. They'd worried he was out in the middle of nowhere, but if nowhere looked like this, with its pristine storefronts and roaring summer waves lapping and teasing their way onto shore, then, nowhere was where he wanted to be.

"She was right." Alethea had told him the ocean had healed her. Who was he to argue when he could feel its pulsating power vibrating up and over the sand and rocks? That briny smell of amplified oxygen, fresh air and promise was as intoxicating as his own addiction to oil, rubber and heat.

That expanse of beach seemed endless, curving its way down toward an outcropping of cliffs, on top of which sat a giant yellow structure that stretched up into the cloudless sky. The Flutterby Inn had become a symbol of the town in recent years, not only as one of the original structures of Butterfly Harbor, but also as a focus for media publications and events. Jason Corwin and his wife, Abby, had gotten married in that inn and even had a TV special about it; his sisters had gushed about it at the time. The inn was frequently used for special events like weddings and anniversary celebrations. It was also rich with the history of the town and had been recommended on vacation websites as a must see for anyone visiting.

The trek to explore the inn further would have to wait for another day. As steady and strong as he was feeling today, walking that far, and up that steep a hill after the day he'd already had, would only set him back. But he added the visit to his goals list, along with a run on the beach.

After resuming his walk, he soon found himself in the heart of the downtown area. Giant metal butterflies had been welded to the top frame of the Butterfly Diner's glass door. The eatery had a giant window that stretched the length of the building, displaying cozy, vintage vinyl booths in bright orange and black. While customers exited and entered, he noticed the steady stream of visitors strolling up and down the street, popping in and out of storefronts and making a beeline across the street to the beach where families, couples and solitary visitors enjoyed the warm summer day on the shore.

Deciding to take an extra few minutes to revel in the late afternoon, he sat on the wall, stretched out his legs and took in his surroundings. Cars buzzed by at low speeds... probably due in part to the sheriff's vehicle parked right outside the diner. When he spotted a familiar blue clunker put-putting its way toward him, he smiled, his cheery mood lifting.

Alethea's car slowed and she rolled down her window, frowned at him from where she'd stopped in the middle of the road. "You okay? Need a ride back?"

"No." He shook his head. "Just taking a walk. Where would I find a bookstore called Cat's Eye?"

"Up that way." She pointed toward the next cross street ahead of her. "You sure you don't need a ride home?"

Need? Probably. Want? Declan pursed his lips. He did now. "I thought I'd do a bit of sightseeing before heading back. You offering to play tour guide?"

Alethea blinked at him, then, checked her watch. She shrugged, drove on and pulled into an open parking space near Harvey Hardware. A few minutes later, purse slung over her shoulder, she crossed the street to join him.

"I've got a few hours to kill. You want to hit the bookstore first?"

"Depends on what you suggest." He leaned his hands back on the wall and looked up at her. She'd taken her hair down, allowed all those black curls to spill over and around her shoulders. With those bright blue eyes of hers she looked like an animated princess brought to life: only with a much sharper edge. "I'm open for anything."

She rolled her eyes. "I have no doubt. I can't imagine you're hungry."

He shrugged. "Depends what you're offering."

"At some point you're going to have to visit

the Chrysalis Bakery. Or there's an ice-cream shop a few doors down. Why don't we start at the bookstore." She grinned. "What have you heard about it?"

"That there is one." He pushed himself up, took a moment to swipe the sand off his jeans while his leg readjusted. Sitting probably hadn't been the best idea; it would take him some time to get going again. "Why?" He saw what he could only describe as a mischievous glint in her blue eyes. "What wasn't I told?"

"You'll see. Let's go."

He tried to take in the variety of shops and businesses he spotted along the way. The hardware store that he'd heard of looked inviting and reminded him of the one in the small town where he'd been born. It was one of the few memories he had of his father, going to the hardware store every weekend to see what new tools were in stock. Little did he know his father, instead of buying tools for himself, had spent what little money they did have on a bar of candy for Declan. The treat Declan looked forward to all week.

Declan cleared his throat, pushing the emotions back down to where they wouldn't choke him. What he knew about his father now compared to what he understood then was mind-boggling. He'd had no idea how bad things were; his father had never let on until there wasn't any other choice. But on those Saturdays when his father bought him that candy bar, Declan's entire world had been perfect.

"You okay?" Alethea's question scraped along Declan's nerves.

"You need to stop asking me that." He kept his tone light. "If I've overdone it or need help, I'll ask for it."

"You're right." She shoved her hands into her pockets and ducked her head. "It's none of my business if you're in pain. I'll wait until you fall on your face before asking again."

"Not to get your hopes up, but I'm sure it'll happen." And that earned him a smile.

Up the slight hill, on the other side of a gaming and comic book store, Alethea stopped. "Here we are." She pointed to the hand-carved wooden sign depicting a cat and books. "The signs say to be sure to look up. I recommend you do."

"What? Why?"

But she'd already pushed open the door and stepped inside.

Declan let out a low whistle when he joined her. "Wow." His sisters were the book fans. He wasn't the greatest reader unless it was to do with mechanics or an instruction manual. Reading fiction made him itchy and jumpy, like he should be out doing something. Marcy had always said that was because he hadn't found the right author yet. Well, he was almost thirty and it still made him jittery. That didn't mean, however, he couldn't appreciate a bookstore, especially an independent and meticulously arranged store like Cat's Eye.

The polished hardwood floor was in the same rich tone as the shelves that stood neatly arranged throughout the store. Along the front near the windows were tables displaying the latest releases or recommendations. The children's section was identified with giant lettering on a sign hanging over a decorated archway with orange-and-black curtains that were tied back with open-winged monarchs.

So many books arranged by category filled the space, from a dedicated current events section to a substantial romance area his sisters would have gushed over. Tables sat at the end of the shelves filled with trinkets and jewelry and candle options for shoppers who were also inclined to be looking for more than books. He saw dozens of different cat-themed objects, from cute pens to statues to plush toys that looked…so real.

"Meow!" He nearly jumped as the stuffed multicolored kitten he'd been admiring greeted him and reached out a paw.

"It is real." The disbelief in his voice had Alethea laughing, but his incredulity faded into shock as he finally did as she'd suggested and looked up. The walls were lined with various platforms and perches, all within leaping distance of one another. Four of them were currently occupied with felines, most of whom seemed unconcerned with any of the humans occupying their space.

"Cat's Eye doubles as a fosterage for cats." Alethea came over and scratched the pretty kitten's head. "There's a lull in demand right now. Sometimes there's as many as a dozen roaming around."

"It's an interesting combination."

"Mandy loves her cats. Come on. I'll introduce you to her dad, aka the owner." She gestured for him to follow her to the front register that sat on a glass cabinet displaying beautiful handmade jewelry and small pieces of artwork. "Sebastian, this is Declan Cartwright."

"Oh, right. Sure." Sebastian set down the book he'd been skimming and smiled. "You're the guy living up at the old Howser place."

"That would be me." Declan wondered if any introduction around town would elicit a surprised reaction. "Great store."

"Thanks. Keeps me out of trouble." Pride shone on Sebastian's face. "Anything in particular bring you by?"

"Actually, yes." Declan continued to glance around. With the holidays coming up, he could get most of his shopping for his sisters done right here. "I'm looking for a repair manual for a '64 Chevy Impala."

"I don't keep a lot of car manuals in stock." He tapped on the computer, frowned. "Let me check something in the back. Just a second."

"Sure."

A teenage girl with long, straight blond hair hopped down the staircase behind the counter. "Daaaa-ad, the group for tomorrow's dive backed out. Monty's going to cancel the charter unless you know someone who— Oh, hey,

Alethea. Sorry." She cringed. "Should have checked for customers first. Hi." She looked at Declan, then, did a fast double take. "Oh, wow. Wowza wow. Aren't you—?"

"Mandy," Alethea cut her off. "This is Declan Cartwright. Declan, this is Mandy. Cat wrangler extraordinaire and part-time fish. Rumor has it she has gills she spends so much time on the water."

Mandy laughed. "I won't get gills until I'm working on the water full-time."

Alethea chuckled.

The shirt Mandy wore displayed the logo for Wind Walkers, the boating and tour company he'd read about.

"My BFF Eleni's a big fan. Big racing fan," Mandy clarified. "She was watching the race when you…well, she watched your last race. She's going to be so bummed she didn't get to meet you." Mandy sighed. "She's on a student study program in Greece this year. Man, wait until I tell her I met Declan Cartwright!"

"Bring it down a notch, Man." Sebastian wandered out of the back, a thick paperback in his hands. "You lucked out. I was about to return this to the warehouse." He handed it to Declan.

"This is great." He thought for sure it would be at least a week before he'd be able to start reading up. Curious, Declan shifted his attention to Mandy. "What kind of diving do you do?"

"Huh?" Mandy blinked.

"You said a group canceled on you for tomorrow. What kind of diving?"

"Free diving. There's a spot Monty and I found not far off the coast. It's got some great kelp forests and sea life to observe."

"If you need someone to grab the reservation, I'd be happy to."

"Really?" Mandy bounced on her toes. "You mean it?"

He could feel Alethea's gaze boring into him. "I do. I did some free diving as part of my rehabilitation. A friend of mine recommended it to help with my breathing control, rebuilding the strength in my lungs." Maybe if he could convince her the activity had a medical purpose, she'd stop glowering at him.

"The reservation is for ten a.m. tomorrow. Is that okay? Lunch is included."

"Is there a minimum age?" Declan asked. Luke had lamented the fact that Simon was preoccupied with only books and screens.

Maybe this was something father and son could do together.

"Considering the number of kids of all ages in this town?" Sebastian answered before Mandy could. "It depends on the individual kid, but typically anyone over ten is fine."

Declan nodded. "I might have another two people who can join. I'll let you know in a few hours if that's okay?"

"More than," Mandy said. "Here's Monty's number." She grabbed a business card off the stack on the counter. "Just give him a call and let him know who to expect."

"Perfect." Declan pocketed the card. "I'll do that."

"Um." Mandy looked suddenly unsure of herself. "Do you think there's a chance you'd be up for promo pics tomorrow? Having Declan Cartwright as a customer of Wind Walkers would be great advertising. If you have time, of course."

"Sure." Declan couldn't start promoting himself too soon when it came to his racing return. Images of him doing something physical like diving was a win-win for both him and Mandy's employer. "Happy to help if you think it will."

"Double awesome. Just head down to the marina tomorrow morning. You can't miss Wind Walkers, but just in case, head for slip seven."

"I will see you there."

He set the book down on the counter, faced Alethea, who he had no doubt had something to say about both his plans and his impulsiveness. Sure enough, the disbelief on her face had every hackle rising inside him.

The second he opened his mouth, something sharp stabbed him in the back of his calf. What the…he didn't want any new pains! He let out a strangled, rather pathetic groan.

"What's wrong?" Alethea demanded as he reached back and down.

When he encountered something furry, soft and moving he nearly jumped out of his shoes. The tiny stabbings made their way up the back of his jeans, into the fabric of his shirt until the kitten he'd met earlier settled on his shoulder.

"Percy." Sebastian sighed and walked around the counter, reaching for the cat. "I'm so sorry. He's usually pretty skittish which is why I let him wander. I want him to get used to people. But not like that." Sebastian continued to hold out his hands for the tiny fur ball. "Come on, little guy. Let's discuss boundaries and personal space."

Percy's claws came out to cling to Declan's shoulder. He mewed and dug his claws in deeper.

"Ow. Ow. Okay, how does something so little hurt so much?" He waved Sebastian off and reached up to gently grasp the cat, who released his hold the second Declan touched him. Declan pulled the cat down and held him up to his face, nose to nose. "You are too curious for your own good."

"He probably mistook you for a tree." Alethea laughed. "He is a cute little thing. What kind is he?" She asked Sebastian.

"He's a tortoise. Tortie for short. Very rare to come across a male. They're almost always female."

Percy mewed again and batted his paws out toward Declan's face.

"I think he's in love." Alethea leaned over and rested her cheek on Declan's forearm. "Look at that face." She reached out to stroke the cat's ear. "Come on, Uncle Declan. Take him home."

"Yeah, because he's so neglected here," Declan joked. "I'm not set up for a cat and I'm only here for a short while." Still… "He'll get lost in that house."

"No, he won't," Alethea urged. "He'll probably be stuck somewhere on you. Forget Percy, name him Barnacle. You can call him Barnie."

Percy mewed as if in approval.

"Torties are fairly hearty," Sebastian added his two cents. "He might look small now, but trust me, they can be bulldozers. With an attitude to match."

"I could send him to one of my sisters' kids once I'm back on the circuit." Or he could find a way to bring the cat with him on the road. Could be an interesting challenge.

"I think you two are made for each other," Alethea teased.

Declan sighed and, surrendering, shifted the cat back onto his shoulder. "I came in for a book and am leaving with a roommate. What were the odds?"

"In Butterfly Harbor?" Alethea asked.

"Better than you'd think," Sebastian answered. "Stay right there. I'll get the adoption paperwork."

"Am I forgiven?"

After leaving the bookshop, Alethea led the way down the hill to Monarch Lane and turned left. "There's a pet store on the next block. They should have everything you need for the first few nights with him. Forgiven for what?" She had to admit, watching a world-famous race car driver being attacked—or rather claimed—by a kitten the size of an avocado had made her entire day. Now here the man stood, a reusable bag with his book in one hand and a cardboard pet carrier in the other, heading off to buy supplies for his new feline companion.

Declan winced. "Forgiven for going diving tomorrow."

"Oh. Right." Just like that, her good mood vanished. "It's none of my business what you do."

"But you disapprove."

"It's not my place to—"

"Alethea." He shifted the bag to the hand carrying the cat and caught her arm, stopping her right in front of the Butterfly Diner. "Maybe it matters to me what you think."

"It does?" She didn't want to know the answer. She didn't want to think of this man—a man who got up every morning ready to jump at any challenge, big or small—as someone she should care about. "It shouldn't. This is what? The third time we've even spoken to each other?"

"Fourth." His grin widened. "I've been keeping count."

She refused to acknowledge the heat in her cheeks. "Fine. The fourth. We're barely friends. We're acquaintances. Just." And it was better for everyone if things stayed that way.

"So maybe I care about what my acquaintances think of me."

"Please. You didn't get to where you are by caring what anyone thinks."

Declan stood a little straighter. She understood him better than he realized.

Alethea pointed to the carrier. "Don't think that you've earned any goodwill because you're taking that little guy home." But he had. More than she cared to admit. Watching him lose his heart to Barnie—the cat's new official name—had been one of the most endearing and entertaining events she'd been witness to. "I'm not your doctor, Declan. If you think you're capable of diving into the middle of the ocean—"

"I am. At least I think so." He glanced up and frowned. "Um. Who are they?"

"Huh?" Alethea turned and found not one, not two, but five members of the Cocoon Club crowded into one of the diner's booths, their noses practically pressed up to the glass. Myra's telltale orange hair matched the booth. "Geez." She could feel the warmth moving up her face. "That's the Cocoon Club. Let's move—"

"We're good here," he said. Alethea looked back at him in time to see him wave at their observers. "Makes you feel like we're in a fishbowl, huh?"

"Something like that." Heaven help her, she could only imagine what that group of gossips was thinking. Or planning to impart to others once they left the diner. "Where were we?"

"You were chiding me for being immature and careless with my safety by going diving tomorrow."

"Right. Yeah. That." She crossed her arms over her chest. "All of that."

"If I were new to free diving, I might agree with you, but I'm not. It's exhilarating, Alethea. It's life-affirming and if there's one thing I've learned in the last year it's to be grateful I'm still here. Someone gives me the chance to go diving in one of the most beautiful spots in the world, darn straight I'm going to take it."

"It's your life. If you want to take a risk like that, feel free."

She suspected he wanted to laugh, but when he inclined his head and his expression turned to one of concern, she glanced away. She didn't need him to see her worry. Her fear.

Her terror.

"Nothing's going to happen to me tomorrow, Alethea."

She tightened her arms. "You don't know that."

"No. I guess I don't. But you don't know anything bad will happen, either. I'll tell you what."

"What?"

"If you're this concerned, come with me."

"Come with you?" Was he out of his mind? "Out on the boat? Out diving?" Like in the ocean? Where her feet couldn't touch the bottom? She shuddered.

"You don't have to dive if you don't want to, but come out on the boat. You have tomorrow off, don't you?"

Her eyes narrowed. "How did you know that?"

"I heard you and the other woman in the food truck talking. Sounds like you taking a day off work is a rare occurrence. How about you make it a special day."

"I have things I have to do."

"Sometimes having to do things needs to take a back seat to unexpected opportunities."

"If you're planning a new career in bumper sticker writing, that one's too long."

He moved closer to her and it took all her resolve not to back away. He was so…she let out a slow breath. He was so good-looking. So charming and funny and alive. So alive it almost hurt. She tried to stay angry, to resent the fact that he was here and someone like Talia was gone, but she couldn't quite manage it. He lifted his hand, stroked her cheek with his finger and tipped her over the edge of indecision. "If you're that worried about me, be there. Keep me on the straight and narrow. Make sure I don't do anything foolish."

"Why do I have the feeling this would be

one of the least foolish things you've done?" He laughed, a soft, gentle, thrilling sound that made her toes tingle.

"You're the one who told me the ocean made you feel alive again. How about you take that extra step and prove it?"

CHAPTER SEVEN

HE'D MADE A MISTAKE. A horrible, terrible, ridiculous mistake he'd be paying for, for the next ten, maybe twenty years.

"Barnie, you need to come down from there." It was after eight o'clock. Alethea was going to be here anytime to pick him up so they could grab breakfast before they headed to the marina. Instead of being downstairs waiting for her, he was stuck in his bedroom, which was filled with cat toys, a small litter box in the closet and an elaborate carpet-upholstered cat castle that made his jaw drop every time he spotted it.

Sitting on the edge of his bed he looked up at the top of the antique armoire taking up most of the west corner of the room. Declan had no idea how he'd managed it—unless kittens had some kind of built-in transporter—but Barnie had gotten onto the very top and was playing peekaboo from behind one of the decorative scrolls.

"Mew." Barnie blinked his gold eyes in a way that pretty much called Declan's bluff.

"Look, work with me," he pleaded with the cat. "I convinced Alethea to come out diving with me. Believe me, that's a big deal. How's it going to look if I have to cancel because I can't keep my cat under some kind of control?"

"Mew." Barnie sighed as if irritated his human didn't realize that control and cat didn't exist in the same universe.

"I'll bring you some tuna when I come home." Like the little guy had a frame of reference for promised tuna. Now, if he only had some in his pocket… "Look, little dude. You need to come down so I have some faith you'll be safe while I'm gone. Come on." Declan stood, and, after giving his stiff back a bit of a stretch, held up his hands in surrender. "Don't make me get the ladder out. That won't end well for either of us."

Barnacle tilted his chin down, looked at Declan's hands, back into Declan's face, mewed and rolled to the side. Declan caught him as if they'd been pulling off this act for years. He set the cat on the top of the three-tier castle on the other side of the room and after rearranging the litter box, and shoving one of his suitcases on top of the armoire to prevent a repeat visit by the cat, he let out a sigh of relief.

He had a bowl of kibble and another bowl of water ready by the door he planned to close while he was gone. If Barnie were left to explore the house on his own, there was no telling where the cat would end up. The timing of the diving trip could be better, like after he and the cat had been trained on their new relationship, but some things couldn't be postponed.

And getting Alethea outside her comfort zone and willing to embrace life instead of turning her nose up at it was definitely at the top of his to-do list.

A car door slammed and Declan grabbed his shoes. Rather than attempting to put them on again—he'd learned the hard way that kittens and shoelaces were an intoxicating combination—he lifted Barnie off his new perch and carried everything downstairs. His leg hitched before he reached the first floor. The pain shot straight up his spine and settled into a dull, annoying throb at the base of his neck.

His knuckles went white around the banister. He drew in long, slow, deep breaths and willed the pain to subside.

The water would help. The diving and swimming would stretch things out. But at the moment he was stuck, waiting for the tingling racing up and down the backs of his legs to stop. He was still standing at the foot of the stairs when Alethea's shadow appeared on the porch.

"Come on in!"

Alethea pushed open the door and stuck her head in. "You don't lock it, do you?"

"Good morning to you, too, sunshine." He shook his head. The bright pink shirt she wore beneath a zip-up hoodie accentuated the blue of her eyes. She'd knotted her hair back, no doubt in preparation for the wind. She looked bundled up enough to go dogsledding, not spend a day on the ocean. "Barnie and I have been coming to an understanding."

"Ooooh, there he is." Alethea hurried forward and held out her hands. "I've been wanting to snuggle him since I got up this morning." She plucked Barnie out of Declan's grasp and rubbed her nose in his soft fur.

Declan watched, wondering how it was possible to feel jealous of a cat. A cat who, given the besotted and satisfied expression on his whiskered face, knew exactly what Declan was thinking.

"You entertain him while I put these on." Slowly, he lowered himself onto the steps and put on his shoes.

"How'd he do last night?" Alethea dropped down and settled Barnie on her knees so she could tickle his tummy.

"Oh, he did great. How a microscopic fur ball can take up most of the bed is beyond me. I kept waking up, afraid I'd rolled over on him."

"You didn't have to let him sleep with you. That castle you bought him—"

"Yeah, it was my *choice* for him to sleep on the bed." Declan rolled his eyes. "Clearly you've never had a cat. Every time I put him somewhere he clawed his way up the bedspread."

"Awww. Poor Declan." She giggled when Barnie's paws shot up in the air for easier tummy access. "And nope, I've never had one. My sister-in-law has one. Ophelia. But she's older and quite independent. My mom's allergic so we didn't have animals growing up. Just as well given everything else she was juggling."

"Anytime you want kitten-sitting rights, feel free. You want to take him back up to the bedroom and get him settled?" The idea of climbing those stairs again was enough to sour his mood. "Second door on the right. I've cat proofed it as much as I can."

"Sure. You need anything else while I'm up there? A jacket maybe?"

"That I have down here, thanks." Grateful she didn't hover and fret, he listened to her talking to the cat, murmuring platitudes and teasing the little guy.

Declan shoved himself up, wincing as that knot in his leg refused to ease. He made his way into the kitchen where he downed one of the painkillers. He hated taking them, but they worked and right now, that was all he wanted.

To ease the upset stomach the medication could cause, he grabbed a hard-boiled egg. He stood there, hands braced on the refrigerator, waiting for the pain to subside.

Alethea bounded down the steps just as he'd swallowed.

"You want to do bakery or diner for breakfast?" She stopped in the kitchen doorway, looked around. "Wow. This is kinda dinky, isn't it? How do you even fit in here?"

"Pure will and necessity." He liked it, actually. The house was cozy. A little too cute for his taste, but that would change once Kendall got her hands on the place. Just in time for him to leave. "I'm not much of a cook so as long as the microwave works, I'm not in here very often."

"Except to get coffee."

"You want some?" He still had half a pot left from the morning brew.

"Depends. Diner or bakery?"

"My answer determines your need for coffee?"

"You haven't had Holly's special blend. And forget it. You waited too long. Diner it is." She glanced at her watch. "We'd best get going. Diner gets busy in a little while and we're on a schedule."

He followed her out of his house, only to hesitate at the door. "You sure the kitten will be okay?"

Alethea shrugged. "We'll find out when you get home. Come on. I'm starving."

Uncertain what had shifted Alethea from reserved and cautious to energetic and excited, Declan decided he didn't care. He'd take Alethea Costas with a smile on her face any time of the day.

"SCRAMBLED EGG WHITES AND VEGGIES for Butterfly Harbor's newest tenant and one eggs bene for Alethea."

"Thanks, Holly." Alethea rubbed her hands together before she picked up her fork. Declan stared down at his plate. Even a simple order like this was presented with polish, right down to the mini fruit salad on the side. His stomach growled just looking at it. No wonder this place was hopping, right down to the half-dozen customers waiting for seats.

"Nice to finally put a face to the name, Declan." Holly set their check on the edge of their table. "I keep telling Luke we should invite you to dinner one night. Help you get acclimated to town."

"It's been a pretty easy process," Declan assured her. "Your husband's been great, letting me lease that house."

"Well, from what I'm hearing you'll be paying him back in spades. He's so relieved to have your help with that house."

"I'm glad I can lend a hand."

"Mama, up! Mama, up up." Declan had to stretch his neck to see the little boy who had toddled over and grabbed on to Holly as if she were a lifeline.

"Hey, it's my favorite little man under two." Alethea dropped her fork and scooted to the edge of the booth.

"Allie!" The toddler relinquished his hold on his mother's jeans and toppled right into Alethea's arms.

"Where's Zoe this morning?" Alethea asked as she avoided a bonk on the head from Jake's excited hands.

"It's daddy-and-daughter day. She loves going into the station with him, so I get this one. You have any free evenings in the next couple of weeks, Al?"

"I'll check my calendar and let you know, but probably. Date night?"

"You got it." Holly reached up and tightened her ponytail. "Don't worry. I know you can't do Saturday because of the baby shower."

"Will you be able to come to that?"

"Yep. Kevin and Twyla are going to run the diner and if there's any problem, they can call me or Brooke. I'd better get going. Have a good day."

"Nice to meet you, Holly," Declan called after her. When he shifted his focus back on Alethea, he noticed her move her plate closer for Jake to grab a crispy potato. "Old friend?"

"I've been babysitting Jake and Zoe since they were born." Alethea snuggled Jake much in the way she'd nuzzled Barnie.

He was about to ask if she liked kids, but the expression on her face was all the confirmation he needed. She didn't just like them; she loved them and from what he could tell both yesterday at the playground and here with Jake, the feeling was mutual. His heart skipped a beat. She was open and relaxed with Jake, not hesitant or uncomfortable in the least and he certainly didn't sense any trepidation or worry where the little boy was concerned. Whatever issues she had with Declan's perceived recklessness didn't have anything to do with the unpredictable behavior that came with childhood. Whatever she was dealing with had to do with circumstances that were much more serious.

"Good morning, Alethea."

"Ezzie, good morning." Alethea held Jake's flailing hands away from her coffee and motioned to Declan. "Declan, this is Ezzie Salazar. She helps with the Cocoon Club."

"Don't tell them that." Ezzie lowered her voice and pointed over her shoulder to the booth of now familiar faces peering back at them. "They like to think they're helping me."

"It's nice to meet you." Declan held out his hand.

"And you. You've accomplished quite the feat, going unnoticed around this town for a few weeks. Oh, hi, honey." Ezzie stepped to the side as a distinguished older gentleman approached. He was tall and on the slender side. His sleek gray hair was as polished and neat as the slacks and dark green polo shirt he wore. "Declan, this is Vincent Fairchild. He's another recent transplant to town."

"Pleasure, Declan. It's Vince, please." He slipped an arm around Ezzie's waist. "I've been trying to be open to new things since I've been dating this one." He tucked Ezzie's head in under his chin. "Sorry I'm late."

"Don't be. I was just going to borrow this little guy for a visit with the club. I'll meet you at our table." Ezzie scooped Jake into her arms and spun him away while Vince pushed his hands into his pockets.

"Fairchild Enterprises made out quite well by sponsoring your team," Vince told Declan. "I was sorry to hear about your accident. Looks like your recovery is going well."

"Beyond expectations." Nerves he hadn't felt in almost a year scampered back into his stomach. "I'm working on a comeback."

"Really?" Vince nodded in approval. "That's excellent to know. Your innovative engine designs were something that caught my research team's eye. Well, they were my research team before I retired. I still maintain an advisory role with the directors. When you're ready to get back on the circuit, let me know if I can be of assistance. Nothing the sports world likes better than a comeback story." Vince held out his hand.

Stunned, Declan returned the handshake. "Thank you, sir. I appreciate that. And I'll take you up on it for sure."

"Excellent." He smiled at Alethea. "You two enjoy your breakfast."

"Vincent Fairchild moved to Butterfly Harbor?" Declan couldn't keep the wonder out of his voice. "Did you know his company was one of the first investors in CatchAll Motors?" He'd been looking at expanding their endorsement deal before the accident. "Didn't I hear there was some kind of scandal earlier this year with his daughter?"

"Depends on your definition of scandal." Alethea had resumed eating, although not with nearly as much gusto as before. "She left her fiancé at the altar. It was a marriage Vincent seriously encouraged at a time when Sienna shouldn't have been making life-changing choices."

"She did a full-on runaway bride?" Declan chuckled. "Boy, I got here just a little too late to witness that, I guess. Never thought a man like that would walk away from a multimillion-dollar business."

"He had a heart attack." Alethea stabbed a potato. "He almost died and when he didn't, he changed his life. Moved here to be closer to his daughter. And to Ezzie." She sounded almost hurt. "Gave up his old life so he could live out this one."

"Good for him." Declan nodded.

"Good for him." Alethea repeated, looking at him with an odd light in her eyes. "But not good for you?"

"Different circumstances. He had his daughter to think about."

"And you don't have to think about anyone other than yourself."

Declan frowned. "That's not what I said." What switch had he flipped that turned off the carefree Alethea he'd watched bounce into his house just a little while ago? "Okay, we've been dancing around this long enough." He pushed his plate forward and rested his arms on the table. "Something about me ticks you off. No." He snatched the check off the table before she could grab for it. "I invited you out today, so it's on me. And you're trying to change the subject. What did I do or say that was so wrong?"

"You didn't do or say anything." She swallowed so hard he could see her throat work. "It's not you, necessarily. It's your mindset. Your impulsiveness. I look at you sometimes and I just get..." She stopped, searching for the words as she waved her hand in the air.

"Angry. The word is *angry*."

"It isn't you," she repeated and looked as

if she wished she hadn't said anything. "It's what you represent."

"Success? Financial stability?" Time to lighten the mood. He'd asked, but he was suddenly wishing he hadn't. Not when the conversation was clearly upsetting her. "Romantic temptation? Come on." He flashed the smile that had landed him on the cover of national magazines. "You've thought about it." He reached across the table and slipped his fingers through hers. He watched as her chin dipped, as she looked at how their hands were joined and he felt her shiver. Just as he felt the chills race up his arm.

Her lips twitched. "Seeing you, being around you is nice, Declan. It's really nice."

"I think it's nice to be around, you, too." There. Common ground. And more easily admitted to than he'd anticipated. Too easily. "There's a but coming, isn't there?"

"A big one." She took a deep breath and surprised him by not pulling her hand away. "Being around you is nice. You're a risk. And seeing how you are, it gets to me. Deep down. You are so lucky. You said so yourself."

Had he? Some days he didn't feel lucky. Lucky would have been walking away from that crash. Lucky would have been not needing skin grafts to heal the burn scars on his arms and legs, or the physical therapy to help rewire his brain. Lucky would have been... He blinked and released his hold on her. "Lucky was probably an overstatement."

"No, it wasn't." She picked up her fork and began to eat again. "Trust me—you're one of the luckiest people on earth." She skewered a potato and when she lifted her fork, he saw the tears shimmering in her eyes. "Because you're alive."

WAS SHE EVER going to get past this?

Walking to the marina with Declan after what had turned into a disastrous and rather silent breakfast felt like a punishment. She'd been determined to prove to him, to herself, that she could take chances, that she could appreciate the unexpected excitement and opportunities life presented and yet...

And yet.

She tucked her hands farther into the pockets of her sweatshirt and wondered how she could extricate herself from the rest of the day without looking like an even bigger fool than she felt. The marina stretched out before and around them, welcoming them into its embrace. She loved being here and watching the boats come and go. But rarely, if ever, did she want to be on one. What was wrong with her that she couldn't leave the past where it belonged? Behind her.

"It occurs to me." Declan spoke easily, so easily she had no doubt he'd been rehearsing what to say. "That we should be focusing on moving beyond acquaintances toward a more solid friendship. We really don't know anything about each other. Other than what you've read about me online or heard on the news."

"Acquaintances don't really have much reason to delve deeper." Alethea stopped walking. "In fact, it's probably best if we keep things in that realm. I don't think I should come along—"

"No." He could have caught her arm, could have touched her in some way that would have made her want to stay with him. But he only blocked her path. "No, this is exactly why you should. I think there's a solution to our situation."

"Do you?" She looked at him through narrowed eyes.

"I might not know or understand a lot about you, Alethea, but I know you're smart and I know you're in pain. There's also something between us. Maybe you felt it that first day. I know I did the second I touched you." He stepped closer, but again, didn't touch her. Simply feeling the warmth radiating off his body was enough to scatter whatever thoughts she still had in her head. "I'm a man who says what he thinks. Probably more often than I should. My sisters say I'm filterless. I think of it more as open and honest."

Alethea ducked her head to hide her smile. She could see both sides of that argument. "Attraction doesn't have to lead to anything." She did not have time for, what would she call this? A romantic complication? "Being friends or even acquaintances is a good thing to be."

"Okay." He nodded as if he'd expected this response. "Okay, yeah, but let's put a solid foundation on our friendship. It would be, should we decide to pursue it, the best way to begin a relationship."

Her head snapped up. "A relationship?" Who...what... Who said anything about...? "You don't strike me as relationship material."

That grin of his was back. "So you have been thinking about me in that way. That's a bit of good news."

She snorted, shook her head. He could lighten up any petrifying topic, couldn't he? "Better tell Monty and Mandy they need a bigger boat. That ego of yours won't fit on any of theirs."

"Not going to argue with that one. Ego is part of what kept me alive. No, don't." Now he did touch her. He caught her chin between this thumb and finger and tilted her head up. "Don't shut the door on me again. Don't make me keep guessing and wondering. I'm not going to apologize for still being here, Alethea. And I'm not going to stop taking advantage of every moment I have. I'm sorry that you lost whoever you lost. But that wasn't my fault."

"I know it wasn't." His words stung, mainly because he was right, and was opening the wound she'd tried so hard to heal with her silence and acceptance. "It was hers." Tears blurred her vision. "And mine."

He let out a slow breath and nodded. "Okay. I think I understand now."

He guided her gently to one of the benches

overlooking the slip where Mandy and Monty welcomed Luke and his son, Simon, onto one of Monty's boats. The wall she'd built around her heart cracked. They must have been who Declan thought of to round out the rest of the diving group. She'd heard Luke and Holly discussing ways to get Simon outside and trying new things. Apparently Declan had heard about it, as well. More importantly, he'd remembered.

Darn it. Beneath all the fame and flirtatious reputation and easygoing smiles, Declan Cartwright really was a good guy.

"We're going to be late." She did not want to do this. She didn't want to talk about Talia. Not here. Not now. And not with him.

"We have plenty of time and if we're late, I'll pay for the delay." He drew her down beside him, rested his arm across the back of the bench: not touching her, but close enough his presence gave her some comfort. "Some things are more important." When she hesitated, he pushed. "What happened?"

She shook her head, not in refusal, but to stop the tidal wave of grief that surged up inside her. It hurt, coming up with the words; revisiting those days physically hurt and yet now, with him, the desire to let go of those emotions, those memories, hammered her determination to keep herself closed off.

"All right, let's start with something easier." There was no impatience in his voice, just care and concern. "Tell me a name."

"Talia." She choked it out, cleared her throat and found the second time saying it was easier. "Her name was Talia and she was my best friend."

He nodded, brushed his fingers against the back of her shoulders and remained silent.

"We were born a week apart. Her family lived across the street from mine. Our moms." She swiped a finger under her eyes to get rid of the tears. "Our moms called us sisters of the heart. We were together all the time. Inseparable. Took our first steps together, first day of school. We even went on our first dates as a double one. The truth is, I don't know that I knew how to do anything without her. When we went to college, there was never any doubt we'd be roommates and we found a school where we could each pursue our own interest. I was prelaw," she added and the idea felt a universe away.

"Talia was scouted, got a swimming

scholarship. She was on track to get to the Olympics. It was like watching a miracle when she swam. And then, just before the end of our freshman year, she was in a bike accident that dislocated her hip. Everything went downhill from there." The tears wouldn't stop now. Probably because she hadn't let them flow this freely in months. "I don't have to tell you how horrible therapy and recovery can be. But she was determined and her folks and me and my family, we all rallied around her. We didn't know...didn't see." She tried to swallow but had to catch her breath. "One of her doctors prescribed an opioid."

"Alethea."

She heard it in his voice, in the way he said her name. He understood. Completely. Without her needing to elaborate. But now that she'd started, she couldn't stop.

"She changed. So much. She was so angry, so volatile one minute and, then, perfectly fine the next. On top of the world. The mood shifts were terrifying and when she was up, I thought maybe she'd beaten it. She insisted she had it under control, that she wasn't an addict. To prove it, she tried to go back to swimming, but couldn't keep up." Watching her best friend's dreams disappear had broken Alethea's heart. Not only because she felt like she was losing her friend, but because she couldn't stop it.

"The school was no help and even made things worse by saying they would have to pull her scholarship." She shrugged, feeling as helpless now as she had, then. "She started forging prescriptions, getting the pills from other students. I tried to convince her to get help. Time and time again, she said she would. That she'd talk to her parents and the dean. Find a counselor."

She sat on her hands, wished the cold would stop seeping into her bones. "One day I came back to our room and found her. She'd overdosed." Alethea tilted her head back to stop the tears. She was so, so tired of crying. "I couldn't stay after that. It was impossible to know if she did it on purpose or if it was an accident." She gulped in a big breath. "Either way, it was my fault. I should have gotten her help sooner. I should have…"

"There are no should haves, Alethea." Declan drew her in, wrapped her tightly in his arms. She found she didn't want to leave. "You did everything you could at the time.

Nothing can change what happened. Nothing." He murmured words of comfort against the top of her head, pressed gentle kisses to soothe her pain.

"If you mean I can't go back? That's obvious," she argued. "I know you're trying to say the right thing but—"

"There is no right thing. I know. I also know you don't want this—to open yourself up about it. Nothing anyone says is ever going to be enough. I'm so sorry, Alcthea. The regret. The guilt. The loss." He pressed his lips against her hairline. "You're going to have to find a way to accept them all and move on."

She shivered against the truth of his words. "How did I not see how bad it was?" And that, above everything, was what haunted her. How had she been so blind that she didn't see her best friend was in agonizing pain? "How did anyone not see?"

He squeezed her tighter. "Because that's how it happens sometimes, unfortunately. But I can't imagine this is how she'd want you to be feeling. Not after..." He hesitated. "How long has it been?"

"Almost two years. And she doesn't exactly get a say, does she?" She pushed away from him, felt his arms loosen and felt the loss instantly.

"It's all right to be angry, Alethea." He nodded and looked her in the eye. "That your friend didn't or couldn't come to you or others for help is very sad. But it's not your fault. You need to stop living like it is. Choosing the safe path, going out of your way to avoid anything risky isn't living. It's existing."

She shook her head. "What's wrong with making safe choices?"

"Nothing. There are plenty of people who live their entire lives without taking one risk. But that isn't you. You know how I know? Because you're here. You're a light in this town. But that spark feels like a fraction of what it should be. Maybe it dimmed when Talia died. Maybe you're afraid to light it again. There's nothing wrong with taking chances. If we don't, then, we're just treading water. And you can't do that forever. At some point, it'll be too much."

He was right about that. The exhaustion to keep her head above water was dragging her under. "Taking chances, taking risks, it seems so selfish."

"Sure." He shrugged. "But I'll tell you one of life's biggest secrets."

"What?"

"Sometimes it's all right to be selfish." He leaned forward, and, after making certain she wanted what he did, pressed his mouth to hers.

She'd wondered what it would be like to kiss Declan Cartwright. She'd wondered about it a lot, but never had she imagined the feel of his lips could literally stitch her heart back together. He was gentle and caring, and so, so slow. And when he pulled away and left her blinking at him again, she knew her life had been changed.

"See?" He murmured when he sat back. "Purely selfish on my part, but I think I see a spark in those eyes of yours." His smile reached in and nudged something inside her awake. Something that had been sleeping for the past few years. "There's nothing I can do that will change what happened, Alethea. There's nothing you can do. But I do have some experience at starting over. If you'll let me, I can show you how to start."

He stood and held out his hand.

Was that all it would take? She swallowed

hard, tried to find her breath. Her courage. Her strength. It felt as if she accepted his offer, she'd be taking a step so big she could never go back and yet…

And yet.

After a long, heartbeat of a moment, she placed her hand in his.

And walked with him to the boat.

CHAPTER EIGHT

"DON'T YOU WANT to join us, Alethea?" Declan treaded water and looked to where she stood stone stiff at the railing. "You wore your bathing suit!" She'd ditched her sweatshirt and jeans, and stood beneath the cloudless, sunny sky in her suit and an oversize Flutterby Wheels T-shirt. Her hair had been tugged free by the wind, her eyes scanning the horizon as her bare feet seemed to have become glued to the deck.

"I got on the boat," she called with a stern eye. "Take your wins when you get them."

Declan nodded. He did take her coming out here as a win. Along with the fact she'd confided about the loss of her best friend. He couldn't fathom what a loss like that felt like and he hated that Alethea had gone through it, was still dealing with the grief and guilt. He pivoted in the water, turned and watched

Luke Saxon nearby, coaxing his twelve-year-old son to join them.

The catamaran rocked and bobbed in the waves a good forty-give minutes from shore. It was a perfect day for diving, a perfect day to be out on the water. Monty was staying low-key, giving Mandy free reign as acting captain as the five of them headed out. From swim vests to flippers, goggles, snorkels and everything else a diving expedition would need, *SeaFarer* was stocked to the gills for a day out on the water.

Alethea's reluctance was nothing compared to Simon Saxon's. The fact that Luke had forbidden his son from bringing any electronics with him had definitely not earned Luke many dad points. The fact Luke had somehow managed to coax Simon into a swim vest seemed a small miracle.

"How're you doing, Simon?"

"Okay." Simon's lanky frame and pale white skin definitely spoke to why Luke was hoping to get the boy more physically active. Given what he'd been through, Declan wished everyone was as active as they could be. "Dad said I should at least try." He sat down on the edge of the boat and dangled his feet in the water. "He also said there aren't any sharks in here." Simon leaned over, peering intently, as if he expected one to jump out at him. He clearly did not believe his father.

"I told you if you read up on this part of the ocean, you'd see that for yourself." Luke swam forward to hold on to the side of the boat. "You research everything else you do."

"Yeah, but everything I do is on dry land. I don't like the water."

"This is the first time—" Luke started.

"I went fishing with you and Grandpa, remember? I threw up twice."

"Oh, yeah, right." Luke grimaced and glanced at Declan. "Sorry. I forgot about that. Still, maybe give this a try, Simon? You might be surprised."

Simon scooted his feet up. "I don't want to be surprised."

"Your sister and brother are going to start swim lessons pretty soon. Are you going to let them get ahead of you?"

Simon's eyes sharpened on his father and he set his jaw. "Yes."

Declan couldn't help it. He laughed.

"He can stay on the boat with me," Alethea

offered as she walked over and crouched behind the boy.

Declan didn't want to push the boy into doing something he truly didn't want to do, but he also didn't want Simon shying away from things that intimidated him. If he did it once, he'd do it again, and possibly with something important. "Simon, I hear you like science."

"Like?" Luke snorted. "Kid's got a Nobel in his future for sure."

The apprehension in Simon's eyes suddenly faded. "Yeah, I like science a lot."

"The ocean is full of science," Declan announced. "And it's all right on your doorstep, so to speak. It's a whole different world out here than it is on land, Simon. If you're curious about it, that is."

"I guess I am." Simon shrugged. "But I don't have to be *in* the water to study it. That's what we have labs for."

"You've told me the best way to solve any problem is to examine it from every angle," Luke said. "I know you think this isn't your thing, buddy. But I'm not going to let anything happen to you. Neither will Declan, Monty or Mandy. Or Alethea."

Simon shielded his eyes and twisted around to look at Alethea. "What do you think?"

"Of the ocean?" Alethea's eyes went wide. "Well, I like being on the water a lot better than in it."

"See?" Simon pulled his flippers off and stood up. "I'll wait here for you, Dad."

"Hang on." Alethea stood up and faced the boy. "Simon, if you really, really don't want to get into the water, that's okay."

Declan frowned, but just as disappointment crashed through him, Alethea continued.

"But if the only reason you aren't going in the water is because you don't know what it's like or that you wouldn't have any fun, maybe you should give it a try."

"Why?" Simon accused. "You feel that same as me and you aren't going in."

Alethea rested her hands on Simon's shoulders. "You know what? You're right. So I'll make you a deal, Simon." Alethea looked out into the ocean, then, down at Declan. He could see the fear, the worry, fighting against that spark struggling to relight itself. "I'll go in if you will."

"Really?" Simon didn't look convinced.

"I know. But sometimes it's important to

do the things that scare you." She held out her hand. "Do we have a deal?"

"I don't have to go in alone, right?" Simon looked back at his father. "You'll stay with me?"

"Always," Luke confirmed. "Promise."

"And you can use one of these diving buoys," Mandy chimed in and handed Simon what looked like an oversize orange plastic football. As if expecting Alethea's offer to Simon, she handed her a snorkel and goggles. "Whenever you're ready." Mandy grinned.

"Right." Alethea took a deep breath and as Simon wedged his feet back into his flippers, she pulled her T-shirt over her head.

Declan, transfixed by the image of Alethea in her bright blue bikini, dived away, determined to defog his mind before Alethea hit the water. When he resurfaced, she was sitting beside Simon, pulling on her flippers and adjusting her goggles.

"Promise you won't let go of me, Dad." Simon grabbed hold of Luke's arm even as the buoy bobbed in the water.

"I promise," Luke said and pushed off the side of the boat. Simon squeezed his eyes shut and gritted his teeth. "Breathe, Simon." The water lapped up against Simon's face and he gasped, sucked in a bunch of water that he had to cough out. "Open your eyes, son. It'll help." Declan moved closer to Alethea and the boat as Luke pulled Simon around.

Declan held up his hand to a wide-eyed Alethea. "Your turn. Don't worry," he murmured. "I won't let you go."

When she placed her hand in his, when she allowed him to pull her into the lapping water and into the depths of the ocean, he realized that his words were entirely, possibly true.

"OH MY GOSH, MOM! That was the best day ever!" Simon raced off the boat with a new pair of sea legs, well after their expected return time. Simon slammed into his mother at top speed. Holly Saxon stood on the dock, her arms filled with her son as the rest of them followed. "I swam in the ocean! Like swam swam. I mean, I had my flippers and my floatie thingie and Dad only let go of me when I told him he could, but it was so cool! When can we go again? I want to learn to free dive like Declan did."

"We've created a monster," Luke muttered and slapped his hand on Declan's shoulder.

"Thanks for the invite, Deck. And for the breakthrough. We'll see you at your place on Saturday." Arms filled with his and his son's things, he greeted his wife with a kiss and an apology for being late.

"Saturday?" Alethea asked.

"That's baby shower day, right?" Declan slipped an arm around her waist, an action that had a whole new set of tingles racing up her spine. When had this become so…comfortable?

"I invited Luke and Simon out to try the rock climbing wall," Declan said.

"Next thing you'll have him diving out of planes and windsurfing." Her teasing tone faded as she realized it probably wasn't a joke.

"Sky's the limit," Declan said. "Hey." Declan nudged Alethea away from watching the family disappear up the gangplank. "You okay?"

"I'm good." A bit dazed, a little exhilarated and a lot shocked by the day's events. Not only had she gotten into the water, she'd stayed in the water. Long enough to feel comfortable taking a shallow free dive while Declan went all in. She'd never seen anyone so fearless before. The water had been smoother than she'd anticipated, and not quite as intimidating as she'd feared.

And nothing bad had happened. If anything, the day had been utterly and completely perfect.

"Mandy, you sure you don't need any help cleaning up?" Declan called over his shoulder.

"Nah, I'm good. Monty's here." Mandy followed them. "Thanks for coming out today and for the tip."

"I appreciated the chance to get back out there," Declan said. "You'll let me know how those pictures come out, right?"

"Will do. Might be a couple of weeks. I'll ask Sienna to play around with them on her computer though she has the baby shower next weekend. Thanks again." Mandy waved them off and ducked back inside the boat.

"That was a long day," Alethea sighed. "Longer than I expected." She eyed him. "How much did the extra three hours cost you?"

He shrugged it off. "It was totally worth it."

"Who knew Simon would turn out to be part fish?" Alethea said. When Declan didn't laugh, she looked at him. "You feel all right?"

"Yeah, just sore." He twisted and pressed

a hand against the base of his spine. "Probably overdid it. Not the first time. You up for dinner?"

"I'm up for a nap." But the idea of extending this day with Declan overrode reason. She did not want the day to end. "How do you feel about pizza?"

"Opinionated."

"Challenge accepted." Alethea laughed as they headed up the gangplank. "Zane's has amazing—"

"Hang on a second." Declan reached into his pocket and pulled out his cell phone. It beeped and buzzed, no doubt rebooting now that they were within cell range. One look at his screen had his arm stiffening around Alethea.

"Everything all right?" That look on his face, she couldn't quite tell if it was concern or panic.

"Everything's fine. I just need to take this." He held up his finger and answered. "Declan Cartwright." He moved away without looking at her.

Feeling oddly abandoned, she tried not to feel out of the loop. One day on a boat did not make for a relationship. She didn't have any right to know what was going on in his life or who might be calling so late in the day. Could be one of his friends from the circuit. Or one of his sisters.

Given the way he paced, nodded and gave short, concise answers she was pretty sure the call wasn't personal. The fact that she felt relieved had her checking herself. Reality, she chanted in her mind. Today had been a fantasy day, an unexpected, romantic, fun day she could never have anticipated.

But the reality was Declan Cartwright had had one foot out of Butterfly Harbor since he'd first arrived. She was not going to be clingy, or having a cliché vacation romance. While they'd definitely moved past acquaintance, she needed to plant herself firmly in the friend lane before the idea of happily-ever-after and falling head over heels for the man wreaked havoc with both their lives.

She tried not to listen, but even from a distance she could hear the tension in his voice. Who on earth—

Nope. She leaned against the wooden railing and clutched her bag and sweatshirt against her chest. She needed to mind her own business and shift her focus on to the busy week she had ahead of her, while holding on to the wonderful day she'd just had.

A day that had brought her so much peace. The temperature was dropping along with the sun. The sounds of boats knocking against the dock and waves lapping against hulls were almost as comforting and hypnotic as the beach. In the distance she could hear buoy bells clanging. Salt clung to the air and coated her skin as the breeze brushed across her face and lifted her hair. She knew she needed to make a decision about school. About her future. But how could she even think about leaving when everything was so...perfect?

When Declan stopped pacing, he glanced at her, his lips twitching in a quick smile. Bolstered, she stood up straighter as he disconnected.

"Sorry. I've been waiting weeks for that call." Whoever had phoned him had obviously unnerved him and ended their perfect day together.

"Bad news?"

"What?" He blinked. "No. Just...unexpected." He glanced at his watch. "Is there an internet café or something around where I can use a computer and printer?"

Considering he'd spent hours in the company of the town sheriff, she could have easily taken him to the station and let him use one of the computers there. Or…she caught her lower lip in her teeth. Or she could take one of those chances that not so long ago would have felt impossible. She shot him a smile as she dug out her phone. "I know a place. I'll call ahead to Zane's for carryout. Let me guess. Veggie heavy?"

He nodded. "Are you sure— "

"Already dialing. Hey, Zane. It's Alethea." She shifted her bag and sweatshirt as they started walking. "I need two large pizzas, veggies only. No pineapple." She wrinkled her nose at the idea. "Who does that?" she mouthed at Declan whose smile appeared forced. "Okay, Zane. Thanks. How long?… Perfect. See you in a few. Ten minutes." She clicked off her phone. "Just enough time to walk there." Determined not to be nosy and push for information, she stopped long enough to tug on her sweatshirt and shifted her bag over her shoulder.

"Aren't you going to ask?"

"About your call?" She glanced at him, her heart skipping a beat. "Do you want me to?"

"I—" He frowned, clearly torn. "I guess I do. But it's all, I don't know another word to use but *complicated*."

"I can handle complicated." Pride in sticking to her decision not to poke at him surged. "When you're ready, and if you want to tell me, I'll be here." *For as long as you want me to be*.

And that thought, when it hit, terrified her more than the thought of diving headfirst into the ocean.

CHAPTER NINE

DECLAN HADN'T BEEN entirely sure where Alethea planned to take him, but his thoughts were jumbled enough that he honestly didn't care.

She drove up the hill, past the wooden fence and trellised old-fashioned gate. Tiny, twinkling fairy lights dotted the fence line, giving off just enough glow to make Dusky-wing Farm visible. When she turned right and wove her way down the gravel road, he found himself thinking he'd been pulled in to some kind of magical world, replete with a stone cottage that looked as if the stones had been plucked from the Emerald Isle itself.

"It looks rustic—I know." Alethea parked behind two other cars, a dark SUV and a bright red truck. "But Calliope installed some wicked-fast internet. Don't ask me what magic she uses to avoid the dead zones, but you won't find a better connection anywhere in town."

"You brought me home." Even he heard the disbelief in his voice.

"Yeah, well." She cleared her throat. Even in the dim light of the car he could swear he saw her blushing. "Tonight was my turn to cook dinner, anyway, and seeing as I'm later than expected, two birds and all. Pizza will earn me a little forgiveness."

Declan shifted his attention to the back patio partially covered with a wooden awning. More lights were strung, interspersed with sparking light catchers and bright colored ribbons dancing in the evening breeze. A tall pregnant woman was lighting candles placed on a large picnic table. The woman was stunning. Long, braided red hair swayed far down her back. A rainbow tie-dyed dress was draped loosely over her figure and brushed against her bare feet. She turned and said something over her shoulder to a man who stepped up to her holding two different wine bottles. A younger version of the woman followed him and carried a stack of plates.

The woman's laughter reached the open windows of Alethea's car moments before the lady noticed them and waved. She grabbed hold of the flowing skirt of her dress and headed over. The scent of roses drifted toward him.

"Perfect timing, Alethea." She leaned in and smiled. "You must be Declan Cartwright. It's a pleasure to finally meet you."

"Thanks." He couldn't help but frown in confusion. When had Alethea called to let her family know they were coming? "I don't mean to intrude. Alethea said I could use—"

"The computer. Yes. It's in the kitchen. Come in, please." She opened the door and stepped back, held out her hand for the man who approached. "Declan, this is my husband, Alethea's brother Xander. Xander, Declan Cartwright."

Declan managed to shove himself out of Alethea's car, barely restraining the cringe as his leg protested. Whatever loosening up the diving had done, the muscles and nerves had locked back up again the second they hit land.

"Pleasure, Declan." Xander's handshake was firm, a little bit tight, but nowhere near as uncomfortable as the expression on his face. Declan hid his grin. As the brother to six sisters he had no trouble identifying the assessing look on the man's face. He had the same dark hair as Alethea, but without the curl. The same skin tone, same nose and definitely the same blue eyes. That dangerous, protective glint in those eyes was enough to make him almost gulp. "Thanks for getting her out of her rut today."

"Please ignore him," Alethea pleaded as she climbed out of the car and retrieved the pizzas and her things. "I'm very happy in my ruts. Make yourself useful, Xan, and take these." She pushed the boxes across the top of her car. "And before you ask, they're both veggie."

"My favorite," Calliope said at Xander's teasing frown. "We'll keep them in the oven while Declan takes care of what he needs to on the computer." She abandoned her husband and entwined her arm around Declan's. "You'll be able to relax once you aren't thinking about other concerns."

"Ah, okay." It sounded more like a question as he let himself be led away, but not before he glanced at Alethea. If she was confused at the odd interaction, she didn't seem to show it. "Thank you for the basket of produce that Alethea delivered," he said as Calliope drew him onto the porch and in through the back door. "I've been meaning to come here myself and stock up, but…"

"It's quite the trek on foot from the Howser house," Calliope said as they entered the homey kitchen. "I'd be happy to give you a tour of the farm after dinner and you can place an order. The delivery service is complimentary for our continuing customers."

"Hi!" The young girl who had been holding the plates was pulling a pitcher of iced tea out of the fridge. She was as barefoot as the others, with the same long red hair threaded with tiny, tinkling bells. "I'm Stella. Calliope's sister."

"Declan." He spotted the laptop on the kitchen table. With the stacks of papers and folders around it, clearly this was where Alethea did a lot of her work. He couldn't help but feel as if he was invading her privacy. But she had offered. And the sooner he got those forms in, the sooner he'd get the approval he needed.

"No password to access it," Alethea said as she came in behind them. "It'll turn on as soon as you open it. Be back in a second." She hurried down the hall and out of sight.

Stella unloaded a bunch of salad fixings.

"Stella, why don't we wait and give Declan some privacy?" Calliope suggested.

"That's okay," Declan said. "I'll be quick. I just need to return some documents before my trip."

"Trip?" Xander stood up from where he'd stashed the pizzas in the oven. "You taking off already?"

Declan spotted Alethea returning to the kitchen. She wasn't fast enough to hide the shock and disappointment from her face. A rush of warmth went straight to his heart. "Not for good. Not yet, anyway. I need to go to San Francisco for a couple of days."

"That's what the call was about," Alethea murmured.

"Maybe Alethea can go with you," Stella suggested and earned a grimace from Xander. "Hey! What was that for?"

"Being perceptive," Calliope said with a knowing look at her husband.

"I won't have much time for sightseeing." Telling Alethea the truth was going to open conversational doors he'd been trying to avoid. "I'll be spending most of the time at the hospital. They want to run some follow-up tests. Nothing serious," he added, hoping it was the truth.

"Does this have to do with the accident?" Alethea asked.

He nodded.

"What accident?" Stella asked.

"Stella, perhaps you should go check on your bees?" Calliope suggested as she nudged her toward the door.

"It's night." Her face scrunched and she ducked away. "They're asleep. What accident?"

"I was in a car crash last year," Declan said. "I drive race cars," he added at her blank look. "The accident was pretty bad and some of the injuries haven't completely healed."

"Oh." Stella mulled that for a moment. "I'm sorry. How fast do you drive?"

"Stella," Calliope said in a warning tone.

Declan found himself grinning. "I've topped out at about a hundred and forty."

"Wow." Stella's eyes went wide. "That sounds dangerous."

"Yes," Alethea said. "It does, doesn't it?"

"Let's take these drinks outside, shall we?" Calliope claimed Xander's hand and steered her sister out in front of her.

"So what kind of tests?" Alethea asked when they were alone.

"The usual. CT, MRI, blood work." A bunch of others he didn't want to bore or scare her with. He was scared enough for them both. "There was some…nerve damage. Hopefully there's been enough regeneration that I can get back on the circuit."

"Is that why you still need your cane? That damage?"

"Yeah." He cringed, dreaming of the day he could ditch that thing once and for all. "I still have some issues with my legs and back. The specialist in San Francisco's been out of the country. She's returned for a few weeks and managed to get me in."

"A nerve specialist seems serious."

Declan couldn't ignore the concern on her face. Nor the truth as it hovered behind his lips. "It is. It can be. But if anyone can get me back on the circuit, it's Dr. Kenemen."

"And that's what you want," Alethea said, her tone a bit distant, cool even. "To get back to racing."

"It's the only thing I want. It's what I need," he added as if that explained everything. "Being behind the wheel, hearing that engine roar, feeling those vibrations zooming through my body…it's the best feeling in the world."

"You seemed pretty alive today," she murmured. "Out in the water."

"Therapy," he admitted. "Just like the shoreline was yours. Hang on. Let me get these arrangements printed before I check out car services."

"It's like a thirty-minute flight from Monterey."

"What can I say?" He grinned. "I love a good drive." He clicked to reserve a driver and car that would pick him up at six Monday morning. "Okay, this will probably work. Fun times ahead." Hardly. He'd hated the long weeks he'd spent in the hospital after the accident. But he was willing to go back in a heartbeat if it meant getting his life on track. "I'll only be a few more minutes."

"Of course. Use whatever you need to. I'm going to get started on the salad for dinner."

"Sounds great." He'd lucked out meeting this woman. In more ways than one. "Thanks for the assist. You saved my life."

"Uh-huh." Alethea's smile didn't come

anywhere close to reaching her eyes as she stood up. "Glad I could help."

FOR THE FIRST TIME since she'd started working for Jason, cooking provided no distraction for her. There were no recipe ideas floating around in her sleep-deprived mind. No inspiration to be found as she surfed her favorite foodie websites.

It was nearing midnight and the only thing she could think about was Declan and the future he refused to let go of. A future that was fraught with danger and risk.

Not wanting her tumultuous thoughts to draw Calliope into the kitchen, Alethea surrendered to the insomnia and brewed herself a cup of her sister-in-law's soothing tea. Rather than taking it into her room and closing herself back up with her thoughts, she went outside into the cool air, curled up in one of the Adirondack chairs beneath the stars.

If the midnight sky couldn't ease her mind, nothing could. The collection of wind chimes accented the night with their tinkling tones. She shivered, wishing she'd put a sweater on over her tank and rooster pajama pants. At least there was Ophelia. When the cat jumped onto the chair and curled up beside her, she tucked into the warmth. She sank a hand into the cat's soft gray fur.

"Take this."

She jumped at her brother's voice, her snappy retort dying as he draped one of Calliope's knitted blankets over her shoulders. She nearly melted in gratitude. "Thanks." She cupped her mug of tea between her hands. "I didn't wake you up, did I?"

"No." Wearing the $E=MC^2$ pajama bottoms Stella had bought for him for Christmas, he sat next to her and popped open a bottle of beer. "Don't tattle on me to Calliope. Since she can't have wine, I told her I'd give up alcohol while she's pregnant."

"Well, you tried." Alethea laughed even as her heart tilted. Her brother loved his occasional beer. That he'd been willing to give that up for his wife was rather endearing.

"Truth." He toasted her and took a long drink. "So. Declan."

She eyed her brother, waiting for the punch line.

"I like him."

Alethea frowned.

"I mean it," he said. "Not exactly the kind of guy you've usually dated."

"You mean hot?" She hid her smile behind her mug when he flinched. "I'm teasing." Kind of. She loved reminding him she wasn't a kid anymore. "I know what you mean. He's a risk taker."

"Doesn't get much riskier," Xander said. "You're worried about him. Which means you like him, too." He twirled his bottle. "More than I've seen you like anyone before."

"Considering I haven't really dated anyone since Bucky Bartholomew in high school—"

"Man, that kid's parents must have really disliked him." Xander laughed and shook his head. "Imagine living with that name."

"Yeah, imagine. *Xander.*"

He toasted her. "Touché. Calliope said I didn't have to remind you to be careful. You know how to do that better than anyone I've ever met. But I do worry about you, Al."

"I know you do." He always had. It was why, in the aftermath of Talia's death, she'd come to him instead of going home to their parents. He never judged. Didn't criticize. He worried, yes. But never to an extreme. He trusted her to know her own feelings and limitations. And that mattered. It also made this conversation particularly odd.

"Declan Cartwright aside, there's something else I want to talk to you about."

"If this is about me wanting to move out—"

"No. Well, yes, but not tonight." He reached behind him and produced the envelope she'd brought home with her days ago. "I want to talk about this."

She swallowed hard and refused to look at the envelope. "How did you find this? I had that—"

"Hidden. With your work papers. As you've never experienced the wonders of little sisters before, it's time you learned that curious kids find all kinds of things belonging to their older siblings."

"Stella." She could never be mad at that kid. Stella's heart was just always so big and open, even when she was being sneaky. "Little snoop."

"She's worried you're leaving. Moving out aside," Xander said when Alethea started to respond. "That's a whole other conversation. I had a feeling since you didn't tell us about this, you've decided not to go."

"It's contingent on an interview and no,"

she decided in the moment. "I'm not going to go."

"Why not?"

She stared down into her tea, ignored the niggling doubt. "It's not what I want."

"Al." Xander clearly didn't believe her. "I stayed up with you while you were putting that business proposal for Jason together. You have amazing ideas for his business and companies and he's literally handing you everything you need to help him see them through. Attending this school could mean huge things for your future."

"Maybe I don't want huge things. Maybe I'm perfectly happy with the way things are." She had been, too, right up until Declan Cartwright showed up and started making her see...possibilities.

"If you want to lie to me, fine." The eyes and kind face that had guided her all her life sharpened. "But don't lie to yourself, Al. Look, I'll be the first to admit I wasn't thrilled with you operating a food truck, but I was wrong. You're amazing at what you do. Attending the academy can open so many doors. The contacts you'd make, the friends.

Not to mention the support you already have from Jason."

"I didn't ask him for any of this."

"Maybe not in words. But in action? Everything you've done the last two years got you to where you are. Why do you want to limit yourself now? Why do you want to be stuck in the back of a truck?"

"I'm not stuck any more than you are," she snapped. "You moved here and got married and are having your family here. Why can't I just keep things as they are and work on the food truck?" Why did everyone want everything to change?

"You can absolutely do that if that's what you really want."

"Good. Conversation over." Her phone buzzed. To shut her brother up, she turned her screen over and tapped open the text message. She snort-laughed before she could stop herself. "It's from Declan." She turned the phone toward Xander, who leaned over to get a closer look.

"What is that?"

"According to his text, it's the contents of two tissue boxes strewn all over his bedroom. And that is a teeny tiny feline butt print in his pillow." She tilted her head and read the follow-up message. I can never leave the house again. Laughing, she texted him back letting him know he had her sympathy. He responded with an emoji sticking out its tongue. "Barnie did not appreciate being left alone all day."

"And you thought Bucky was a ridiculous name. Who names their cat Barnie?"

"Actually, I named him. It's short for Barnacle" She beamed with pride. "That cat may as well have suction cups on his paws when it comes to Declan."

Xander looked at her for a long moment. Long enough that she squirmed in her chair.

"What?"

"You really are all grown up." He took another drink and got to his feet. "Such a coincidence, isn't it, that Declan has to go to San Francisco next week. And here you have someplace wanting to interview you for a spot in their school."

Alethea took a deep breath. That hadn't escaped her notice. "Don't, Xander."

"Don't what?"

"Don't tell me that since I have a valid reason to go to San Francisco myself that I should offer to drive him." If Declan wanted her help, he'd ask for it. Wouldn't he?

"Man, you guys are two peas in one very small prideful pod." Her brother shrugged. "I don't have to tell you. You're already thinking it. Nothing's a done deal until it is, Al. No one's forcing you to go to school."

She smirked. "Sure seems that way to me."

"What I'm saying is don't make a decision without having all the facts and you can't have all of them if you won't even check the place out and do what it takes to get in. If you decide not to go, fine, but don't not go because you're scared." He rested a hand on her shoulder. "One of these days you're going to have to accept that as tragic as it was, it was Talia who died, not you. You have a full life ahead of you, Alethea. A different life, but still a life." He bent down and kissed the top of her head, the way he used to when she was little. "Maybe that's something you and Declan can discuss on the drive."

CHAPTER TEN

"NOT SURE YOU coming up to look around is going to do any good." Declan followed Matt Knight and Luke as they circled the outside of the workshop, making sure to give the deputy and the sheriff some room. "Whoever broke in was long gone by the time I got out here. I didn't see any point calling you sooner."

"Without you seeing him, we can't prove it was Russo." Luke clicked on a flashlight and shone it into the trees at the edge of the property. "But we haven't had any reports of other people lurking in the area. Next time, if there is a next time," Luke told him. "Don't wait. We need to get an idea as to where he's holing up."

Declan knew he was right, but an eight in the morning call to the sheriff seemed plenty early enough to him.

"If Russo's up this far out of town, it's like looking for a pine needle in a stack of pine needles," Matt added. "He's had almost two months to get used to the terrain. Probably knows the wooded areas better than we do. At least he didn't try to set fire to anything this time. Guy nearly blew up the construction locker at the sanctuary site a while back. You at least missed seeing him. Jo Bertoletti and her dog weren't so lucky."

"Was she hurt?" Wait. Wasn't Jo the woman Alethea and her friends were throwing a shower for this Saturday?

"They both were. It was touch-and-go for Jo and the baby for a while, and Lancelot, that's her dog," Luke added, "got injured protecting her."

"Nothing like that's going to happen again," Matt stated. "Our flyers around town surely mean everyone knows his face."

Luke nodded. "We've got the construction sites loaded with security, too. But if he's starting to break into homes at night, he's getting desperate. Which means he'll make a mistake. You mind if we take a look inside the workshop?"

"No, of course not." Declan turned and walked the way they'd come, careful of where he stepped since he'd left his cane in the house.

In the days since he and Alethea had gone diving, his body had finally begun to ease up on him. The internet company had saved him from boredom by finding a work-around to install a connection. It had taken most of a day and two workers, but he was back in the land of emails and binge-watching and, since he'd been spending most of his time flat on his back in bed to give his body a break, catching up on the shows he'd discovered during his time in the hospital.

Barnie had been in seventh heaven having his favorite plaything, aka Declan, at his beck and call. And speaking of calls, he'd been texting with Alethea like some lovesick teenager. While he'd have loved to have seen her again, taken her to dinner, visited her at the food truck during lunch, he wasn't sure he could venture far from the house without taking medication and he wanted those painkillers out of his system as much as possible before his tests.

"Whatever Russo's done, seems he was hungry. Not that I had a lot to steal. Pantry staples mostly. And my can opener." He needed to get another one at the hardware store when he picked up some new locks. "I have no idea how long he might have been out here."

"I was really hoping to have found him by now," Matt chimed in.

"Me, too." Luke clicked his light off and stashed it in his utility belt. "We definitely don't need any complications with the mayoral election coming up. And Gil could easily accuse us of playing candidate favorites if we let this Russo thing go on much longer."

Declan pointed at the busted lock on the workshop's metal door. "I haven't touched that. In case you want to dust for prints."

"I've got it." Matt headed back to their sheriff's vehicle.

"Why would Russo be an issue for the election?" Declan asked Luke.

"Christopher Russo is Gil Hamilton's half brother," the sheriff said as he wrenched open the door. "No idea on the family history, but given what's happened over the past few months, Russo's nursing a personal vendetta against Gil. But there's no use speculating until we have Russo in custody for questioning."

"Family issues." An unsolvable maze of

emotions. "Makes me grateful I'm not dealing with any of those at the moment. Unless you count a half dozen overprotective sisters."

Luke chuckled and Declan joined in.

A cursory inspection of the workshop proved what Declan already noticed. Some of the tools he'd found in the junk were gone. A hammer, a couple of screwdrivers. An ax that Declan had placed by the door. "If he'd broken in a day later, he'd have found this place empty. Irving Drummond's coming by later to haul most of this away. I bet Russo's building a kind of shelter."

"Most likely," Luke said.

Matt bagged up the dust-covered metal lock. "Got a couple of good sets. I'll need to print you for elimination purposes."

"Oh, right. Come on in the house." He was already halfway through his second pot of coffee. It was the last he'd be drinking for a while. Like with the medication, he wanted his system as clean as possible for those tests on Monday and he didn't want caffeine skewing any results. When Matt was done taking his prints and Declan was washing up, he asked the deputy, "Did Luke talk to you about bringing Leo out tomorrow for some rock climbing?"

"He did, actually. And we're definitely in. Leo's getting some serious mileage out of that bruise Charlie gave him." Matt shook his head. "Lori is definitely getting a crash course on raising a kid. Meanwhile, he doesn't let anything stop him from trying. Climbing will be good for his agility. Wish I'd thought of it when I lost my leg."

Declan's gaze immediately dropped. "I didn't realize—"

Sure enough, Matt reached down and knocked his knuckles against the prosthetic. "Afghanistan. IED. Same accident that burned Kendall."

Pieces of the Butterfly Harbor puzzle dropped into place. Everyone seemed drawn here but for different reasons. He and Matt headed back outside.

"This shop would make a great indoor activity center for kids," Luke suggested. "Once you're not using it as an auto shop. Speaking of. Rumor has it you're going to restore that Impala."

"Is that what's under the tarp?" Matt shifted

closer to it. "That could be a sweet ride for sure."

"That's what I'm counting on."

"You need any help, just call," Matt said.

"I'll do that."

Declan was almost inside the house after his guests had driven off when two big pickup trucks turned onto the property. Declan glanced at his watch, noted the junk dealer and thrift store owner was right on time. Closing the door to the house so Barnie wasn't tempted to join them, he walked over to greet his latest visitor.

"Mr. Drummond."

"Irving, please." The large man who slid out of the front truck offered his hand. Wearing old, faded jeans and an even older blue-checked flannel shirt, he looked like the kind of man who both stood out and fit in wherever he went. Big, bushy gray eyebrows matched the fuzzy quality of his hair. "Getting your call was music to my ears. Been wondering what treasures Ms. Howser was keeping to herself up here. This here's my son, Eddie. Fair warning, he's a bit of a fan."

"He's afraid I'm going to be unprofessional." Eddie tapped a finger against the brim of his broken-in baseball cap and walked around the front of the truck. He was a younger version of his father, and looked as if he'd be earning his Drummond eyebrows any day. "It's great to meet you. And it's even better to see you on your feet. That mean you'll be racing again soon?"

"I hope to." It had been hard these past few days, not to dwell on the possibilities of next week. He was close. So close to getting back to his life. The time couldn't go fast enough. "Appreciate you guys coming out. I've gone through things as much as I can. I kept what I wanted, which wasn't a lot. Luke gave his permission for you to haul away what's left. You can send him the bill."

"Done and done. If you got stuff to do, go on. We'll be as quick as we can." Irving was lumbering his way toward the workshop. "If we come across something special, I'll let you know. C'mon, Eddie. Let's get to haulin'."

Father and son disappeared into the workshop. Declan had no sooner made it up the porch steps than two more vehicles entered the property. "When it rains it pours," Declan muttered and went back down to welcome Kendall and her partner, a very pregnant Jo

Bertoletti. "Wasn't expecting you for a couple of hours," he called.

"That's my fault. These days I never know when I'm going to be able to go anywhere. This baby could arrive at any moment." Jo, an attractive woman with wavy streaked blond hair and an open expression, gave him a smile before she stepped back and whistled. The large German shepherd mix that leaped from the vehicle might have looked intimidating were it not for the stuffed purple dragon clenched between his teeth. "This is Lancelot. He's harmless."

"Unless you're a dragon." Declan approached slowly, keeping eye contact with the dog before he reached out his hand for a sniff. Lancelot nudged Declan's hand up for a pet. "Well, you're a gentle soul, aren't you? Anything I can do to help you two?"

Kendall joined them, wearing her familiar black cargo pants and tank top. Today she had on a baseball cap with her hair pulled through the opening at the back. "Once we get inside, for sure. I showed Jo your list and ideas."

"They make a lot of sense and I'm pretty certain everything will be doable. Thanks for letting us look the place over again." Jo glanced over at the other trucks. "Irving's here?" Her eyes went wide. "That means you have junk."

"Lots of it in the workshop."

"Ooooh, it's like Christmas." Jo's eyes sparkled. "Come on, Lancelot. Kendall, give me a few."

"Yep." Kendall rolled her eyes but her lips twitched. "More like an hour. I'm going to go grab that ladder of yours."

"I've got coffee and iced tea in the kitchen. Help yourselves to it. The place is yours. Bathroom especially. I have six sisters and have many nieces and nephews," he explained.

"An educated man," Kendall said. "You're a dying breed. You want to walk around with me or—" She stopped, stared over Declan's shoulder. "What on earth is he doing here?"

"He who?" Declan turned as a shiny, pricey classic car drove in. The driver parked and the door popped open, revealing a tall, sun-blond man who looked as if he should be carrying a surfboard rather than a pair of designer sunglasses.

"Morning, Kendall," the newcomer said.

"Gil." Kendall shoved her hands in her pockets and rocked back on her heels. "Declan, this is our current mayor, Gil Hamilton. Gil, Declan Cartwright. If you two will excuse me?" She headed toward the house, crunching through the decaying flora.

"Great to finally meet you." Gil offered his hand. "Sorry I haven't been up to welcome you personally before. Luke suggested giving you your privacy."

"Guests are always welcome." Declan shook the man's hand. "Good timing, though. Irving's here to haul away the first load from the workshop and Jo and Kendall are doing a walk through."

"I don't want to interfere with progress," Gil said, then, moved closer and lowered his voice. "I heard through the grapevine someone broke in last night." It was evident by the expression on his face he was hoping the information was wrong.

"About four this morning. Nothing major was taken. Just some food staples, some tools out of the workshop. Whoever it was raced off when I got downstairs."

"So you didn't get a look at who it was."

"I did not." Declan couldn't tell if Gil was hoping the intruder was or wasn't his half brother. "Luke and Matt are running some prints, but other than that, there wasn't anything to be done."

"Well, I hope that disturbance won't drive you away too soon. No pun intended," Gil added with a strained laugh. Beneath the polish and shine and wound-too-tight smile, the circles under the mayor's eyes were all too familiar. The man was stressed.

"I've got coffee inside, if you're interested."

"Ah." They both glanced up as Alethea appeared on the path, a small wicker basket looped over one arm. Gil slipped his glasses back on. "I think you're about to have your hands full. I'll take a rain check, okay?"

"Sure." Declan had no doubt he'd be seeing the mayor again. "Well, hey there." Just the sight of Alethea lightened his already good mood. It was the first morning in a while that he didn't hurt and that he hadn't needed his cane. Seeing her now, ready to tackle the day with her bright green food truck T-shirt and knotted-back hair made him realize how much he'd missed her.

"Calliope sent this over. A bit early, I know." She patted the collection of purple cauliflower and bunches of kale. "But seeing as you're heading out of town for a few days, she broke your order into two deliveries."

"Smart woman." He reached for the basket, but she stayed just out of reach. "Everything okay?"

"Yeah." Her nod was a bit shaky. "Yeah, I was going to call, but I needed to talk to Jason first, then, I saw the basket and…" She blew out a breath. "Okay. Scratch all that. Here." She pulled a folded-up flyer out of her back pocket and handed it to him.

"It's for a cooking school. In San Francisco." He arched a brow. "You thinking about applying?"

Her gaze skittered to the side. "Jason gave me a few days off so I can go be interviewed for acceptance. I figured since we both have to be in the city, we should go together. Xander said I could take his car, so we don't have to worry about mine dying a gasping death on the side of the road. And, also, you won't be doing this thing alone."

He grinned. "You're worried about me."

"No." She planted a hand on her kicked-out hip. "Not exactly. Okay, yeah, maybe a little. But I do have a legit reason for going with you. See?" She tapped her finger on the paper. "I have a flyer and everything."

"Yes." He folded it closed and handed it back to her. "I do see. You sure about this? The two of us going off together, staying at the same hotel—that's bound to get around town."

"Whatever." She waved off his concern. "What time do you want me to pick you up on Monday morning?"

"I need to be at the hospital by nine, so six? To avoid traffic."

"It's the Bay Area," she scoffed. "There's no avoiding traffic. But six is good. I can pack a breakfast for—"

"No food." He laughed at her shock. "I have to fast for the tests. But when I'm done, we can enjoy the city. Oh, wait." He snapped his fingers. "I was going to ask you to take care of Barnie for me while I was gone."

Her smile was smug and proved she'd thought ahead. "Calliope and Stella said they'd watch him."

"Well, okay, then." He'd run out of reasons for her to change her mind. "I guess we have a date."

She beamed at him and handed over his basket. "I guess we do."

CHAPTER ELEVEN

WHY HAD SHE CHOSEN TO approach Declan about going to San Francisco so far ahead of time?

She had *days*, no, make that days and *nights*, to overthink, worry and tamp down her excitement about the trip that bubbled up to the point of overflowing at times. Thankfully, between work, her other obligations and Jo's baby shower, her time to overthink was limited to those few hours when she was alone and awake, although she had caught herself daydreaming a time or two and in one instance, overheated the fryer and nearly set the food truck on fire.

If anyone noticed her preoccupation with Declan and their journey to San Francisco, they certainly weren't commenting. But she had been on the receiving end of numerous knowing smiles and whispers. Although according to Harvey at the hardware store, Declan had gotten an earful himself when he'd stopped in to buy new padlocks and a can opener.

She was counting on Jo's shower being the distraction everyone needed and if the beautiful late summer day was any indication, she was going to get her wish. The back patio of Calliope's house, which had been redesigned specifically to host outdoor group and catered events, was an explosion of yellow, lavender and baby green. The playful scheme of hot air balloons, fluffy clouds made from sewing batting, and cartoony, cute giraffes wearing Seattle Seahawks caps, an ode to Jo's lifelong football obsession, had turned the cottage's backyard into a baby wonderland. Picnic tables were draped with colored cloths. Baby bouquets of miniature pink roses and baby's breath were placed at each table setting. A large round table was set up by the punch bowl and was quickly filling up with gifts as guests—men, women, kids, toddlers and babies—flowed into Duskywing Farm.

"The place looks great." Holly Saxon, carrying a sleepy looking Zoe on her hip, handed off the large gift bag to Alethea. "Almost makes me want to have another baby."

Zoe let out a wail that had Alethea wincing.

"Almost," Holly sighed. "Clearly I'm going to need to track down the father-to-be. Ozzy works magic with this one when she's cranky."

"Juice," Zoe demanded. "Zo, juice."

"We've got a juice bar for the kids set up over there." Alethea tried not to laugh and directed Holly toward the buffet table. They'd used the food truck to transport the catered offerings, along with the plates, flatware and other necessities. Jason and Natalie, who had become indispensable to her during the past few days, had offered to oversee the food so Alethea could fulfill her responsibilities as one of the shower organizers.

When the van carrying the Cocoon Club arrived, Alethea moved through the crowd to find Sienna, Leah and Brooke, who were putting the finishing touches on some of the surprises they had planned.

"Where's Ozzy?" Leah asked. "Has anyone seen him?"

"He went to greet Ezzie and the gang," Alethea said. "Don't worry. The party will go off without a hitch."

"Is it okay if I sit instead of stand?" Jo's

sudden appearance had the group of them jumping. "What?" Jo looked down at her unlaced work boots, her black leggings and the oversized football jersey. "Don't give me grief for wearing the only things that fit me, okay?"

"You look great." But Leah still tried to re-arrange Jo's hair. "I'm sure the photographer can find your best angle."

Jo snorted. "I don't have angles anymore. Have you ever seen someone so round?"

"I've never seen anyone so happy," Alethea countered.

The banner over their heads displayed a cheery "Welcome, Hope" and Alethea couldn't think of a better name for the baby Jo thought she'd never be able to have. A name Ozzy, apparently, had chosen for the infant.

Joy and happiness pulsated around every inch of the farm as the festivities began, starting with the lunch menu Jason had suggested she run with.

"She could have at least let us play a few more games," Sienna sighed and sank into the seat beside Alethea when Jo settled in to open her gifts. Jo's aversion to cutesy, sometimes embarrassing shower games had been on the top of her "don't even think about it" list her friends had promised to adhere to.

"When it's your turn for a shower we'll play dozens of them," Alethea promised as she looked at the crowd. Holly had indeed found Ozzy and handed off little Zoe, who was trying to snatch the "Daddy To Be" hat off Ozzy's head. Abby walked with baby David in her arms, who gurgled and pointed at everyone in sight, while Calliope welcomed latecomers Frankie Bettencourt and Kendall MacBride, who had Phoebe in tow.

"Sorry we're late," Frankie said, still wearing her regulation cargo pants and fire department T-shirt. She lifted and twisted her red hair, and stuck a plastic knife into the knot to secure it to the top of her head. "Last-minute call and Roman had car issues. Is it too late to eat? I'm starving."

"Buffet's still open. Help yourself," Sienna said. "Hey, Phoebe. You're right on time."

"Phoebe, come on!" Charlie Bradley, wearing a pair of bright purple pants and pink shirt, raced over. Jo had presented her with an honorary big-sister sash at the beginning of the party and she was wearing it as proudly as she did her crooked pigtails. "Jo said you can help with the presents."

Phoebe turned to Kendall and asked, "Can I?"

"Absolutely." Kendall smoothed a hand down the side of Phoebe's face. It was only then Alethea noticed the tears on the little girl's cheek. "Go on."

"Is she okay?" Alethea asked when Phoebe was out of earshot.

Kendall nodded, accepted a bottle of beer from Sienna, who had just refilled her own punch glass. "Rough morning. It's her mom's birthday."

Alethea nodded, remembering again that Kendall wasn't Phoebe's birth mother. Kendall's husband, Hunter, had gained custody of Phoebe when his sister and brother-in-law had died in a car accident a few years prior. From what Alethea had witnessed, Kendall, who had suffered her own losses, had been instrumental in helping the little girl heal.

"We threw a bouquet of her mom's favorite flowers into the ocean, sang happy birthday," Kendall told them. "It's a new tradition we started after Hunter and I got married. I'm not sure who the day is more painful for, though, Phoebe or Hunter."

Alethea bet it was Kendall who had the most difficult time. When it came to her husband and adopted daughter, the former soldier's empathy knew no bounds.

"Positions, everyone!" she called to the group. Sierra and Brooke came over to stand next to her. While Brooke's pregnancy had been confirmed, she was still leery about making any official announcement. At least until after she landed solidly in her second trimester. "Ozzy's up first."

"Shouldn't the father give his gift last?" Kendall asked.

"Depends on the gift," Alethea whispered.

Kendall's silent "oh" had Alethea practically bouncing on her toes.

With the photographer in place, and everyone else taking their seats, Ozzy handed Zoe Saxon off to Calliope and retrieved one of the boxes on the gift table. After Jo was settled in a wicker fan chair covered in yellow-and-lavender streamers, she took the box with a surprised smile.

"He's hoping to cut out early to go rock climbing with the boys," Jo told her guests.

The laughter added a healthy pink tint to Ozzy's cheeks. He knelt down beside Jo as she tore open the wrapping. Inside the box she found…another box. She glared at him. "Really? You're going to tick off the mom to be?"

"Up to a point," Ozzy said. "Keep going." Two more boxes, and a lot more attitude later, Jo stared into the peeled back wrapping. Before she could lift out what was inside, Ozzy did. He produced the velvet ring box. "I thought it was time we made this official."

Even from a distance, Alethea could see the tears in her friend's eyes as Ozzy held the ring out to her.

"Jo Bertoletti, I love you more every day. Will you marry me?"

"Yes." Jo's voice cracked as he slipped the ring on her finger. "I can't believe it fits!" She laughed and before she even looked at it, she caught Ozzy's face in her hands and kissed him. "Yes, yes, yes!"

"Aw." Sienna patted her hand against her heart as the guests erupted into applause. "Let's see who tops that gift."

"Me," Alethea promised. "Hey, a marriage proposal is one thing, but unlimited free babysitting? I've got it in the bag." Tears misted her eyes. She'd seen this level of happiness before in Butterfly Harbor. On so many of her friends' faces. All of whom had overcome so much to be where they were today. Once upon a time she'd dreamed of what Jo was experiencing: being cared for, being loved. Belonging with someone.

Belonging made her think of Talia. And everything she wouldn't be able to share with her friend. Though, even now, she could feel her dreams beginning to take root again, sprouting among the warm, giving community she'd found in this wonderful, amazing town.

She also had Declan. Somewhere, somehow, he'd managed to claim a piece of the heart she'd been determined to keep locked and protected. But he'd found a way in and she wasn't in any rush to say goodbye.

She put her fingers to her lips. For the first time in almost two years, the promise of the future didn't feel like a wound to the heart. It felt like…

Alethea looked at the banner over Jo's and Ozzy's heads and smiled through her tears. It felt like hope.

"YOU CAN DO IT, BOYS. Remember to concentrate," Luke said as he and Matt chugged water while their sons attempted to conquer the rock climbing wall,.Declan gave the boys a thumbs-up and, then, folded up the tarp that had been covering the Impala and set it aside.

"Can't believe you talked Cal into coming up and moving that for you." Matt toasted him. "Didn't think the man picked up a phone anymore."

"It took some convincing." And a pretty big check, but Declan had managed. Barely. This would be his reward for getting through the unending wait of the last few days. But as anxious as he was to have the medical tests over with, he was looking forward to spending time with Alethea, away from Butterfly Harbor and the hundreds of prying eyes.

He'd done some quiet investigating, contacted a couple of people and after calling in a few favors had some surprises in store for the woman who had almost managed to end his idea of a return to the racing track.

He hoped her interest in the cooking school was genuine. Her food was fantastic; she had a lot to offer the culinary world. But whatever the truth might be, the future was definitely opening up in front of him with a giant checkered flag poised to drop. The question was…could he have everything he wanted?

Or would he have to choose between racing and a possible future with Alethea?

"How are you going to get anything done on the car with that beast on your shoulder?" Matt teased, pointing at Barnie, who had settled into his favorite place.

"I'm getting used to him." Declan reached up and scratched the little guy's head and smiled at the resulting purr. "He had an interesting encounter with Lancelot the other day. Ever seen a fur ball back a German shepherd into a corner before?"

"You should have recorded it and put it online," Luke said. "Probably earn you more followers than your racing career."

Declan laughed. "Oh, we're going there, are we? Okay, just for that, you don't get lunch."

"Heard you and Alethea are going to San Francisco together," Luke countered. "What's going on there?"

He'd lost count of how many surrogate big brothers Alethea had. It didn't surprise him, and in fact, seemed a testament to who she was that so many people cared about her. But that tone in Luke's voice had him thinking maybe his old friend didn't trust him with Alethea's feelings as much as Declan would have thought.

"I like her." Declan didn't tend toward having revealing conversations about his feelings, but he owed Luke for a lot of things. And that included an honest answer. "More than I've liked any woman in a long time." More like ever, if he were honest with himself. "And before you go all bodyguard, I reserved separate rooms for us." Alethea had enough going on without adding the complication of worrying about their overnight arrangements. "She's coming along for moral support and to check out that cooking school."

"Oh, yeah. I'd heard she got in," Matt said.

"Wait. She got in?" Declan set down his bottle of water. "I thought she was just going for an interview."

Matt's gaze flew to Luke's. "She is but Jason said it's pretty much a done deal. She's been accepted starting in January. She didn't tell you that?"

"No," Declan said slowly. "She didn't."

Why wouldn't she have shared that important bit of information?

"Alethea rides on the quiet side of things," Luke said. "Maybe don't make a big deal out of it, Dec. If she wants to tell you about it, she will."

Declan nodded. "Sure." Still, it seemed like big news not to have shared with him, especially since he was going with her. "Oh, hey, Leo, hang on there." Declan removed Barnie from his shoulder and dropped him into Luke's hands. Simon was hanging on to the balance rope for Leo as he climbed, using the holds, but Simon's feet had begun to lift off the ground. Declan seized the rope just before Simon went up and Leo went down. "Let's try this again. Matt? You want to help us out here?"

He checked Simon's harness and motioned for him to climb. "How about you try it together. Matt and I will spot you."

"How far up can I go?" Simon asked, tilting his head back so far he nearly fell over.

"As far as you want. Matt, grab those mats over there, will you?" They arranged them on the floor where the boys would be climbing above as an extra precaution. "Okay, here we go. And up!"

"Remember, no flying in those harnesses!" Luke ordered, standing next to Declan. "You going to give us bigger kids a go at this?"

"Whenever you want."

"Great." Luke grinned at him, then, down at the cat. "Twenty bucks says I can beat you to the top."

"Twenty? Please." Declan snorted. "Make it fifty."

"Deal."

"ALL PACKED FOR TOMORROW?"

Alethea glanced up from placing a few last-minute items into her overnight bag. "Yep. Thanks again for watching Barnie while we're in San Francisco."

"My pleasure. I think." Calliope slid into the chair by the door, one of her unreadable expressions on her face. Ophelia slinked in behind her and jumped onto Alethea's bed to explore her suitcase. "I'm not sure Ophelia will forgive me for adding a new cat to the family, but she'll find a way to cope. Won't you?" She bent down and drew her hand down the cat's sleek fur. "What hotel are you staying in?"

Alethea rattled off the name, frowned at Calliope's raised brows. "What?"

"It's a lovely hotel. One of the nicest in the city. Beautiful views of the bay, four-star, rooftop restaurant. Quite romantic."

"And separate rooms," Alethea added. "In case Xander sent you in here to ask."

"Your brother understands the boundaries of your personal life, Alethea," Calliope said with a knowing smile. "But he will be pleased to hear that information. How are you feeling about the interview?"

"Fine." She didn't want to get too excited about it. Accepting the admittance meant so many things would change, maybe too many and she'd had a lot more to think about in the last few weeks that didn't involve changing every aspect of her life.

She had started thinking about the what-ifs. And almost all of them circled back around to Declan. Why did everything have to land on her at once? "I haven't decided to go."

"That's better than saying you aren't going. Keeping your options open is always a good idea. You'll know if you belong there. Stella?"

She leaned over as her sister's bedroom door across the hall popped open and quickly shut again. "What are you still doing up?"

"Nothing."

Alethea and her sister-in-law exchanged looks.

"Stella, it isn't nice to eavesdrop," Calliope said. "Especially in secret."

"Especially when she's so bad at it," Alethea joked.

"Something we're all grateful for," Calliope agreed. "Stella, please, come out here."

Stella opened her door again and did as she was told. "I'm sorry." She grabbed a braid of her hair and twisted it around her fingers. The pale yellow nightdress she wore was dotted with tiny, buzzing bees. "Are you really going to go away to school?" she asked Alethea as Calliope drew her close.

"I don't know," Alethea said. "But maybe. It's a big change. And a big investment. In time and money."

"If it's the tuition that's stopping you—"

"No." Alethea held up a hand to stop Calliope from offering. "I appreciate the thought, but if I'm going to go, I'll manage it myself." Although, she'd be lying if she didn't admit to spending a good amount of time crunching budget numbers.

"But I thought you were saving to buy a house here?" Stella said. "You can't do that and go to school, too. I like you living with us. I like having another sister."

"I'll still be your sister wherever I live, Stell." Alethea zipped up her bag and sat on the edge of her bed. "Nothing's going to change that. San Francisco isn't that far away. And depending on whether I do full-time or part-time classes, it could be as little as a year."

"Sounds like you've given this some thought," Calliope said.

"Yeah, well." Alethea plucked at a thread on her bedspread. "It would be pretty selfish of me not to, given the trouble Jason went to. I hope you feel better now, Stella."

"I guess. I just—"

"Stella, this is Alethea's decision to make." Calliope's voice was sterner than usual. "You, we, all need to let her make it in her own time. And we will all support her when she does."

Alethea opened her mouth to respond, but

shut it when she sniffed the air. "I smell popcorn."

"Xander's making popcorn?" Stella raced out of the room and down the hall.

Calliope stood, held out her hand for Alethea to take. "I meant what I said. Whatever you decide to do, we'll be right behind you."

"Pushing me out of my comfort zone?" Alethea asked.

"Partly." She pulled Alethea out of her bedroom and toward the kitchen. "And partly to break your fall should you need it."

CHAPTER TWELVE

"ARE YOU SURE you don't want some moral support?" Alethea pulled into the patient drop-off area of the hospital parking lot, grateful to be out of freeway traffic. At least, for a while. The usual two-hour drive had come in closer to three thanks to Monday morning traffic and she was anxious to get out of the car and stretch her leg muscles. "I'm happy to be a distraction."

"A distraction is exactly what you'd be." Declan reached for his backpack, the one Alethea had snuck a few after-test snacks into. "Besides, aren't you due at the school in a little while?"

"I have time." The closer they'd gotten to San Francisco, the jumpier her nerves had gotten.

"Well, I'm due to check in now." He unhooked his seat belt, popped open his door. "Thanks for the lift." He leaned back and, after flashing one of his toe-tingling smiles at her, gave her a quick kiss. "I'll have to make that last all day."

He really did have a talent for short-circuiting her brain. "Call me when you're done," she told him.

"I will." He brushed his thumb across her lips. "Good luck."

She almost called "good luck" before he closed the door, but she wasn't entirely sure what that meant for him. Or for her. He headed inside the sliding doors, waved over his shoulder and disappeared. Guilt knotted low in her stomach. If his test results came back promising, chances were he'd head right back to the racing circuit as soon as he was allowed. The thought of him driving one of those cars, however, made her feel slightly sick.

On the other hand, the tests could reveal less positive results and that would devastate him. And as much as she wanted him safe, she wanted him whole. She wanted him as he was now, full of promise and hope and fun. She wanted him happy.

Take away his dreams, take away anyone's dreams, and what would be left for them?

"Okay, you need to stop." The command she gave herself was a practical one. There was no guarantee they were anything other than, well, two people testing the romantic waters during a tumultuous time in both their lives. There was no guarantee Declan was thinking about anything other than his future in a sport that had always sustained him. In the scheme of things, Alethea probably didn't factor in much at all. Thinking she might have a place in his future was definitely getting ahead of things.

She pulled back into traffic and drove toward the Embarcadero.

She'd be lying if she didn't admit she had feelings for him. Feelings she couldn't quite define. How could she? She'd never been in love before. Never...

In love?

"Oh, that can't be right." But even as she denied it, that uncertainty circling inside her settled into a heart-thumping rhythm of promise. Now was not the time for emotional epiphanies. Not with her future in question. Now was not the time to fall in love.

But the more she tried to argue against it, the more right the realization felt.

Was she even emotionally equipped to love a man whose entire existence was based on thrill, risk and a live-till-you-die mentality? She'd be existing in a perpetual state of fear and while she may have already been existing in that realm for other reasons, she didn't believe she'd find long-term happiness there.

Declan was a leap-before-you-look devotee while Alethea not only looked, she microassessed all possible outcomes and chose the safest route. Finding common ground given those two mindsets didn't seem impossible; it was wholly improbable. His lust for life both terrified and inspired her. She hoped the tests provided the answers he wanted, the answers he needed.

But there was no denying that his greatest wish could prove to be her biggest heartache.

She took a deep breath and sighed. If they did pursue a romance, they could never be more to each other than a sweet, unexpected diversion while he waited for his life to start again. All the more reason she needed to look toward her own future, explore all her options. And keep an open mind as to what they might include.

This early in the morning, affordable park-

ing wasn't difficult to find. She left the SUV
in a lot near the Ferry Building, which had
become a destination for food fans from
around the world. The ACT had recently re-
located to the area, and was within walking
distance from Bierman Park, one of Alethea's
favorite picnic spots for when she visited the
city. While Fisherman's Wharf and Pier 39
were the typical tourist attractions, there were
dozens of other restaurants and businesses
to explore, including some amazing seafood
restaurants that had her stomach growling in
anticipation.

Shoulder bag in hand, she climbed out of
the car and headed toward the Ferry Building that was already bustling with activity.
She had plenty of time to kill before heading
over to the school for her interview. Besides,
this time of year, early holiday offerings were
starting to pop up in shops. She could easily
start her Christmas shopping and get ahead
of the game.

Two hours later, she was loaded down with
goodies and surprises for a number of people on her list. She'd only checked her phone
a half-dozen times but Declan hadn't called,

except to text her a few times to let her know he was between tests and just touching base.

He didn't want her to worry. Alethea smiled and dropped her packages off in the car.

She scrubbed her damp palms against the front of her floral-print dress. The matching blue sandals and sweater made her feel a bit flirty, a bit girlie and just a bit chilly. Far more than she felt back home. Home. She looked around.

Could she feel at home here? Away from everyone she cared about? Even for a little while?

With the crisp bay air swirling about her, she headed up the block and had just turned the corner onto Washington Street when her phone rang.

The disappointment she felt not to see Declan's name was tempered only by the surprise of the name displayed. "Melissa?" she answered. It had always seemed odd to call Talia's mother by her first name. "It's so good to hear from you. How are you?"

"Some days are harder than others," the woman who had been like a second mother most of her life said. "I didn't want to bother you, but your mother said it would be all right to call."

"You're never a bother." Alethea could see the school from where she was standing: a smartly renovated warehouse structure that took up a good chunk of real estate. Classic touches of elegance amidst the history of the city. Tingles raced up her arms as she wondered about the promise she would find inside the modern building. "How have you been?" She crossed the street to the park and took a seat on one of the benches facing the ACT. "How's Martin?"

"Spending most of his time tinkering in the garage. He's building one of those van homes. I hope he doesn't think I'm going to go gallivanting around the country in that thing, because that will not be happening in this lifetime."

Alethea laughed. "I'm not surprised he's building one. Camping with you guys was one of my favorite..." She broke off, looked at her watch, saw the date and felt the blood drain from her face. "I forgot. Oh, Melissa. I am so sorry." Her breath caught in her chest as the tears squeezed her throat shut. No wonder she'd called Alethea. "I can't believe I..."

She shook her head. "I should have remembered."

And here she'd spent the day wandering blissfully around town wondering what to do with her feelings for Declan and debating her plans for the future.

"There's nothing to apologize for, Alethea." The kindness in Melissa's voice made her feel worse. "That you've moved on and don't dwell on things we can't change is good. It means you're healing. I just thought I'd call. Hearing your voice makes things a bit better, you know?"

Alethea nodded, then, remembered Melissa couldn't see her. "I miss seeing you." But she didn't miss the onslaught of memories and the guilt that struck whenever she went home and she looked at the house Talia's parents still lived in. "Tell me what you've been up to? Tell me about Martin's van. Catch me up."

"I don't want to keep you," Melissa said.

"You're not." Alethea crossed her legs and tucked her arms in tight around her and ignored the time. "Catching up seems a good way to honor the day. Let's have it. Did you get that dog you talked about?"

"We did. He's a retriever rescue. We named him Tucker."

"Tucker." Alethea ducked her head and willed the pain to stop. "You'll have to send me pictures." Unable to sit still, she focused all her attention on Melissa, stood up and moved deeper into the park.

Leaving ACT, her interview and all thoughts of her future, behind.

"THANKS FOR THE RIDE." Declan climbed out of the sedan, tapped the app on his phone to pay and stepped onto the sidewalk in front of the ACT.

Backpack slung over his shoulder, he glanced up at the sign over the door. Dr. Kenemen and her staff had been ruthlessly efficient in running the tests she needed. What he'd anticipated taking most of the day had only required a few hours. He was scheduled to go back tomorrow to discuss the results and his options, neither of which Dr. Kenemen had been willing to theorize on now. She'd know when she looked at the labs, end of story.

The fact he'd only have to wait twenty-four hours to find out what the future held for him was a blessing and a curse. One of the perks to seeing a world-renowned specialist. Tomorrow he'd take that first step toward racing.

Declan decided to wait and surprise Alethea when she was done, rather than possibly interrupting her tour. He checked his watch. Anxious to see her again, he headed inside, climbed the short staircase to the lobby. The walls were a deep, rich gold and accented with photographs of graduates, recent and going back the fifty years the academy had been around. The polished wood and marble floors seemed far more sophisticated than he expected a culinary academy to be. He could smell fresh-baked bread and the hint of herbs wafting through the air. The aroma made his stomach growl even more than it already was.

A few students wearing their starched, white cooking jackets and tall matching hats walked down the hall, books clutched under their arms before they ducked into a room. Declan headed for Reception.

"Hi. I'm looking for Alethea Costas. She had an interview scheduled with the dean of admissions today."

"Oh." Behind the desk a middle-aged woman with rhinestone-dotted cat-eye glasses blinked at him. "You're a friend of Ms. Costas?"

"Yes." More than a friend, he wanted to boast, but he wasn't sure how Alethea would feel about that. All he knew was that right now he couldn't wait to see her so they could celebrate their progress in his case, and her good news. But the confused expression on the receptionist's face dulled his good mood. "Is something wrong?"

"Just a moment." She held up a finger and picked up the phone. "Yes, Mr. Windam. I have a friend of Ms. Costas's at Reception. Yes, of course." She hung up. "Mr. Windam will be right out."

"What's going on?" The back of Declan's neck prickled. "Where's Alethea?"

"Mr. Windham will fill you in," the woman said as she rose to her feet as a man approached them. "Mr. Windham…"

"Thank you, Eleanor." Only a few years older than Declan, the man was dressed casually, with his shirtsleeves rolled up, no dress jacket and cotton slacks. The lapel pin on his collar depicted the logo for the academy, but it was the concern in his dark eyes that had Declan on alert. "You're a friend of Ms. Costas?"

"Yes. Declan Cartwright." He shook the man's hand. "I was hoping to meet her here. Is there a problem? Is she all right?"

"Please." Mr. Windham motioned to the seating area. "I'm afraid Ms. Costas never arrived for her interview, Mr. Cartwright."

"Never arrived?" Had she been in an accident? She hadn't said anything the last time they'd texted. In fact, her last message had said she was heading to the ACT. He checked his phone just to be sure. "Did she call?"

"No. I assumed something came up. Eleanor had been attempting to reach her, but her phone goes straight to voice mail."

"Okay." Declan shoved the worry aside and forced himself to think logically. "There must be an explanation to this. She was excited about the opportunity." Wasn't she? Or was this why she hadn't told him she'd technically been accepted? Was that why whenever he brought the topic up she changed the subject? Had she lied to him? "I hope her not showing up doesn't change your mind about potentially admitting her?"

"I'm afraid it does put me in the position of having to reconsider," Mr. Windam said. "Reliability and responsibility are an important part of what this industry is about. If she is unable to keep a simple tour appointment, well, we do have a long list of students waiting for admission."

"Of course you do." Declan glanced at his watch. "Mr. Windham, I can only assume something important came up." Or had she been in an accident? It was all he could do not to bolt and do what he could to find her. "I realize you don't know me, but I'm sure you agree that Jason Corwin never would have recommended Alethea for the school if he didn't think she was deserving of admission."

Mr. Windham nodded. "Jason's enthusiastic endorsement definitely played a part in our decision."

"Let me find her. Let me talk to her and see if we can turn this around. Please," Declan urged. "I promise you, she's worth the added effort."

"All right." Mr. Windam checked his

watch. "All right. I have a class at four, but if she can be here well before then—"

"Thank you." Now all Declan had to do was find her. He got to his feet and shook the man's hand again. "You will not regret this."

He hurried out of the building, stood on the street and got on his phone. No sooner had he started to dial than he glanced up and across the street. The park stretched a number of blocks, and people were milling about, picnicking on the grass; adults and kids, plus a few dogs, were going along the path toward the playground he could see in the distance.

And that's when he spotted her.

The bench. There, under a giant tree in the park, overlooking the playground. He saw Alethea sitting, legs crossed, face blank, her phone clutched between her hands.

Relief swept through him, but rather than run to her, he phoned her. And watched as she glanced down at her screen and declined the call.

"Definitely something's wrong." He didn't wait to think it through, didn't try to reason it out. He just wanted to make sure she was okay. The fact she didn't see him coming until he was practically standing in front of her sent that feeling of relief out of reach.

Her face was pale. She didn't speak when he sat next to her.

"How did your tests go?" Her voice sounded distant, detached, but still she forced a smile.

"I'll find out in the morning." He set his backpack on the ground beside her purse. "What's going on, Alethea?" He wanted to touch her. To hold her. He wanted to convince her that no matter how bad she thought things were, she was going to get past it. "I went to the ACT to surprise you and they said you didn't show up for your interview."

Her lips twitched into a tight smile. "Yep. Messed that up big time, didn't I?"

"What happened?"

"It's Talia's birthday today." She cleared her throat. "I got so wrapped up in you and in school and my life that I totally forgot. It took her mother calling me…" She lifted her cell phone. "I forgot my best friend's birthday." When he didn't respond, she turned on him and he took the accusation in her eyes as a good sign. "Aren't you going to try to convince me I'm wrong? That I have nothing to feel guilty about?"

"Would it change your mind?"

"No."

"I won't ever say what you're feeling is wrong, Alethea. I haven't been through what you have." Because he couldn't stop himself, he reached over and put his hand on top of hers. "What did Talia's mother say? About you forgetting?"

"That she understood. That it was probably a good thing in the sense that it meant I was moving on with my life."

Declan breathed easier. Thank goodness Talia's mother had brought empathy to the table instead of more guilt.

"We were supposed to take these big life steps together," she whispered. "School, work, everything was supposed to be shared." Her gaze, when she looked up at him, was filled with a surprising amount of frustration. "I was not supposed to be doing this alone."

"You're not alone, Alethea." That she didn't seem to realize this was a source of his own irritation. He'd never seen any place filled with more love, caring and compassion than Butterfly Harbor. The town was just overflowing with support and community and Alethea was a part of that. "You have your brother and Calliope and Stella and from what I can tell all of Butterfly Harbor is with you. And I'm right here." He sat back, lifted her chin with his finger. "Talia's here, too. You carry her with you. I know you still feel a connection to what happened to her, that you can't forget it. But maybe it's time to try something different."

"Like what?" She scoffed.

"Like forgiving yourself." He trailed his finger between her brows to erase the frown. "Nothing any of us says is going to change how you feel or help you forget. Forgiveness is your way forward, Alethea. I think maybe, given everything that's still holding you back, it's the only way."

She stared at him for a long moment, then, looked up at the sky. "That sounds like something Talia would have said. And, then, she'd tell me to get over myself. I am not the center of the universe, or so she would remind me," she added with a small laugh.

"I feel certain I would have really liked Talia." He slipped his arm around Alethea's shoulders and pulled her close. "Although

I'd argue that last point. You're an amazing woman, Alethea Costas." He pressed his lips against her temple. "You can do anything you set your mind to, and that includes being able to move on and embrace the life you still have."

"Said the man who's been given a second one." Alethea rested her hand against his heart. "You're a good man, Declan."

Her words brushed against his soul and made him think, made him wish…no. Now wasn't the time. She had so much to deal with already. She didn't need to add in his untimely realization that he'd fallen in love with her. "You'd have been a great addition to ACT's student body," Declan said, grateful she wasn't looking at him, since he was a terrible liar with zero poker face. "Too bad you blew the interview."

"Well." She sighed. "I was just sitting here thinking that, too. I didn't want to do it. Not at first. And not until recently. Not until after I offered to drive you up for your tests."

"So you did offer only to keep me company."

She shrugged, let out another laugh and this one sounded lighter. And more like the woman he loved. Love. He couldn't stop looking at her. He loved her. Every single, frustrating, entertaining, cautious part of her. Imagine how scared she'd be should he admit his feelings?

"You don't know what you've lost until it's gone," she said. "Apparently it's a mistake I have to keep learning. Jason's going to be so disappointed in me."

"What Jason thinks doesn't matter," Declan said. "What do you think?"

"I think I'm tired of being scared." She sat up, brushed her fingers under her eyes and pinched her cheeks. "I think it's time for me to take at least one chance and ask them to reschedule me for that interview."

"So you want to go to the ACT?"

"They have to accept me first, but yes." She nodded, and seemed to let out a breath of relief. "I want to go. I think… I think Talia would want me to." She popped up off the bench and grabbed her bag. "What?" she asked when he sat back and tilted his head.

"I think if you simply apologize for being late the dean of admissions will be happy to interview you today. At least that's what Mr.

Windham said when I spoke with him a little while ago."

"You spoke…" She balked, blinked and, then, smiled. "You used that charm of yours, didn't you? You had them reschedule my interview."

"I said that only something important would have kept you away. Second chances don't come up too often, Alethea. We both know that. Why don't you go on ahead? I'm going to hit up that food cart—"

She smiled. "You haven't checked your backpack, have you? I snuck a boxed lunch in there before we left Butterfly Harbor. Lots of protein for you to get you through the rest of the afternoon."

Something inside him shifted, as if centering his entire being into place. A new emotional state. A new hint of promise. "You do think of everything. Thank you. Now leave." He smiled back. "I'll be waiting here when you're done."

"I'm the one who should thank you." She stepped in and caught his face between her hands, pressed her mouth against his. "You make me feel like I can be the best version of myself, Declan Cartwright."

He watched her walk away and grinned when she opened the door of the ACT. Standing in the middle of the park, he glanced up just as an enormous fluffy cloud passed overhead. The shape reminded him of a butterfly: a sign, he thought. Of new beginnings. "Happy birthday, Talia."

CHAPTER THIRTEEN

"I CAN'T BELIEVE you did all this." Alethea smiled at him as the waiter pulled her chair out when she returned to their table.

Declan had chosen the hotel not for its elegant ambiance and proximity to the hospital, but for the renowned four-star rooftop restaurant. With its glass walls and ceiling, eating here was truly like dining under the stars, and tonight, a night that was as clear as he could have hoped for, allowed for a glorious, perfect view of the city. They could see the lights of the Golden Gate blinking in the distance.

Alethea grinned. "I just had the most amazing tour of the kitchen. And eating at Chef Antoine Pervus's private table? Do I even want to know how you managed to make all this happen?"

He'd have done anything to make it happen if it meant keeping that smile on Alethea's face. "I have my secrets," he teased and poured her a second glass of wine. The decor was simple classic chic, from the black tablecloths to the small copper bowls flickering with tea lights. The silver-trimmed white china and matching flatware made the scene sparkle all around them.

Gone was the sullen, remorseful, stressed woman he'd found on the park bench. To say she'd been walking on clouds ever since her interview was an understatement. She hadn't been content to go back to the hotel and rest before dinner. She'd wanted to go everywhere and see everything possible. Her enthusiasm had kept his own spirits from dipping when, by the time they'd headed to Fisherman's Wharf, he'd had to return to the car to get his walking stick. The pain in his leg he'd hoped had been gone for good decided to make a return visit. And almost, almost, ruined the rest of his evening.

"I take it you enjoyed yourself?"

"It's a culinary amusement park back there," she gushed and reached for the dessert menu, frowned when he pulled it out of her hand. "Hey, I walked enough today to earn some serious sugar."

"I've already taken care of it." He signaled

to the waiter, sat back in his chair to enjoy the frustration playing across her face. Her simple black wraparound dress and heels had knocked him speechless. He particularly loved that she'd left her hair down, instead of tying it back. All those curls spilling down around her shoulders and framing her face had him wishing he could sink his hands into the silky depths and draw her to him. But it was the light in her eyes—the sparkling life he found in the blue irises—that had him humming. "Have you decided which culinary program you're going to choose?"

"That'll be the difficult part." She sipped her wine and eyed the remaining crusty bread in the basket. "There are a lot of options and a lot of things to consider. Part-time means it'll take longer, but I like the idea of three days here and the rest at home. They're even offering online extension classes, which could help keep costs down. The tuition will eat into my house fund—"

"You have a house fund?"

"Yeah. I've been saving for my own place. Once Xander and Calliope's baby gets here, that house at Duskywing is going to get super crowded. Plus, I do my best cooking at night and I don't think Calliope and Xander will appreciate me banging around in their kitchen at all hours. Oh, here it comes. What did you do this time, Declan?"

He smiled as their water set down a silver domed serving tray between them, lifted the lid and watched Alethea's face glow in wonder.

"Tiramisu chocolate bomb cake," the waiter said. "Can I get you anything else, sir? Madam?"

"No, thank you, Sean. This will be great, thanks."

"'Congratulations, Chef Alethea.'" Alethea read aloud the words written in white chocolate across the top of the dessert's shiny shell. Then she shifted her gaze to the plate. She dabbed at the corners of her eyes. "You're going to make me all sloppy." But her smile didn't quite tip to sad. "It's been a really good day, hasn't it?"

"One of the best," he agreed. He lifted his wine as she lifted her fork. "Here's to tomorrow being even better." He saw it, then, a flicker of discomfort or…was that fear? "What?"

"You really miss racing, don't you?" She pushed her fork into the dessert, cracked open the chocolate and went wide-eyed at the flood of coffee-scented chocolate that spilled out. She ditched the fork and opted for her spoon instead and had him unable to look away as she scooped up an enormous mouthful.

"More than I'd miss air to breathe," he admitted.

"Why?" She seemed genuinely confused by it. "It's so dangerous. I mean, you of all people know—"

"It's the only place I've ever felt alive." He'd spent years joking in the media, with his family and friends, about his love of the sport. About the rush it gave him. But it wasn't until he'd lost the ability to climb behind the wheel, to hit that gas pedal, and explode down the asphalt that he understood just how much racing was a part of him. "We had rough patches when I was growing up. We didn't have a lot of money and my parents... They spent most of their lives scrambling for everything they could get for us. My dad took a job at a gas station and garage after he'd been laid off the last time. It was the only job he could get, even though he didn't know anything about automobiles. He'd spend hours online, watching videos, reading articles. He didn't just teach himself how to fix them. He taught himself how to understand them. And he taught it all to me. He inspired me. Don't get me wrong, though," he added when she smirked. "He taught my sisters, too. Most of them still change their own oil and do their own tune-ups."

Alethea grinned. "I love that."

"My dad earned himself quite a reputation as a mechanic, made a lot of friends in the racing world. One of his customers gave him a pair of tickets to a race. I was eight. I can still remember holding his hand when we walked across the parking lot to the stadium. The roar of those engines hurt my ears, and the smell. Diesel and determination." He shook his head. "It got into my blood. Watching those drivers get into those cars and push their boundaries with every gear change, it was like a switch got flipped inside of me. My dad loved those races. I could tell, even from that age, he wished he'd taken a different path. That he'd lived that life. So instead of being able to do it himself, he instilled that love in me." Declan forked up a bite of dessert, but couldn't taste anything beyond grief.

"He had me taking apart engines and rebuilding them with him starting the next weekend. Two years later he was gone."

"Declan." Alethea's hand touched his, her fingers soft and comforting.

"Racing, it's not just about the cars, Alethea." He wanted, no, he needed her to understand. "It's more than that. It's about connecting. To the fans. To my team. To my family. It's something we all are a part of. The money's nice and it's been great, especially the last year, but when all is said and done, it's about getting out on that track and pushing myself to the absolute limit."

"And it's about your dad." Her voice was quiet, filled with awe. "He's there with you. In the car. In the pit. The people we love are always where we need them to be."

"That, I believe." He turned his hand over, slipped his fingers through hers. "I know it's scary," he said. "I know the idea of me or anyone racing around at hundreds of miles an hour sends chills down your spine—"

"But it's where you belong." That light he'd been enjoying all evening dimmed now.

Maybe it was the candlelight, maybe it was the hope inside him. There was no way she was ever going to accept what he did. But if he wasn't Declan Cartwright the race car driver, then, who was he?

"I hope you get what you want tomorrow, Declan." Her voice sounded strained, and the smile on her lips was tight. "I hope you get what you need."

He let out a shaky breath. "Me, too. I was going to ask if you'd come with me to hear the results, but if you'd rather not—"

"Of course I will." She gripped his hand harder and the tears in her eyes receded. "Whatever she tells you, and whatever you decide to do, it'll be the right thing."

"For me, or for us?"

Her eyes went wide, as if she'd assumed her feelings had been one-sided.

"I care about you, Alethea." Throwing caution—and his own reservations—to the wind, he tightened his hold on her hand. "From the moment I met you, I've known…this is something special. Between us." He sounded like a complete sap and he didn't care. "I'd like to see where it might lead."

"I care about you, too, Declan." Rather than the hope he wanted to hear, doubt rang clearly in her voice. "Let's not talk about this tonight, okay? Let's finish this amazing meal and take a walk in the rooftop garden and enjoy the rest of this trip. Tomorrow…" She shrugged and pulled her hand free. "Let's see what tomorrow brings."

"No, Lou, SERIOUSLY, you do not need to…" Declan stopped pacing Dr. Kenemen's office and froze. "You cannot be serious?"

"What?" Alethea asked from her seat in front of the doctor's desk. They'd been waiting more than fifteen minutes for Declan's test results, after spending an oddly tense morning in the hotel lobby drinking far too much coffee.

She'd barely slept last night. If only she was capable of dealing with life's twists and turns or going with the flow. Dodging punches. Embracing change. If she could do all that she wouldn't be sleep deprived and she wouldn't be wishing her heart hadn't staked a claim to one Declan Cartwright.

Whatever excitement she should have felt about being officially accepted into the ACT had been dampened by their surprising and frank conversation over dinner. Just when she'd thought her life couldn't get any more tied up in knots, Declan had to tell her how he felt about her, about them. It would have been so much easier to continue to believe this was all on her, and that somehow she could find a way to work through, and get over him once he returned to his old life.

It was so much easier when she believed there was no hope for a future between them.

"What's wrong?" she asked again when Declan seemed to stammer.

He paused on the phone and spoke to her. "My sisters Lou and Hilda are coming out to Butterfly Harbor. Wait, what?" He talked into the phone again.

Despite her rampaging thoughts, she couldn't help but smile at the helpless expression on his face. He really had no idea just how devastating he really was, did he? All that charm of his…it wasn't an act. It was purely and utterly Declan. And she loved him for it.

"You're already on your way? What, are you calling from the plane?… Oh. Great. No, yeah, um, I should be back by dinner time." He rolled his eyes. "Sure. Yeah. Five o'clock at the Flutterby Inn. Okay. See you then." He clicked off and dropped his chin to his chest. "Awesome."

"Moral support?" Alethea guessed. Only family could put that much tension on someone's face.

"Something like that," Declan grumbled. "Hilda's my sister-slash-manager-slash agent and she has been chomping at the bit to find out what the doctor thinks. Apparently she's got news she can't share over the phone so she and Lou decided to make a girls' trip out of it." He resumed his pacing. "Sorry. Not what you signed up for today, I know."

"Why don't you sit down?" She held out her hand and waited the extra beat he took to decide to take it.

"Thank you for coming with me."

It was on the tip of her tongue to ask where else she'd be, but since it was the absolute truth, it had her emotions clogging her throat. She'd gone and done the impossible. She'd fallen head over heels in love with the man. "You're almost there, Declan. It won't be much longer…"

The door behind them clicked open and

Declan spun around in his chair. "Dr. Kenemen."

"Good morning, Declan." The fiftysomething woman with close-cropped silver hair and gold-framed glasses offered them both a smile. "And you're not alone this time. Hello, I'm Dr. Kenemen. You must be Alethea."

Alethea blinked. Declan had mentioned her? "Yes, I am. Nice to meet you."

"And you." Dr. Kenemen set a paper tablet on her desk and took a seat. "Sorry to keep you both waiting. I wanted to get all your options lined up before we spoke." She folded her hands and, as she smiled, Alethea's stomach dropped. "Let's go over the good news first, shall we?"

Declan's hand went cold around hers. "I guess that means there's bad news." He attempted to pull free, but Alethea held fast, keeping her attention pinned on the doctor.

"I'll be honest, Declan. I expected it to be worse. Your recovery has far exceeded most expectations. With the current medication regime, I believe the chances of not recovering from the nerve damage are on the low side."

"How low?" Declan asked. "Low enough that I can drive again?"

"A regular vehicle? Yes. On the circuit?" Dr. Kenemen's eyes sharpened. "I'd want to run another round of tests in about six months to confirm."

For the first time in hours, Alethea felt as if she could breathe.

"So that's a no to this season." Alethea could feel the sense of defeat radiating from him.

"The nerve damage to your legs and spine was more extensive than originally believed. However," she added and held up a hand to pause him when he leaned forward anxiously in his chair. "In your tests I see some promise at regeneration, and I believe you're an excellent candidate for an experimental surgery I've developed."

"How soon would I be—"

"Declan, let her finish," Alethea said softly.

"Right. Sorry." He flashed that eye-twinkling smile. "Getting ahead of things."

"I'm fairly optimistic we can alleviate the pain you've been experiencing with this procedure and stimulate the connections needed to get you close to, if not back to where you were before the accident."

"Has the pain been that bad?" Alethea asked Declan, who shrugged in typical laid-back fashion.

"I've been managing it," he told her without looking at her, which sent warning bells clanging in her head.

"Right now, the nerve damage is causing the pain and the pain is making it so the nerves can't heal," Dr. Kenemen went on. "It's a cycle this new procedure can break. I won't go into details now, but the surgery itself is rather delicate and will take serious recovery time. We're talking weeks, perhaps months in rehab. Also, and it's important for you to hear me on this, Declan, it would not be a guarantee of anything."

"If it gives me a shot to get back on a racetrack, I'm in," Declan announced. "When and where?"

"Hold on." Alethea tugged her hand free from his. "What are the possible outcomes?"

"There's only one outcome I care about," Declan said.

"Well, I'm not you," Alethea tried not to snap. "I don't think your family would appreciate you diving into this without knowing exactly what else could happen." She turned her attention to Dr. Kenemen. "What are the odds that if the surgery is successful, he'll be able to race again?"

"I would put the odds at about fifty percent."

"That's better odds than I had without the surgery," Declan confirmed. "Without the surgery, I'm out of luck. Odds are one hundred percent I'm done."

Done, but alive. Knots tugged in her belly. "What could go wrong?"

"As with any surgery, there's always the possibility of—"

"Death," Alethea supplied when the doctor hesitated. "He could die." Because he couldn't let go of the life he'd once had.

"Frankly, yes."

"I should have died in the crash," Declan reminded them. "I shouldn't be sitting in this office right now talking about this possibility. In my mind, that increases my odds."

"By that logic, the two of us never should have met and I shouldn't be sitting here, either." He glared at her. Anger, frustration, hurt overwhelmed her. She'd been so close... they'd been so close to finding common ground and maybe finding a path through this wild, unpredictable world together, but now... Now what? "I take it he could also wake up with partial paralysis."

"Yes."

She appreciated the doctor's candor. "And if he didn't have the surgery at all? What's his prognosis?"

"It doesn't matter—"

"It matters to me, Declan. And if you were thinking more clearly it would matter to you, too," Alethea said around a too tight throat. "Please, Doctor."

"If he continues on his current path, chances are he'll see more healing, but the nerve damage will become permanent. At some point, he could possibly lose the ability to walk. The pain will become less tolerable and he'll need stronger medication to manage it."

Alethea glanced at Declan as his jaw tensed. She knew him well enough to understand he'd take any risk he needed to prevent that from happening. She could see it all over his handsome face. In the clenching of his hands. In the way he stared straight at the floor and not at her. Her being here didn't matter. Not really.

He'd already made up his mind.

He loved his life; he loved the excitement and adventure. He loved racing.

More than he could ever love her.

"The bottom line is I either take the chance to reverse the damage." When Declan spoke, it was with such conviction, her heart clenched. "Or I do nothing and lose everything."

Dr. Kenemen frowned. "I wouldn't go that far, Declan. You can live a full, vital life for years, possibly decades. And even after that—"

"No, Dr. Kenemen," Declan said. "I didn't get this far in life by pulling my punches. My entire career was a fluke, all because I took a chance. I'm not going to change how I do things now. Send me all the information on the surgery."

"All right."

Alethea shivered when he looked at her. "You're really going to do this? You don't want to talk to your sisters or—"

"This is my decision, Alethea." He stared at her and for the first time, all hint of the easygoing charmer she'd fallen for was gone. "And I've made it."

"You're right." She nodded even as the tears threatened. "It is your decision."

It was also, she thought later, the most painful way he could have ever said goodbye.

CHAPTER FOURTEEN

SHE'D NEVER SPENT a longer two hours in a car with someone in her entire life. They'd skipped any last-minute tourist activities and were on the road home before noon. She could have make that *should* have offered to let him drive. Considering he'd been given the all clear to operate a motor vehicle again it probably would have been something positive to end their trip on.

But he hadn't asked and she didn't offer. Just as well. She needed something to do, something to concentrate on rather than accidentally on purpose say something they would both regret.

How could he just agree to that surgery without thinking it through? Without weighing all his options. She could see where her opinion wouldn't carry much weight, but she couldn't imagine his sisters were going to be pleased at his impulsiveness. Then again, they'd had almost thirty years to get used to his mindset. She'd only had a few weeks. It wasn't that she didn't think the surgery was a good option and, given his doctor's experience and confidence, it probably was. It was just the "do it and we'll see what happens" mentality that had her stomach threatening to revolt.

Now, as they passed the turnoff to Monterey and Pacific Grove, she found her foot pressing harder on the gas. Almost home. Almost home.

"This one's nice." Declan held out his cell phone, but barely long enough for her to get a glimpse of the white sports car he was ogling online. "What do you think?"

I think anyone who drives one of those should think twice or wonder what they're really trying to prove. "Maybe you should go with something a bit easier to get into? Dr. Kenemen said you're looking at months of PT. Crouching into that machine would probably compress your spine." Or knock his head off his broad shoulders. "It also looks like a mutant robotic space soldier with poor aim."

"You're probably right." He scrolled through to another page. "An SUV like this one might be good. Just slide in and out. I can always trade it in later. Oh, hang on. Got a call. Hey, Hilda… Yeah, we're almost home."

Almost home. Alethea blocked out the rest of his conversation with his sister, even as she caught words like *sponsorships, commercial deals, return to the track, interviews and profit margins* that made her cringe.

Wow. Alethea pulled herself back. Cringing or not, she sure needed to get herself under control.

"Well, that solves one problem." He clicked off his cell and glanced out the window. "Hilda put me on their rental car agreement, so when they head back home, I can keep that car until I figure out what to do about one."

"That's great." She may have given herself a cavity with that response. "Things are working out already, then." Eight more miles. Just eight more miles until she was back where everything made sense and she could regroup. "I'll drop you off at the inn, check in with Jason, then, head home to get Barnie. Call me when you're home and I'll come by." She flashed what she hoped was an optimistic smile.

"You don't want to join us for lunch? But I wanted to introdu—"

"I have an early day tomorrow." She cut him off. "And I have a ton of prep to do." A lie. She was well aware Natalie already had the week's menu and their schedule well in hand. "Besides, you haven't seen your family in a while and I don't want to intrude."

"You're not an intrusion, Alethea."

He reached over, covered her hand with his. She knew what he was trying to say—without more words. But she didn't want to know it. Instead, she reminded him, "You need to talk to them about what Dr. Kenemen told you and how it relates to all the plans you and Hilda have."

"Okay. How about dinner tomorrow night? My treat? Maybe check out a movie and Zane's. I remember seeing that they're showing a retrospective of *Bullet* this week."

The last thing she wanted as entertainment was a car movie. "I'll let you know." The idea of spending more time with him right now felt like a recipe for heartache. Before she took that on, she needed to know exactly where her thoughts, her feelings and her future lay.

She took the ramp for Butterfly Harbor at

top speed, earning a frown from him as she veered into town and down Monarch Lane.

"You have an appointment you're late for I don't know about?" Declan half teased.

"I need to catch Natalie before she leaves for the day." She saw Charlie Bradley and Phoebe MacBride walking down the hill from the Flutterby Inn, backpacks swinging behind them. She returned their waves, gunned the car forward, parked at the far end of the circular drive and hopped out. She shivered. The weather was turning, inching its way toward fall, bringing to mind roaring beach bonfires and fresh apple cider brewing on Calliope's stove.

"Alethea." Declan caught her arm when she tried to speed past him.

"What?" *Please don't say anything. Please don't make this harder than it already is.*

"Alethea, talk to me, please. I know you don't approve of my decision, but—"

"Like you said in the office, it's your decision. Not mine." It shouldn't matter so much. It shouldn't hurt that he didn't care what she thought. And yet, it did.

"I didn't mean it like that," he insisted. "I just meant—"

"Declan!" The sharp female voice shot at them from behind. They turned and saw two women heading down from the memorial bench overlooking one of the most picturesque spots in all of Butterfly Harbor.

"I'm not going anywhere, Declan," Alethea said quietly when she looked back at him. "But I have work to do and arrangements to make." Arrangements that did not revolve around him. "The sooner I get to things, the more time I'll have to play." She reached up, touched his face and felt her fingers tingle against his skin.

She stepped back far enough to put distance between them to settle her nerves.

"You're early." The taller of the two women hurried over and stretched out her arms, offering a smile to Alethea as she embraced Declan. "It feels like forever since I could do this." She squeezed hard, rumpled his hair as if he were six years old. "It's disgusting how you get more good-looking while the rest of us Cartwrights age, right Hilda?"

Shorter, stouter, and with a cloud of dark blond hair that seemed to have its own zip code, Hilda Cartwright slid in to duplicate her sister's greeting. "You got here fast. Some habits are hard to break, huh?"

"I wasn't driving," Declan admitted. "Hilda, Lu, this is Alethea Costas."

"Hi." Alethea stepped forward, then, found herself enveloped in Lu's rib-crushing hug. "Oh, okay," she laughed.

"It is so great to meet you. Declan's told us all about you and we can't thank you enough for driving him to that doctor," Lu said.

"I'll double that," Hilda gushed, but instead of hugging Alethea, she nodded to her. "Our boy's going to be on the track soon and it'll be all because of you."

"I don't think that's true," Alethea said with a pointed look at Declan. "In fact, I had absolutely nothing to do with it. It was nice to meet you both. I need to, um." She pointed behind her to the inn, backed away slowly. "Declan, I'll see you later."

"Yes, you will."

She knew what he meant; they weren't done with their conversation.

Even though she could think of nothing left to say.

"FOR ONCE YOU were not exaggerating." Lu linked her arm around Declan's as he retrieved his overnight bag and cane from Alethea's SUV and stashed it in his sisters' rental. "She really is a knockout."

Yes, Declan thought. *She is. In more ways than one.* "You two did not have to come all the way out here. I told you everything was fine." He tugged Lu closer, slipped an arm around her shoulder and reveled in the feel of family. "But I'm glad you did."

"Uh-oh. He must be sick." Lu put a hand against his forehead as if to check his temperature. "Hilda, call the doctor."

"Don't think one will help." Hilda had been watching Alethea's retreat into the inn. "Marcy and the gang send their love." She glanced down. "How's the leg?"

"The leg's all right." Despite being cooped up in the car for a few hours, the pain was negligible, but it felt good to be able to stretch and move. "Better. I just carry the cane around most days for security. Sorry about you staying at the inn. The house I'm in is a bit cramped for three."

"Are you kidding?" Lu pointed at the expansive wraparound porch and veranda. "This place is amazing and look at that view!"

"They gave us oceanside rooms," Hilda said as they strode into the lobby. "Just because. We were passing the time, waiting for the restaurant to open for lunch. I'm finally going to eat at a Jason Corwin restaurant and I'm not going to even count my calories."

"Wait till you try the diner in town," Declan added.

"Oh, we went there for breakfast," Hilda said. "This town's so cute."

"And friendly," Lu added with an arched brow. "I've never been on the receiving end of such a thorough yet innocent inquisition. You've clearly started another fan club, Dec."

Declan chuckled. The revelation struck a stronger chord than he expected.

"Let's sit." Lu motioned to a grouping of wingback chairs beside a bay window. A few guests milled about, getting fresh brewed coffee from the complimentary tankard that remained full at all times. A selection of cookies and pastrics sat beneath glass domed lids, offering constant temptation for paying guests as well as visitors. "We want you to fill us in on your appointment," Lu ordered in her typical second-oldest big sister manner.

Declan shrugged, declined a seat and waited for them to get comfortable. "I told you everything on the phone."

"Not quite everything," Hilda murmured.

Lu shot her a look. "Did they schedule you for surgery?"

"Dr. Kenemen said she can get her team in, in about two weeks."

"Two weeks?" Hilda's silver-gray eyes widened as she pulled out her phone. "Whoo boy, you don't waste any time. I need to start making some calls."

"That can wait," Declan suggested. "What was your news, Hilda? The news that brought you halfway across the country?" he added at her blank stare.

"Oh, right." She jumped when Lu kicked her. "Well, I might have been exaggerating on how big...okay, okay." Hilda sighed. "NexSport Corp is showing interest in sponsoring your comeback season. It would be enough to keep the team in place and going another twelve, maybe eighteen months depending on when you hit the track. With the sponsors who are still on board, that puts us in a good position moving forward."

"What's the bad news?" Declan asked for the second time that day.

"And—" Hilda shrugged "—we lost another two sponsors. But we were expecting that," she said in a rush. "Considering you're less than frivolous with your income—"

"You are the family squirrel who's very stingy with his nuts." Lou smirked.

"True." Hilda nodded. "Comebacks are huge opportunities, Declan."

"I'm not in this sport for profit." No. He was in it for the rush. The risk. And the burst of adrenaline that, when all was said and done, probably added to his desire to get onto the circuit again. "And I'm set up just fine money-wise." Even if he never drove again, he had more than enough money at his disposal to choose whatever future he deemed right for himself. A future that, should all go as well as he expected, would put him into the life he'd been living before his accident. A life that only in hindsight had been missing something.

No. It had been missing some*one*.

He glanced toward the restaurant doors. He'd felt the distance in the car. The walls going up between them were no doubt of his own making. He shouldn't have been so dismissive of her thoughts in the doctor's office. He had, after all, asked her to come with him. It just hadn't occurred to him that she wouldn't see the surgery as something positive for the two of them. Was he wrong? Did he have his priorities messed up? Had he missed an element he hadn't factored in or considered?

Hilda's voice faded into the background as his thoughts that had been organized and controlled moments before fragmented into a new puzzle. A puzzle he couldn't quite see the complete picture of. The relief and excitement he'd felt upon hearing the prospect of returning to the track shifted, and left him wondering if, by agreeing to the surgery, he really was headed down the right road.

"NexSport's been expanding their funding of sports programs for students, haven't they?" Declan cut his sister off. "Rebuilding gyms and reestablishing physical education programs in certain school districts."

"They have." Hilda's brow veed. "Why?"

"Just wondering if they'd be willing to have a conversation about what else can be done. Racing isn't going to be an option for me forever, Hilda. My crash last year is evidence of that. I need to make plans for what'll happen in the future." There was going to be a future, too. The surgery was only the beginning.

"All the plans we've made hinge on you getting back behind the wheel," Hilda said as if he needed reminding. "You do that, even once, and I bet NexSport will offer you the moon."

"Lu, ease up. Your bankbook is showing." Lu kicked her again with her booted foot. "Stop playing manager and act like the big sister that you are. You're overloading him on info and he's getting that bored look."

"I am not." Declan frowned, but he glanced away just in case she was right. "This is all what brought you two out here, isn't it?"

"Not exactly," Lu said slowly with a side-eyed glance at her sister. "Tell him already."

Hilda played with a frayed piece of yarn on her light pink sweater. "I don't really think—"

"For the love of Pete, either you tell him or I will," Lu ordered.

"Tell me what?" Sister exhaustion crept over him. Normally he was immune to his siblings' bickering, but it was especially nerve grating when all he wanted to do was find Alethea and have a long, important, soul-bearing conversation about where she fit into his life.

"Okay, okay. So, Declan." Hilda planted

her hands on her knees and smiled up at him. A smile he recognized as both uncertain and determined. "You remember Freddie Tornacci?"

"How could I forget?" Declan shifted, stretched a bit to get the kinks loose. "That guy sent me flying off the track in Charlotte. Minor concussion and a broken finger."

"But he apologized and bought you and your team drinks that night," Hilda reminded him.

"Okay, so the guy's tolerable. Why? You didn't sign him, did you? Ah, jeez." He rubbed a hand across the back of his neck. "You aren't his agent now, are you? Tell me you aren't repping him."

"Not exactly," Hilda hedged. "We're kind of…well, we sort of—"

"Oh, for cripes' sake," Lu cut in. "They got married."

Declan gaped. "Excuse me?"

"Lu, I said let me tell him!" Hilda practically shrieked.

"I would have, but at this rate I'd die of starvation and they just opened the doors for lunch. Freddie and your sister eloped last week," she added after the fact, as if that wasn't the important part of the discussion.

"Huh. Well." Declan, who had spent most of his life shouting over other voices for attention, had often wondered what it would take to rob him of the ability to speak.

"Well?" Hilda asked. "Is that all you're going to say?"

"I'm engaging my filter." Any rivalry aside, Tornacci was a good guy. And an even better driver. He had a stellar reputation for treating his team and his friends well and that always told Declan more about a person than anything. Hilda had always been unlucky in the relationship department and, as she was closing in on forty, had lamented her unwitting devotion to spinsterhood. The idea that she would have taken a chance on Tornacci said a lot about their relationship. "Do you need me to have a brother to new husband talk with him?"

"Please." Hilda rolled her eyes and flipped a few strands of loose hair behind her shoulder. "You're five years younger than he is."

"Which makes him five years younger than you," Lu teased. "Go, Hilda!"

"Are you happy?" Declan asked and earned a look of surprise from Lu.

Hilda smiled warmly and twisted one of her rings around to display the set he hadn't noticed. "I really am. I just don't want it to be weird. For any of us. I mean with you and him competing—"

"That shouldn't have anything to do with it if you love him, Hilda." For Declan, it was as simple as that.

"You mean it?" She sagged in relief and patted her heart. "Oh, that's good to hear. I told him you'd be okay with this, but he wasn't so sure and well." Her smile widened and reached bright, excited eyes. "It's been hard enough getting used to being involved with a race car driver. It's not an easy thing," she stated. Whether she meant to look toward the restaurant doors or not, that's where Declan saw her gaze fall. Again, he thought of Alethea. "It's a lot of worry," Hilda went on. "But when he comes back to me after the race and he's safe? He gets the checkered flag as his rush. The other's mine."

"It's not like this is all new to you," Lu said and stuck her thumb out at Declan. "This one's had us in training for that for years."

"It's different when it's someone you care about romantically, Lu." Hilda, usually filled with vim and vigor, eased back and got serious. "Until that race is over, I'm not convinced I'll be whole again. But, then, it is and I am." She shook her head, and just like that, she was back to her usual self. "Not that I have that much experience with relationships or racing beyond spreadsheets and marketing calls. And hey, who knows how other people might feel about dating a driver. Just throwing that out there." She stood up, touched Declan's arm before she moved to the desk. "Just in case it comes up in a future conversation for you. Okay." Hilda shot to her feet. "Who's ready for lunch because I am starving!"

THANKFULLY, ALETHEA'S VISIT with Jason was easy. After she filled him in and confirmed that she would be attending the ACT beginning in January, they agreed to set aside some time in the next few weeks to figure out her schedule and new official role in her boss's company. With the food well in hand with Natalie's expertise, all she had to do tomorrow was turn up and jump in.

She left the Flutterby Inn by the back door.

It was a coward's move, but she'd embraced enough change the last couple of days. Stashing her belongings in her car, she climbed in and headed down the hill. Instead of turning right and heading home to the farm, she turned left and, a few blocks later, parked across from the one place she knew would help clear her head.

She walked across the street and headed down the wooden deck leading to the beach. Shoes in hand, the second her feet sank into the cool sand, everything inside her began to shift into place.

This was her favorite spot. It was where she'd come the day she'd arrived in Butterfly Harbor almost two years ago. It was where her sadness and worry had been drowned out by the tide roaring in her ears. Her healing had begun here, thanks to the ocean. Thanks to Calliope and Xander who had welcomed her with understanding and care. As had the entire town. She'd thought herself whole. She'd thought herself happy.

And, then, she'd met Declan. Now she knew she hadn't even been existing in the same universe as happy. Which begged the question, what would it be like without him?

She walked toward the glorious cliffs stretching out beneath the Flutterby Inn. Autumn was on its way, leaving behind the dreams of summer fun and frivolity until next year. Butterfly Harbor would soon shift to celebrating its annual monarch festival, which would mean the opening of the brand-new sanctuary and with it, more hope and promise for the town.

Butterfly Harbor itself had healed and was just on the cusp of recovery. And she would be a part of it. Had been a part of it.

The beach was dotted with people. A few families here and there. Several kids darting in and out of the playful waves. The scent of seaweed, salt and pure oxygen coated the breeze and filled her lungs with the ease and relaxation she'd longed for. This place never, ever disappointed her.

Up ahead lay the outcropping of rocks that led to the tunnels and caves below the cliffs that had caused concern and excitement a few years back. Then eight-year-old Charlie Bradley had been caught in high tide in one of those caves and was rescued by the man who would eventually become her dad. She'd been in search of a magic wish box. Alethea smiled, shook her head. Even if such a thing existed, at this point, she wouldn't know what to wish for.

Water lapped at her feet and she bent to curl up her jeans. When she stood, she saw a solitary man sitting on one of the rocks. Someone so wholly unexpected she thought perhaps she was imagining things. And yet there he sat, his gaze locked on the horizon.

She hesitated, uncertain whether to say something or leave without disturbing him. Mayor Gil Hamilton wasn't a person she'd spent a lot of time with; she'd only met him on a few occasions, but despite the rumors and the stories she'd heard, she liked the guy. She couldn't imagine the weight he carried on his shoulders, not just from trying to lead and protect the town, but from the burden of troublesome history his family was rumored to have caused.

"I didn't think you'd be into meditation," she called, throwing her hesitancy into the wind and approaching.

He looked at her and, for a moment, she saw the familiar ghost of grief hovering in his blue eyes. His smile flashed, that familiar smile that was plastered all over town on his campaign posters and flyers. The same smile he offered whenever he accepted his lunch at the sanctuary site. "Hi, Alethea."

"I don't mean to disturb you." She pointed behind her. "I can leave you alone—"

"No, please." He motioned with his hand. "Pull up a rock. Take a seat. I was just re-grouping."

She dropped her shoes onto the sand as she sat. The second her gaze followed his, she sighed. "You've found the perfect place."

"My father brought me here once when I was little. Five or six." He resumed staring at the ocean. "It was one of the few times I remember him doing something fun. Almost frivolous. It's probably why it sticks in my head so clearly."

"I haven't heard a lot about your father," Alethea admitted.

"Nothing good, anyway," Gil said with a forced laugh. "That's okay," he said when she looked at him and cringed. "It's taken me a long time to accept the fact that he was not a good person. He caused a lot of people a lot of pain. Pain I thought I could fix by becoming mayor."

"Fixing other people's pain isn't an easy

thing to do," Alethea said. "And sometimes it isn't even the best way to solve the problem."

"No, it's not." He shook his head, tossed a rock into the ocean. "Half the town hates me because of what he did. And the other half hates me because of what I've done. Funny thing is, neither side is wrong."

Whatever she'd been expecting to hear, it certainly wasn't this. "You're worried about the election."

"I'm worried about a lot of things, but today? No. Right now I'm worried that my brother's coming up with a new way to wreak havoc on me that might hurt someone else."

"Christopher Russo." Alethea was familiar with the name and that the gossip surrounding it recently revealed the man to be a long-lost son of Gil's father. "You think he's dangerous."

"I think he's another person my father hurt and it might not be repairable." Regret shone on his face. "It takes talent to create chaos from beyond the grave. Leave it to my father to have mastered that ability."

For a man who prided himself on presenting the perfect appearance, and who was always seemingly in control, she'd never seen anyone look quite so...defeated. "Can I ask you a question?"

"Sure. Shoot."

"Do you even want to be mayor again? Or are you running for reelection because it's what's expected of you?"

He smiled, and let out a sound that could have been a chuckle. "That is a question I've asked myself a million times." Gil scooted forward and pitched forward off the rocks. He landed solidly and brushed sand from his jeans. "Maybe this election will give me the answer once and for all. I need to head back to the office. Can I walk you somewhere?"

"Um, yeah, sure." She got up and together they walked and talked about the upcoming festival, the completion of the sanctuary and what the holiday season would bring. For all her time in Butterfly Harbor, Gil had always been described as this arrogant king lauding it over the goodwill of the town. Like some evil villain waiting for his chance to strike and wipe away the happiness of all who lived here. A mayor who was determined to cling to his powerful position by whatever means necessary.

And yet, now, watching him leave after

he kindly escorted her to her car, she had to wonder if maybe Gil Hamilton was in need of help the most.

She climbed back into the SUV and headed down to Monarch Lane, then, up the hill to the farm. By the time she parked, hauled her stuff into her room and, then, made it to the kitchen, she found Calliope, Xander and Stella, who was entertaining Barnie with a collection of spare yarn, getting ready for an early dinner.

"You're home!" Stella raced over, abandoning Barnie to the yarn. Wrapped up in little girl hugs, Alethea felt the pressure inside her release. "Did you see the school? What did you think? Are you going to go? Where's Declan?"

"Questions that can be answered all in good time." Calliope came over and unwound Stella's arms and scooted her back to the table. "You're earlier than I expected. Have you had dinner?"

"Not yet, no." Unable to resist temptation, she scooped up Barnie and gave him a snuggle, touching nose to nose. "How did he do?"

"He did great," Xander said as he set aside his tablet. "My shoes on the other hand—"

"Barnie chewed off one of the tassels to his loafers." Stella giggled.

Alethea giggled, too, and cuddled the kitten close. "He's so naughty." And so perfect for Declan. "I need to take him back after dinner. Sorry, Stell."

"Awww." Stella planted her chin in her hand and pouted. "So soon?"

"Stella, you've proven yourself a capable caretaker," Calliope complimented her sister.

"Really?" Stella brightened. "Does that mean I can have a new kitten of my own?"

Ophelia stuck her tail up in the air and pranced out the back door.

"It means we'll discuss it," her sister confirmed.

"Awesome. I'll get the salad."

"Who cooked?" Alethea asked, then said, "Never mind. It smells great."

"Meaning not me," Xander admitted, chuckling. He quickly sobered. "So. Let's have it. How did the trip go?"

"It went." She hesitated, felt the tension of three pairs of eyes on her. She could drag things out, keep them guessing. Or put them out of their misery. "I loved it and yes, I've decided to go."

"Aw, man." Stella pouted and earned a stern look from her sister.

"I'm leaning toward the part-time schedule, so I can work for Jason at the same time. It'll take longer, but it'll be easier to pay the bills. Jason was right. And so were you, Xan. I need the education if I'm going to help build Corwin Enterprises into something really special." And earn the chance to oversee the new pub-inspired restaurant he was thinking about opening in town.

"I would say this calls for a celebration." Calliope pulled a bottle of sparkling cider out of the fridge.

"Planned ahead, did you?" Alethea teased.

"I hoped." As they poured and toasted, celebrated and ate, talked and laughed, Alethea found her heart beating in rhythmic time with the heartbeat of her family: the heartbeat of home.

The only thing missing was Declan.

CHAPTER FIFTEEN

DECLAN PARKED THE rental car and, after turning off the engine, sat back and sighed. Finally.

He'd spent four hours with his sisters before longing for the solitude—and quiet   of the Howser house. After spending his life among the chaos and noise of a multisibling household, there was nothing better sometimes than ear-ringing silence. With his sisters exploring every nook and cranny of Butterfly Harbor's main drag of shops, businesses and offerings, he'd had the uncontrollable itch to finally, after more than a year, slide behind the wheel of the car—of any car—and see where it took him.

He'd driven up the coast a bit, taking in Monterey and meandering over to the iconic 17-Mile Drive. It wasn't speed he wanted, it was to reconnect, to know that he was in control of a car when not so long ago he'd been convinced he never would be again.

The wonder and beauty of the Pacific Coast swirled around him, offering unmatched views and the pristine air that only the ocean could provide. Funny. He'd worried about feeling trapped when he'd first come to Butterfly Harbor. That the small town would feel suffocating, making him anxious to be on his way and yet... Declan sighed again.

And yet...

Declan's thoughts returned to the present. He shoved out of the car and gathered his things, realizing he was looking forward to seeing Barnie—and Alethea—again.

He approached the porch, but stopped and turned toward the workshop. The rustling sound was distinctive. Something—or someone—was inside.

He set his belongings down and moved quietly to check the lock on the door. Secure. He peered into one of the windows on the side of the building. Someone scrambled out of sight, diving around the tarp-covered Impala and heading for the opposite window.

Declan pulled out his cell phone and hurried around the building. Just as he hit Luke's number, the glass in the window exploded and a dark figure hurtled right at him. There was nowhere for Declan to go. The man's momentum sent Declan flying off his feet. He landed hard on his back, stunning him even as he heard Luke's voice echo from the phone.

Declan groaned, tried to move and, for one awful moment, thought he couldn't. Pain shot up and down his leg and spine. As much as he wanted to catch a glimpse of the intruder, as much as he wanted to follow, all he could do was lie on the hard ground and wait for the pain to pass.

"Aren't you supposed to be taking Barnie over to Declan's?" Calliope asked Alethea. But Alethea knew what her sister-in-law was really asking her. She appreciated Calliope's subtlety and her offer of a friendly ear.

There wasn't an inch of Duskywing farm that Calliope didn't understand. And that included Alethea and her pointed retreat after dinner to seek out the calm, quiet garden beneath the stars.

Standing beneath the twilight sky, Alethea was struggling. For a bit of comfort, she hugged her arms around herself and looked up, wishing she could get lost in the coming darkness. "I just needed some time first."

"I was glad to hear your interview went well." Calliope bent to pluck a sprig of lavender, held it to her nose and drew in a breath. "And that you've decided to take those steps forward."

"It was ironic I decided to do that on Talia's birthday. Yesterday," she added at Calliope's questioning look. "I forgot, actually. Her mother called as I was heading to my interview."

"Ah. That would be one of those complications you mentioned at dinner." Calliope's bare feet rustled in the small pebbles of the path. "I take it you had help making your way through that particular challenge."

Alethea smiled. "You know I did."

"I've not spent a lot of time with your Declan, but I did sense he's one who chooses his words and his intentions carefully."

"You're kidding, right?" Alethea practically snorted. "Calliope, the man drives a race car for a living. He free dives in the ocean. I bet mentioning the Monterey sky diving club would have him joining in a heartbeat."

"Perhaps he's more careful and deliberate

with the things and people he cares about. Did something happen in San Francisco?"

"You mean other than his doctor telling him he could have his whole life back the way it was if he has specialized surgery that may or may not work?" She squeezed her eyes shut and took a deep breath. "Oh, and I think I'm in love with him."

"Think?" Calliope stood beside her now, a gentle, comforting hand on her arm. The nighttime breeze slipped around them, lifted their hair in a tandem dance of summer warmth. "Anyone looking at the two of you together and they'll see it. Alethea." The sympathy in her voice scraped against Alethea's nerves. "There's nothing wrong with being in love with someone."

"I know that." She ground the words out like glass under her feet. "But I don't want it. I don't want this. I thought I did. Seeing everyone at the baby shower, watching Ozzy and Jo, seeing you and Xander every single day." Tears burned her eyes. "I don't want to be part of someone else. Not yet. Not when I'm just figuring out who I am on my own."

Calliope's expression didn't change as she led Alethea over to the stone bench at the end of the path. "When you first came here, you were so—"

"Fragile," Alethea supplied.

"No." Calliope sat, urged her to do the same. "No, you were never fragile. You were hurt. Wounded. But you never once turned your ability to love off. Paused it, perhaps. Closing yourself off now, just when a new and exciting world is opening up for you, how is that good?"

"I didn't say it was good." Now came admission time. "But it is safe."

"Safe? And yet here you've been so bold, choosing to begin a fresh, challenging chapter in your life. But not including that love you have for Declan? You can take one chance but not another?"

"That surgery could have no positive effect. There's no guarantee it'll work." How did she make Calliope understand when everything was so muddled in her own mind? "How can I say I love him and not want him to have what he needs? And he needs to race, Calliope." She swallowed the bitter tears. "How he talks about it, how his entire being lit up when he heard there was a fraction of a possibility that he could... I was so hurt, so angry.

I wanted to scream at him not to do it. How is that love?"

"How is it not?"

Alethea sighed. Circles. They were going in typical Calliope-induced circles. "Talking with you is so frustrating sometimes."

"Yes, I know." Calliope offered her a gentle smile. "So Declan knows how you feel about him having the surgery. Does he know how you feel about him period?"

"I don't know how he doesn't."

"As perceptive as people can be sometimes, folks can also be closed-minded and determined to ignore what's right in front of them."

"I can't be with a man who's determined to take chances with every breath he takes. That would suffocate me, Calliope. Living in that constant state of fear of losing him."

"You don't feel that way about Xander. Or me, or Stella. Or your parents. Not even your father, and his health has been in decline for as long as I've known you and your family."

Alethea frowned. "That's different. You're all different," she argued, even as Calliope's point struck home. "None of you are purposely reckless and besides, it's just a given, loving all of you. I don't have a choice. It just…happened." She blinked. "Love just happens."

"Especially when you least expect it to." Calliope shifted and stretched her back, rubbed a hand over her rounded stomach. "Your brother showed up at a difficult time in my life, Alethea. A complicated time. I was dealing with my mother and struggling to find a balance between Stella and the farm and life. The last thing I thought I needed was an arrogant architect who insisted he knew what this town needed. He made me all the more confused. But I've since come to realize that often love presents itself when it's needed most. Whether you've been meaning to or not, you've been embracing fear. Perhaps it's time you stepped back and let whatever it is you feel for Declan simply…happen."

"And the rest?" The racing, the surgery, the distance when he returned to his real life. What did she do with all of that?

"When you start with love, the rest can be worked out, with a little patience and a lot of understanding." She took hold of Alethea's hand, pressed it to her belly as the baby kicked. "Your nephew agrees with me."

"It's a boy?" Alethea gasped. "Have you told Xander?"

"He won't let me. He wants to be surprised. We live with so many regrets in this life, Alethea. You already have some where Talia is concerned." Calliope's face glowed in the rising moonlight; her sister-in-law looked at her with encouraging, understanding eyes. "Do you really want them with Declan?"

"FOR SUCH A little thing you make an awful lot of noise." Alethea patted the top of the cardboard pet carrier encouragingly. Barnie, along with all of his belongings, was on his way home.

And Alethea, heaven help her, was ready to face Declan. She loved him. It was as simple as that. Whatever happened next, she'd just have to figure that out, wouldn't she?

The second she crested the hill, she slammed on her brakes. The BHFD engine sat idling, lights spinning, near Declan's property. Heart hammering in her throat, she tried to breathe, tried to think. "Declan." The whisper barely escaped her lips when she spotted Jasper O'Neill emerging from the path toward the house. "Jasper!" She shut off the car and jumped out of the driver's seat to hurry toward the probie firefighter. "What's going on?"

"Break-in." The young man retrieved a first-aid kit from the engine. "We're figuring it was Russo again, only this time he caused some damage. I'm sure it's okay for you to drive on in," Jasper added as he headed back. "Just park as far away from the emergency vehicles as possible. Luke and Fletch are here, Roman and Ozzy, too."

"Okay, great, thanks."

Shaking, she raced back to her car and parked as Jasper suggested. She couldn't leave Barnie in the vehicle, so she took a chance and dropped the cat off in the main house before she sprinted to the workshop where she could see broken glass and splintered wood everywhere. The west-facing window of the shop was gone. "Declan?" She turned and found herself surrounded by firefighters and deputies.

"Over here, Alethea."

Fletcher and Ozzy stepped aside. Declan was on the ground, sitting up, his bare arms dotted with cuts and scrapes.

"What happened?"

"Guy leaped at me like a panther," Declan grumbled, pushing off the oxygen mask Roman attempted to place over his nose. "I don't need that, dude. I'm fine."

"He won't let us call an ambulance," Ozzy told Alethea under his breath. "We all saw him crash on the track. We know what his injuries were."

They didn't know the half of it. "Declan." She crouched down and took his hand. "Can you stand up okay?"

"I don't think—" Roman began.

She shot him a look, then, returned her attention to Declan. "If you can stand on your own, without help, and without pain, I'll back you up." She shifted so he had no choice but to look at her. "Can you?"

He shifted his legs, his hips, and flinched. He tried to cover, then, turned worried eyes on her. "No."

"All right. Hospital it is." Her tone sharpened. "End of discussion, Declan. If for no other reason than you need to be sure this doesn't change your surgery options. Roman?"

Roman Salazar, who served as co-fire chief with his wife, Frankie, nodded. "We're calling right now. Get this on him for me?"

He handed her the oxygen mask and moved off to speak with Luke and the others.

"Don't you dare put that thing on—"

She snapped the elastic behind his head and pushed the mask onto his face. "These people are trying to help you, so you do what you're told. I can't believe you scared me like this. And you aren't even on a racetrack."

His lips twitched as he breathed in, then out, then in again and sat up straighter. "Ridiculous. Got flattened by a flying panther."

"You said that before," Ozzy stated and moved closer. "Can you describe the person?"

Declan nodded. "It was the guy in your sketch. I saw his face for only a few seconds, but I'm sure of it."

"Great. Thanks." Ozzy straightened and got out his cell.

The ambulance, with its siren blaring, could be heard roaring up the hill. Declan groaned. "This is silly."

"This is you taking care of yourself." Alethea held on to him. "You're going to do whatever they say without an argument. Because that's the only route you have to getting back here where we can talk."

"You're willing to talk to me now?" Declan's brow arched. "If this was all it took I should have had the guy tackle me earlier. Alethea?" He caught her hand as the ambulance appeared through the trees and brush. "Don't you dare ditch me. Not now. Not yet."

Alethea backed away as the EMTs quickly hopped out of the ambulance and headed toward them. "Everything they say, understand? I'm going to follow you to the hospital."

He grabbed her hand again. This time he tugged her close for a moment, but rather than saying anything, he simply looked at her.

"I'll be there, Declan." She touched his face. "I promise."

"THIS WASN'T MY FAULT," Declan insisted. He shifted on the squeaky emergency room bed as his sisters stood there, glaring at him.

"It's never your fault," Hilda muttered. He could see the concern fade from her eyes the longer she looked at him. "Well, seems like you're in one piece." She poked him in various places until he slapped her hands away.

He tried his other sister. "Lu, please."

"It's not like this is our first time getting that call, Dec." Lu shrugged and dropped her purse onto the chair Alethea had vacated only seconds before. "Same day, different hospital. Remember when you fell out of the tree house and broke your arm?"

"Or jumped off that roof and broke your ankle?"

"Shocker he hasn't tripped over a feather and bruised his ego." Alethea strode forward, a tray of coffee cups in her hands. "Cappuccinos for you two ladies and one triple shot espresso macchiato for me."

"Hey, where's mine?" he asked.

"Oh, yeah." She plucked the final cup free of the tray and stuck a paper straw through the hole in the lid. "One fruit juice for you."

"Fruit juice?" He sipped, almost gagged and sagged back against the pillows. "This nightmare won't end."

"Thanks for calling," Lou said to Alethea. "We should have known he wouldn't."

"No problem. So. Broken arm and ankle. What else?"

"Hilda, you forgot about the ones your husband caused," Declan grumbled. "Alethea, when am I getting out of here?"

"I talked to Paige. They're waiting on the X-rays. Should be any time." She offered what he thought was a weak smile and worried more. "Whatever the number, his beats mine. Only had the one." She wiggled her pinky finger. "I slammed it in an industrial freezer last year. I howled nonstop for an hour."

"So you're a daredevil after all," Declan teased and earned a grin. The humor didn't quite reach her eyes. But she was holding steady. More importantly, she was here. And that fact made him sappy.

"Oh, yeah? Watch me wield a chef's knife. Did you enjoy your dinner at Dreams?" she asked his sisters.

"Gorgeous dinner and a special tour of the kitchen," Hilda said. "That Jason Corwin's a sweetheart. And we got to see his baby boy. I could just squeeze him."

"I frequently do," Alethea said. She sat beside Declan on the bed, rested one hand on his knee as if it was the most natural thing in the world. He wished it was; it set his heart to racing.

She had no idea how entrancing she was. Entrancing, captivating and positively perfect. For him. He'd seen the fear in her eyes when she'd first gotten to the house. In that split second, he realized he never, ever wanted to see that expression on her face again.

And if he did, he certainly didn't want to be the cause of it.

"Should have known the hotshot race car driver would be having a party in here." Nurse Paige Bradley had her blond hair tied back from her face and wore wrinkled scrubs in shades of pink and green. "All right, mister. You're in the clear. No damage to your spine or legs. Blood work's clean. Hot showers and no exertion for the next few days. Agree and you're good to go."

"About time," he grumbled and rolled his legs to the side of the bed. Now when he moved most of him cooperated without protest.

"Excuse me, would you like to repeat that?" Lu asked him in a way only a big sister can.

"I meant, thank you very much for your assistance, Nurse Bradley. I appreciate your help."

Paige beamed. "I need to keep you fine women around for good. Here." She handed over a slip of paper. "Prescription for painkillers. You can fill it at the pharmacy on your way out."

Declan purposely avoided Alethea's gaze. "I won't take them."

Lu cleared her throat.

"But thank you." He accepted the prescription and set it on the bed, then, he gathered his clothes. "Would you ladies excuse me? I'd like to get dressed."

"No excuse necessary." Lu shrugged. "We used to diaper that butt."

Paige and Alethea laughed. Declan glared.

Hilda promptly got to her feet and reached for her sister's arm. "Okay, fun older-sister embarrassment time is over. Let's you and I hunt down that pie Jason told us about at the diner."

"Blackberry's her best," Paige said as she left. "Guaranteed to change your life."

"Sold. You good, kiddo?" Hilda stopped in front of him.

"Are you taking me home?" he asked Alethea.

"Yes."

"Then I'm great. Thanks, Hil."

"Looks like he's in excellent hands," Lu said. "And I'm craving pie. See you both tomorrow. You." She pointed at him. "No more excitement for a while, all right? That includes her."

Declan chuckled at the instant flush on Alethea's cheeks.

"Don't worry," he said. "I never do what she says. Give me a few minutes, all right?"

"Sure." Alethea hugged her coffee to her chest. "I didn't overstep, did I? Calling them? If it were one of my brothers—"

"If you hadn't, they might never have forgiven me when they found out. It's fine. Now go. So we can get out of here."

It took him longer than he'd have liked, but he managed to get dressed. Five minutes later, and he was walking up to Alethea's tiny car. By the time he was in front of his house, unfolding his limbs from a small car—for the second time that day—he realized how correct Alethea had been when she'd commented on his choice of vehicle.

"Where's the furry guy?" he asked when they were inside the house. He made his way down the hall and into the kitchen.

"Upstairs. Want me to go get him?" Alethea turned on the lights.

Declan sat at the kitchen table and breathed a sigh of relief. Finally. Home. "Thanks. It might be a while before I can make that climb and I've missed him."

"Awww." Alethea giggled. "If your sisters could hear you now. Their little brother and his kitty cat."

"Scat," he ordered even as he laughed. Barnie was one thing he had not told his sisters about for just that reason. He waited until Alethea was upstairs, calling for the kitten, before he shoved himself up and walked to the fridge.

The pain wasn't bad, but he didn't want it getting worse. The prescription Paige had given him in the ER wasn't necessary. Not when he already had what he needed here. He poured a glass of water, downed one of the pills and stood there, waiting for the initial effects to kick in. He didn't realize he'd zoned out until he heard her coming down the hall.

Panicked, he fumbled for the bottle, yanked open the closest cabinet and threw it inside, slammed the door shut just as she walked into the kitchen.

"Here he is." She handed the kitten over to him. "Listen to that purr. That's just for you, I think."

"Hey, fella." Declan cupped the cat in his hands and tucked him close. "Sorry I was gone so long. That won't happen again for a while. Speaking of a while." Now was as good a time as any. "Alethea, are you ready for that talk?"

"Nope. Not tonight." She poked her nose into the open fridge. "You need a delivery from Duskywing. I'll bring it by tomorrow. Okay if I have some tea?"

"Go for it." He sat again, breathed a sigh of relief as the pain that had been threatening to descend didn't. "Glasses are in that cabinet…" He trailed off, dread pooling in his chest. "You know what, I'll just—"

She danced around him as he started to stand. "I've got it." She opened the cabinet, reached in. And froze.

"Alethea, let me explain."

She set a glass on the counter and, then, he saw her reach for the pill bottle. She scanned the label, looked at him. "When was the last time you took one?"

It never occurred to him to lie. "About five minutes ago."

"When you were talking to the doctor." She frowned, as if puzzling things out. "I didn't realize the pain was bad enough for these."

"It's not. Not all the time."

"But some of the time." Hurt slid across

her face, the kind of hurt that was mixed with shock and realization. She stepped away.

"Okay, hang on. No, Alethea, don't." He barely managed to catch her arm as she swept past him. "Please. I can't hang on to you and the cat. Just…" Desperate to keep hold of her, he shifted Barnie to his shoulder, who clung for dear life. "I promise you, Alethea, I am very careful with how much I take," he said.

"I've heard that before." Tears pooled in her eyes. "I can't do this again, Declan. The racing, the danger… I think I could have pushed past that, but this?" She tugged her arm free. "I can't fight this again. Not even for you."

"I didn't accept the prescription from Paige. Remember?" He dug into his pocket and threw the unused crumpled note on the table. Barnie, never having seen that before, dive-bombed and landed four feet splayed right over it. "Darn it, cat. That's…oh, never mind." Barnacle batted the paper and sent it soaring to the floor. "That prescription they gave me was for double the dose I have now. And I didn't want it."

"Because you already have plenty. For now. How long before you did fill it? How long before that one pill isn't enough? How long before you lie to me about it?" It was as if the past few weeks hadn't happened. She stared at him as if he were a stranger.

"I'm not Talia." He said the words with every bit of strength he had. "Alethea, I know you can't see that now, but I'm not her. I've got this under control. I can handle it."

He stood there, helpless, hopeless, as she closed the front door behind her.

CHAPTER SIXTEEN

"Order up! Two pork tostadas, one chili mac and cheese, and one spicy corn dog." Alethea spun back to the grill before the burgers overcooked.

"Take a breath, Alethea," Natalie half teased. "You're spinning like a top."

"Just trying to keep up." She'd been like this for days, unable to stop moving, driving herself to exhaustion so she could sleep and not think. Between her hours on the truck and working out her plans for school, along with her living arrangements, she was doing a good job keeping ahead of the reality nipping at her heels.

A reality that had her friends and family concerned, she knew.

Word was definitely out that she and Declan had hit a serious speed bump and broken up. Speculation was running rampant as to the reason. Even his sisters, before they'd left town, had stopped by for lunch in an attempt to eek out the truth. She flat-out told them that Declan was aware of the reason and if they had questions, they could ask him.

She had little doubt they would.

"Did Jason talk to you about the new schedule for next week?" Natalie asked as she tacked up another two orders. "We'll be doing a late two-hour shift at the Howser property while Kendall's crew is working there."

"Right." It barely computed. She'd worry about that when she had to. Next week. For now, she had something else on her mind. She caught sight of Jo Bertoletti making her way slowly from the lunch area to her tiny house on wheels. "You okay here for a while?"

"Yeah. Here." Natalie tossed her a bottle of water. "Hydrate. And maybe eat something?"

"Later." Alethea jumped out of the truck and hurried toward Jo and Lancelot, who as usual, held his comfort dragon in his mouth. "Hey, Jo. You have a few minutes?"

"I do. And you are just in time to lend a hand." She pulled open her door and waved the dog and Alethea inside. "Pull me in, will you?"

Alethea carefully hauled her friend up the steps.

"Thanks, hon. That won't be possible much longer." Jo fanned her face with one hand and cradled her stomach with the other. "What's up?"

"I heard you and Ozzy are buying a new place together."

"We're moving in next week." Jo sighed. "It'll be nice to have a place where I don't bump into everything."

Alethea had spent quite a bit of time in this forty-two-foot house on wheels. It was all one level, with a bedroom and bathroom at one end, and an ample living area and office space in the other. But it was the kitchen that appealed to her the most.

"I can hear the gears spinning in your head, Al. Out with it." Jo hoisted herself onto one of the stools at the kitchen counter, attempted to raise her feet, then, gave up. "Grab me a water, will you?" She motioned to the fridge as Lancelot settled nearby.

Alethea poured her friend a large glass of cold water and spent a moment checking out the kitchen. "I take it you heard about me going back to school in January."

"I did." Jo took a long gulp of her water. "San Francisco's not cheap to live in."

"I've got leads on apartments. Other students looking for roommates. It'll work out." Optimism and desperation went surprisingly well together. "It'll only be a few days a week and I'll still be here a lot. On the truck and with Jason."

"Okay. Waiting on the punchline, Al."

"I want to buy this house."

Jo stopped mid-drink, lowered her glass. "Really?" She looked left and right, and, then, frowned.

"It's perfect. Lots of kitchen space so I can cook and it's small and private. Plus, Calliope said I can set it up on her property, so I'll be close to the family and not bug her with my midnight cooking." She shrugged. "I don't know how much it's worth, or how much you'd be asking, but I might—"

"Stop." Jo held up her hands. "Breathe. Give me a sec to catch up." She took a moment, then, said, "That could work, actually. You'll need the right kind of car to transport it."

"Unless I plan to plant it," Alethea countered. "But considering I'm going to have to get a new car for commuting, anyway, you could help me with that, right?"

Jo's brow arched. "Wouldn't Declan be a natural choice for car shopping?"

"Don't." Alethea swallowed hard.

"Oh, honey. Sometimes it helps to talk about it." Jo reached for her hand, but Alethea pretended to examine the cabinets.

"What happened is, it's over and I don't want to discuss it." She could barely let herself think about it, let alone dissect the details. "If you don't want to help, that's okay. I can—"

"I didn't say that and you know it. And Ozzy says I'm cranky."

"I'm not cranky," Alethea snapped.

"No, you're in love and miserable about it. Been there. Done that." Jo toasted her with her water. "Now. Since you don't feel like girl talk and I like to strike while the iron's hot, let's get to business and start haggling." Jo put down her empty water glass and slapped her hands together. "Hit me with your best offer."

NINE DAYS. He had nine days before his surgery and Declan was still hoping to figure out how to get Alethea to talk to him.

"It's like being trapped in the worst epi-sode of a soap opera ever." The charming small town had closed ranks, protecting one of their own as Declan had attempted to pil-fer information as to how he might best reach her. She wasn't taking his calls and she wasn't answering his texts, other than to ask him to please go live his best life.

Succinct and to the point. And also utterly useless considering he didn't want a life—or a future—without her in it. Now his sis-ters were ticked at him because he'd clearly messed things up with the one woman they'd approved of. Approved of? Heck, Lu had flatly said if they had a choice they'd gladly take Alethea over him.

Obviously the only way to prove the pills weren't going to be a problem was to get him-self off them once and for all.

It was something he'd called Dr. Kenemen about and together, they had a plan in place as far as how to deal with his pain management for the short term and what else he could do in the long term.

Alethea had been right to voice her fears, but he was determined there was still a way forward for them. He believed in her, in them, and he hoped underneath what was holding her back, she felt the same about him. Now he needed to show he was willing to do something about it.

Please don't let it be too late.

He had a few irons in the fire, irons he had no intention of taking out of Butterfly Harbor. And he only had one more meeting to pull everything into place.

"Mr. Fairchild." Declan shoved himself up and out of a booth at the Butterfly Diner. "Appreciate you meeting with me."

"Any excuse for a slice of Holly's pie. And it's Vince, remember?" Vincent Fairchild, former CEO of Fairchild Enterprises and a one-time sponsor of Declan's team, slid into the booth across from him. Dressed in slacks and a wrinkle-free polo shirt, the man looked ready for a round of golf rather than the boardroom he'd occupied for most of his adult life. "Your business proposition sounds interesting. And promising," Vincent said before Declan could find the right words to begin. "Promising enough that I've already made some calls."

"And? Oh, sorry. Hi, Twyla."

"Hey, Declan." The tall, slender waitress

with a streak of neon blue in her hair gave him one of her trademark winks. "Your usual, Vince?"

"Please. With a scoop of vanilla ice cream."

"Just the coffee." Declan indicated the cup he'd been nursing while he waited. "Thanks." He could only imagine what the caffeine was going to do to his already racing heart. "So. What did your calls produce?"

"They've decided to go with my recommendation and accept your offer. Or I should say, we'd appreciate you accepting ours. On one condition."

"Let's have it." He hadn't felt this exhilarated since he'd seen his last checkered flag.

"We want a five-year deal," Vince said. "Five seasons of sponsorship, with the commercial and advertisement ready to begin concurrently to your racing schedule."

"Five years…" Declan sat back, his excitement deflating. "You're saying this deal is only going forward if I can commit to racing five full seasons?" He hadn't even had his surgery yet. How could he commit to something this big, this important, without knowing what the outcome would be?

Vince nodded. "You're asking for a large

investment. A risky investment. I need to know you're serious about committing."

Oh, he was serious all right. Just not in the way Vince thought. As much as it pained him, Declan said, "I'm sorry, Vince. I can't—"

"They gave me the option of offering you a seven-figure signing bonus. Payable the instant you sign that contract with us."

Seven figures. As comfortable as he was, that was a life-changing amount. But what would he be giving up in exchange? What would he be turning his back on? Everything, he reminded himself. "I can't do it. One year is my first and final offer. I've made a promise to myself, a promise I can't break. If that means walking away from this, so be it. I'll find another way to make this happen." He sat back with a sigh. "I appreciate you taking the meeting and for going to your board. But this is something that's more important to me than money."

When Vince's pie arrived, he picked up his fork, then, set it down again. He reached behind him and pulled a folded document out of his back pocket. He handed it to Declan, then, began eating.

Declan, frowning, opened the paper and

scanned it. His heart skipped a whole minute's worth of beats. "I don't understand. This is…" He looked at Vince. "This is the deal I asked for."

"It is. I needed to hear for myself exactly where your heart was. You see—" he took a bite of pie, almost swooned and swallowed "—earlier this year I came face-to-face with a lifetime of mistakes. I missed so much time with my daughter, Sienna. And I almost left this earth without having admitted how much I regretted that. What you want to do? What your plans are? Those are the types of projects I want to work on. So, while you'll be getting that signing bonus I offered…"

Declan swallowed hard. This couldn't really be happening, could it?

"You're also getting a partner. Me," Vince said with a quick smile. "It'll be enough to keep my feet in the business world and also do some good with the name my family's built up over the years. What you want to do to help communities rebuild, Declan? The way you want to preserve histories that would otherwise be forgotten and lost? That is definitely something I want to be in on the ground floor of. As long as you only race for no more than one year."

"One year." Declan's smile felt as if it reached his ears.

"You think you can convince her to agree to that?" Vince held out a pen.

"I sure plan to try." Declan flipped the document open, accepted the pen and signed on the dotted line.

"ALETHEA, THERE'S A CUSTOMER out here demanding to speak with the chef."

Alethea pulled her face away from the steaming pot of boiling chicken stock and slammed her spoon down. She'd been waiting weeks for another shot at covering for Jason at Flutterby Dreams and she had yet to find her footing tonight. The restaurant was packed, one of the servers had called in sick and the entire night's menu had to be reworked because their main refrigerator had died overnight.

"They'll all be lucky not to get a lettuce leaf and a piece of bologna," Alethea muttered. She tossed an apologetic smile to Natalie, who was serving as her assistant. The two of them had found a really good rhythm, one Alethea didn't want to interrupt.

"Say it with a smile," Natalie teased. "Don't worry about the orders. I've got them."

Alethea headed to the door, tightened the band in her hair and, trying not to slam her hand too hard, pushed into the dining room.

Familiar faces greeted her. Myra, Oscar, Ezzie and Vince represented the Cocoon Club in high style as they dined by the window. Lori and Matt Knight were clearly enjoying date night, while Holly and Luke Saxon were doing the same, albeit in a quieter corner than everyone else. It was as if Butterfly Harbor had sent its best and brightest to the dining room of the Flutterby Inn.

She caught the server's arm. "Who—never mind."

She saw him, standing by the door, looking as devastatingly handsome as he had in any print add or TV commercial. "Declan." Her overly wide smile made her teeth ache. "I don't know what's going on, but I don't have time—"

"You're due for a break." Jason popped up from a nearby table, circled around his chair and nudged them toward the door. "I'll help Natalie out. You two get some air."

"What? Where did you come from? Now hold on…" She hadn't realized she'd raised her voice until the entire restaurant went silent. "You're all in on this, aren't you? You've corrupted my town," she accused Declan.

"Yep. Come with me, please."

"Go," Jason urged when she started to refuse. "Or you're fired."

"You wouldn't." She gaped.

"After the last week of working with you?" Jason snorted. "Try me. She's all yours. For as long as it takes."

Alethea was still agog when she stepped into the lobby of the inn. Xander and Calliope rose from their seats. Xander held out his hand for her chef's jacket while Calliope draped a thick sweater around her shoulders. She gave Alethea a quick squeeze.

"I can't believe you did…whatever this is," Alethea said once they were outside. "I told you I didn't want to talk to you again. I told you I can't."

"I know. And I accept that." He led her to a beautiful new silver SUV at the base of the stairs. "I don't want you to talk. I want you to listen."

"Semantics!" she hollered at him over the hood of the car, then, as she settled in, she realized it was her first time in a car with him driving. "Keep it under the speed limit, buster."

"Yes, ma'am." He headed out slowly and proceeded down the hill, then, pulled into a parking space in front of the diner. When he climbed out and extended his hand, she ignored him, unwilling to let her heart soften even the tiniest bit. They crossed the street and walked down the pathway to the shore. She knew what he was doing and she loathed him for it. This was her place: her place of solace and healing and darn it if he wasn't going to use it against her.

If she'd thought ignoring Declan Cartwright for the past few days was going to make her fall out of love with him, she'd been wrong. If anything, the feelings she had for him had only intensified, adding to her frustration, her anger and her guilt. But she was not going to cave. There were lines she couldn't cross. Situations she could not allow herself to be put in again. Nothing he said was going to change her mind.

Absolutely nothing.

"You were right."

She closed her eyes. Except that.

Alethea folded her arms across her chest and turned her face up into the cold. "About what, precisely?"

"The pills. I honestly believed they weren't a problem—"

"You didn't just stop taking them! That isn't right, either. They were genuinely helping you, Declan." She held on to him tight.

"I know. I called Dr. Kenemen, anyway." He cupped her face in his hands. "She's got me on a new program. One that will be worked into my recovery from the surgery. One that's based on holistic treatements."

"That's good news." He was touching her. He was so close. So perfectly, warmly close and she couldn't feel more further away from him. "I'm glad for you."

"But you still don't want me to have the surgery." There was no judgment in his eyes. No accusations.

"I want you to do what you need to do to

have the life you want," she admitted. "That's all I've ever wanted, Declan."

"I hope you mean that. Because if the surgery takes, I'm going back to racing."

She gave him a sad smile. "Spoiler alert. That's not the right thing to say to win me back."

"No? How's this, then?" He stroked her lips with his thumb, pressed his mouth to hers as the evening tide crashed up onto the beach. "I love you, Alethea Costas."

"Declan." Her whisper could have broken both of their hearts. "Declan, I love, you, too, but that doesn't change anything."

"On the contrary. It changes everything. I'm having the surgery. Not because it's my only way back to the circuit. But because it's my only way out of the pain. I want a future with you, Alethea. I can't do that as I am now. I need to know I did everything I could before we have a shot at moving forward."

"I don't need you perfect," she told him. "I just need you alive." Triumph flashed in his eyes and she narrowed hers. "You tricked me."

"No. I love you." He kissed her again. "I'm

having the surgery and, if it works and I'm given the all clear, I will race again."

Tears flooded her eyes.

"For one year. One, Alethea. Enough to make a comeback and secure endorsements I need that to establish my new foundation and charity."

"Your new...what?" She blinked. How long had she not been listening?

"I've talked it over with Hilda and my sponsors, and picked up a new partner. Vince Fairchild. We're going to locate historic gas and mechanic stations and rebuild them. Reopen them. Make them part of the communities again. Small towns, big towns, all across the country. And we're going to train and teach a new generation of auto repair people. Whoever wants to learn. All ages. And we're going to start with the garage here, right in Butterfly Harbor."

"Cal's place?" She shook her head. "I don't under—"

"I bought it. Signed the papers this morning. Cal is officially retired and his auto shop and gas station are mine. And I know exactly how I'm going to refurbish them."

"Like the place your dad worked in. Darn

it, Declan." She rested her forehead on his chest and breathed him in. "This isn't fair."

"Give me one year, Alethea. You take your year to go to school. I'll take mine to race and after that…" He shrugged as she lifted her head. "After that we'll settle down here, you as one of the best chefs in the country and me as a retired race car driver turned small-town mechanic. I can make this work—I promise you. Give me the chance. Have enough faith left in me to at least give me that chance."

"You're honestly going to give it all up, the racing, the fame, the fortune—"

"The racing, yes. But I'll still have a commercial deal to endorse Fairchild Enterprises products as well as CatchAll Motors, the official suppliers of our new gas stations. And in case you're wondering, both came with a pretty nifty signing bonus."

"This isn't about money, Declan. I don't care about that. It's about being able to trust my heart. And being able to trust my heart with you."

"Xander and Calliope. Abby and Jason. Jo and Ozzy. All of them take the risk to love each other every single day. Why won't you take that same risk with me?"

"Because you scare me," she admitted on a laugh. "Because you do wild, silly things—"

"I'm not going to stop living for you, Alethea." He stared into her eyes. "What I'm asking is for you to live it all with me. I love you. Nothing is going to change that. I'm home. With Butterfly Harbor. With you. Please. Barnie and I need you. Say you'll take the chance."

Standing here, in her special place, in the place that had started her healing two years before, she felt the last bit of her heart shift and join up. She hadn't let herself believe she could have everything she ever wanted, a home, a family, professional success. A man who looked at her the way Declan was looking at her now.

A man who was willing to change his entire life to be with her. How could she not take a chance on a man like that?

"I guess since you already got the entire town on your side, I don't really have a choice, do I?" She sighed dramatically, shrugged as if her entire being weren't surging with happiness. "I don't suppose you thought about giving me a ring for this year-long engagement, did you?"

His smile lit up the final dark corners of her soul. "I might have." He reached into his pocket, pulled out a ring that made her beam.

"That's my grandmother's ring," she whispered. "The one she passed down to my mother when—but how—"

"I got your brother's approval and his help." He kissed her and as they stood there the evening waves lapped at their shoes as the moon breathed its first nightly breath across the sand. He slipped the ring on her finger. It fit perfectly. "Well?"

Her world, along with her heart, settled.

"I've never been so happy to have made a wrong turn in my life," she said with a nod. "Let's do this, Declan." She took a deep breath, and when she released it, she felt healed. "Let's do it all."

EPILOGUE

One week later

"THEY'D BETTER GET HERE soon otherwise that cake is going to be gone." Alethea gently tapped little Leo Knight's fingers away from the yellow rose icing on the edge of the board. "There's ice cream at the truck! Ask your mom," she yelled when he raced off.

She nearly yelped when a pair of arms encircled her from behind. She reached up and touched Declan's head, turning her face for a kiss. "You're supposed to be resting before your big day."

"Surgery isn't until the day after tomorrow." He lingered against her lips. "And now might be a good opportunity to tell you my sisters' plan to help with the wedding. I think it's time to admit they like you better than me."

She laughed. "They're just happy I'm taking you off their hands." She glanced up at the sight of Ozzy's SUV pulling into the parking lot. "They're here!" She shot out of Declan's arms and hurried over. Most of the town had accepted the invitation to celebrate the arrival of Hope Leah Lakeman, Jo and Ozzy's beautiful little girl. Skipper Park was filled with folks having late summer barbecues. Family and friends, residents alike, were ready to ring in the fall and bid goodbye to the heat. Even as they welcomed one baby, the town was already gearing up for the next one, Brooke and Sebastian's, who would arrive in the spring.

Alethea spotted Gil Hamilton who was pulling out his cell phone even as he accepted a beer from Harvey. She watched as Gil waved Luke Saxon over, who abandoned refereeing a game of softball among the children. A flood of guests surrounded Ozzy's car to get a first look at the baby Alethea had had the pleasure of holding yesterday, shortly after her birth.

"Where are you going?" Declan grabbed her hand and tugged her toward the car. "Baby's this way."

"I know. Just a second. Hey." She'd made it a point to continue her growing friendship with Gil and wanted to take a moment to check in with him. "Everything all right?"

"Better than it was," Luke said.

"That was Sheriff Brodie from Durant," Gil told them.

"That's the next town over, right?" Declan asked.

Gil nodded, looking a bit dazed and confused. "Christopher was arrested breaking into a convenience store after hours." He flinched. "He's in rough shape, but he's in custody. He wants to see me."

"You going to go?" Alethea asked, wishing she could erase that wrinkle of concern from his brow. The man she'd spoken with on the beach was in there somewhere: maybe one day he'd let that man shine a little more.

"No." Gil shook his head. "No, not now. Not yet, anyway. This is a big day for Ozzy and the town. It's a day to celebrate. Not regret." He offered Alethea a grateful smile. "Besides, I haven't had any cake yet."

"Right." Alethea turned and the quiet cheers of welcome erupted as Jo cradled Hope in her arms. "And we'll celebrate this in another few weeks, after your surgery, when you're back home and have recovered."

Declan slipped his arm around her waist and they walked over to join the welcoming committee.

Where they were embraced by their friends and family.

Together forever.

* * * * *

More Butterfly Harbor romances by Anna J. Stewart are available from Harlequin Heartwarming!

Visit www.Harlequin.com today!

Get 4 FREE REWARDS!

We'll send you 2 FREE Books plus 2 FREE Mystery Gifts.

Love Inspired Suspense books showcase how courage and optimism unite in stories of faith and love in the face of danger.

FREE Value Over $20

HARLEQUIN SELECTS COLLECTION

19 FREE BOOKS IN ALL!

From Robyn Carr to RaeAnne Thayne to
Linda Lael Miller and Sherryl Woods we promise
(actually, GUARANTEE!) each author in the
Harlequin Selects collection has seen their name on
the *New York Times* or *USA TODAY* bestseller lists!

YES! Please send me the **Harlequin Selects Collection**. This collection begins with 3 FREE books and 2 FREE gifts in the first shipment. Along with my 3 free books, I'll also get 4 more books from the Harlequin Selects Collection, which I may either return and owe nothing or keep for the low price of $24.14 U.S./$28.82 CAN. each plus $2.99 U.S./$7.49 CAN. for shipping and handling per shipment*.If I decide to continue, I will get 6 or 7 more books (about once a month for 7 months) but will only need to pay for 4. That means 2 or 3 books in every shipment will be FREE! If I decide to keep the entire collection, I'll have paid for only 32 books because 19 were FREE! I understand that accepting the 3 free books and gifts places me under no obligation to buy anything. I can always return a shipment and cancel at any time. My free books and gifts are mine to keep no matter what I decide.

☐ 262 HCN 5576   ☐ 462 HCN 5576

Name (please print)

Address   Apt. #

City   State/Province   Zip/Postal Code

Mail to the Harlequin Reader Service:
IN U.S.A.: P.O. Box 1341, Buffalo, NY 14240-8531
IN CANADA: P.O. Box 603, Fort Erie, Ontario L2A 5X3

---

*Terms and prices subject to change without notice. Prices do not include sales taxes, which will be charged (if applicable) based on your state or country of residence. Canadian residents will be charged applicable taxes. Offer not valid in Quebec. All orders subject to approval. Credit or debit balances in a customer's account(s) may be offset by any other outstanding balance owed by or to the customer. Please allow 3 to 4 weeks for delivery. Offer available while quantities last. © 2020 Harlequin Enterprises ULC. ® and ™ are trademarks owned by Harlequin Enterprises ULC.

Your Privacy—Your information is being collected by Harlequin Enterprises ULC, operating as Harlequin Reader Service. To see how we collect and use this information visit https://corporate.harlequin.com/privacy-notice. From time to time we may also exchange your personal information with reputable third parties. If you wish to opt out of this sharing of your personal information, please visit www.readerservice.com/consumerschoice or call 1-800-873-8635. Notice to California Residents—Under California law, you have specific rights to control and access your data. For more information visit https://corporate.harlequin.com/california-privacy.

50BOOKHS22R

Get 4 FREE REWARDS!

We'll send you 2 FREE Books plus 2 FREE Mystery Gifts.

BRENDA JACKSON
Follow Your Heart

ROBYN CARR
The Country Guesthouse

RICK MOFINA
SEARCH FOR HER

B.J. DANIELS
FROM the Shadows

FREE Value Over **$20**

Both the **Romance** and **Suspense** collections feature compelling novels written by many of today's bestselling authors.

YES! Please send me 2 FREE novels from the Essential Romance or Essential Suspense Collection and my 2 FREE gifts (gifts are worth about $10 retail). After receiving them, if I don't wish to receive any more books, I can return the shipping statement marked "cancel." If I don't cancel, I will receive 4 brand-new novels every month and be billed just $7.24 each in the U.S. or $7.49 each in Canada. That's a savings of up to 28% off the cover price. It's quite a bargain! Shipping and handling is just 50¢ per book in the U.S. and $1.25 per book in Canada.* I understand that accepting the 2 free books and gifts places me under no obligation to buy anything. I can always return a shipment and cancel at any time. The free books and gifts are mine to keep no matter what I decide.

Choose one: ☐ **Essential Romance**
(194/394 MDN GQ6M)

☐ **Essential Suspense**
(191/391 MDN GQ6M)

Name (please print)

Address

Apt. #

City

State/Province

Zip/Postal Code

Email: Please check this box ☐ if you would like to receive newsletters and promotional emails from Harlequin Enterprises ULC and its affiliates. You can unsubscribe anytime.

Mail to the Harlequin Reader Service:
IN U.S.A.: P.O. Box 1341, Buffalo, NY 14240-8531
IN CANADA: P.O. Box 603, Fort Erie, Ontario L2A 5X3

Want to try 2 free books from another series! Call 1-800-873-8635 or visit www.ReaderService.com.

*Terms and prices subject to change without notice. Prices do not include sales taxes, which will be charged (if applicable) based on your state or country of residence. Canadian residents will be charged applicable taxes. Offer not valid in Quebec. This offer is limited to one order per household. Books received may not be as shown. Not valid for current subscribers to the Essential Romance or Essential Suspense Collection. All orders subject to approval. Credit or debit balances in a customer's account(s) may be offset by any other outstanding balance owed by or to the customer. Please allow 4 to 6 weeks for delivery. Offer available while quantities last.

Your Privacy—Your information is being collected by Harlequin Enterprises ULC, operating as Harlequin Reader Service. For a complete summary of the information we collect, how we use this information and to whom it is disclosed, please visit our privacy notice located at corporate.harlequin.com/privacy-notice. From time to time we may also exchange your personal information with reputable third parties. If you wish to opt out of this sharing of your personal information, please visit readerservice.com/consumerschoice or call 1-800-873-8635. **Notice to California Residents**—Under California law, you have specific rights to control and access your data. For more information on these rights and how to exercise them, visit corporate.harlequin.com/california-privacy.

STRS21R2